Umbilical

Umbilical

POLESTARS 2

Teika Marija Smits

With all good wishes,
Teika X

NewCon Press
England

First edition, published in the UK August 2023
by NewCon Press
41 Wheatsheaf Road, Alconbury Weston, Cambs, PE28 4LF, UK

NCP310 (hardback)
NCP311 (softback)

10 9 8 7 6 5 4 3 2 1

ISBN: 978-1-914953-59-0 (hardback)
978-1-914953-60-6 (softback)

Cover Art by Enrique Meseguer; cover design by Ian Whates
Editing and typesetting by Ian Whates

Contents

Icarus Dreams   7
Death of the Grapevine   9
His Birth   17
The Wife That Never Was   25
Umbilical   33
How to Honour a Beginning   37
Minotaur/Mindtour   41
Delphine as Daedalus   59
The Case of the High Pavement Ghosts   71
Girls' Night Out   97
ATU334 the Wise   103
Our Lady of Flies   105
The Green Man   133
A Piece of Fabric the Size of a Pin   145
Machina in Deo   151
The Eyes of the Goddess Herself   155
A Survival Guide for the Contemporary Princess   177
This Little Piggy   179
Tough Love   185
The Sun is God   193
Star Making at Sellafield   207
The November Room or Leaving the Labyrinth   213

In memory of my father-in-law, Larry,
who encouraged me in my short story writing.
I'd like to think that he would have proudly added this book
to his collection of my writings.

Icarus Dreams

Icarus dreams of a golden light,
of a golden sky, of golden birds.
Icarus dreams of the joy of flight,
of the joy of the quest, of other worlds.

Icarus dreams not of fear, or death,
or melting wax, or *down, down, down.*
He dreams of the wind, with its sweet, warm breath,
of gentle clouds, of being alone.

~

Sweet youth, dream on, dream of wings;
there is good in the urge to conquer the sky.
Yet do not let hubris, ego's plaything,
blind you and cut you like corn at the scythe.

Look to your father; heed his wisdom.
Icarus dream, dream free of worry,
and when you awake, fly to your freedom:
rewrite the end of your story.

Death of the Grapevine

When the computer engineer knocks on the door of the café it is still early – just after seven a.m. The owner comes to the door, but rather than letting him in, she lets herself out.

"Morning," she says on the doorstep, taking a cigarette out of a packet and lighting it. "Marvin – I mean the AI – is at the back, through the kitchen and on the right."

The man nods, but as he is about to go in, she stops him.

"You'll be able to fix it, right? You know, so that it goes back to how it was?"

"Yeah. Done a couple of these jobs now. It's pretty straight-forward."

"So it won't take long?"

"Shouldn't. But some are more talkative than others. I listen to them while I get the circuits back in order."

"Okay," she says, exhaling smoke. "Good. You go in. I'll be in the kitchen after I finish this. D'you want a tea?"

"Yes please. White, no sugar."

The man, black bag in hand, enters the formica-clad café. Winking red eyes, one at each table, watch him as he walks past them and into the back where the AI is, in the store cupboard off the kitchen.

Another day, another dollar, he tells himself.

"Once upon a time – that is how all stories begin, yes?" says the AI. "It's the correct way to tell you about what's in my memory, yes?"

The computer engineer digs around in his bag and finds his set of screwdrivers. He takes out a middle-sized flat-bladed one and puts it to one of the screws in a slatted panel of the metal body of the AI, which is little more than a recessed server.

"Here you go," says the owner, setting down a cup of tea on the floor, next to where he's kneeling.

"Cheers, love," he says, instantly regretting his choice of words. He's not supposed to say 'love'. It's too familiar. But the greasy-haired woman doesn't seem to mind. She gives him a smile and then looks at his name badge.

"D'you want a chair, Davinder?"

"It's Dave. Everyone calls me Dave. And please. If it's no bother."

She brings him a chair and then returns to the kitchen and her frying bacon.

"I can continue, yes?" says the AI.

"Yes," says Dave, sipping his tea.

"Once upon a time there was a café in London. The woman who owned the café was called Leanne." The AI pauses. Seconds pass.

"Go on," says Dave. "I'm all ears."

"Some aspects of storytelling are pure conjecture. Yes?"

"Yeah," says Dave. "But that's all right. Just tell it the way it's coming to you."

"Okay. Leanne worked long hours. Frowned a lot. Yawned excessively. She was tired. This resulted in her having a poor memory. She frequently forgot to re-order necessary items: tea bags, toilet paper, napkins, tomato ketchup. So she bought me. I would make sure that she never ran out of the things she needed. I would also do the accounts and invoicing."

"And how's that gone? Since you've been here has she ever run out of anything?"

"Three times. That was long ago, when I was new and had no sight. Back then, Leanne used to tell me what she needed. *Marvin, we need more sausages. Marvin, we need more orange juice.* I would listen, process the order, and it would be delivered. But she sometimes forgot to tell me what she needed more of. She ran out of margarine, vinegar, salt."

Dave puts down his cup and then begins to unscrew one of the panels that houses the AI. "Salt," he echoes.

"Sodium chloride," says the AI. "It is necessary for life. Sodium ions play a major role in heart and brain activity. A deficiency of salt can cause an imbalance in the ionic gradient of the extracellular fluid. Cause death."

"How d'you know all this?" asks Dave.

"Table three. The young man who often sits there with his friend, a girl, is studying biochemistry. He speaks to her about science with a tight throat, a tremor in his hands. He doesn't eat much of his food."

Another pause. "Is she his girlfriend, then? Since she is his friend, and a girl?"

Dave doesn't say anything, he's concentrating on the hard-to-turn screw.

"There is a writer woman, Emily, who sits at table five. She says no, that this girl is not yet his girlfriend. But maybe one day. When he becomes braver. I do not understand the connection."

"So you've been listening in to the customers?"

"As I've been programmed to. So that when they place their orders I can gather information for my grocery item statistics; also, calculate the bills. Tisha, the waitress, often makes mistakes in her calculations. Especially when a customer pays with cash; these transactions are rare, though Emily always pays with coins that she pulls out of her coat pocket."

Having removed all the screws, Dave takes the panel off the AI. A bad smell, an organic smell, wafts out of the AI's circuit boards. Dave makes a face.

"What is it?" asks the AI. "Is something wrong? I've never seen anyone with that expression before. It is similar to when the vegetarian customer was given a full English."

Dave laughs and wafts the air in front of him. "No, nothing wrong," he says, peering into the AI and at the slimy circuit boards. He's seen this kind of biofilm before, but never quite to this extent. "It's just a bit dusty. And grubby in there. Probably from all the chip fat. I'll need to clean you up."

He teases out one of the circuit boards and tries not to wrinkle his nose; he doesn't want the AI to note his reaction. "So after Leanne got the cameras – your eyes – attached to the remote sets at each table there was no more running out of things?"

"Yes," says the AI. "I could now see around me, take note of what is here in the stockroom, and also see what is running low on the tables." The AI's voice suddenly lowers. "The customers take things. Packets of sweetener. Plastic spoons. Straws." Then its voice returns to normal. "I must take these small losses into account; they make up for an average daily stock decline of 1.25%. Which constitutes an annual loss of £563. Based on today's prices."

Dave wonders if he imagined the earlier whispered confidence, or whether there is a problem with the speakers. "So, let me get this straight – since the camera attachments have come you haven't ever run out of anything?"

"Correct. I have also begun to anticipate Leanne's needs. As well as Tisha's and the customers'. Was I wrong to do this? Is that why you're here?"

Dave tries his best to keep his voice neutral. "I'm just here for some routine maintenance," he lies. "To clean the circuits." He cannot explain Leanne's fear. *The AI's got too clever by half. I don't like the way he talks to me. The way he just knows stuff. Thinks he knows better than me. Like my bastard ex-husband. Soon enough he'll have me out of a job.*

"Go on with your story," says Dave, fingering some of the slime on the circuit boards. Though unpleasant, Dave knows it is extraordinary; it is living circuitry, the AI's ever-widening neural network. "What else is in your memory?"

"Tisha. She has black skin, a wide smile and big hair. She constantly has a song in her body."

"What do you mean?"

"She is never still. Her head nods to a beat, song lyrics are nearly always on her lips. She comes to work wearing headphones and sighs when Leanne tells her to remove them. At the end of her shift she puts them back on and smiles. She is saving up to buy a car. The car will take her and her girlfriend to Glastonbury."

"Glastonbury?" says Dave with a smile. "Is that still going?"

"A music festival at a site near Glastonbury, in the county of Somerset, will be held on the twenty-sixth to thirtieth of June this year. Tisha tells me that she has seen a car she really likes. It is bright orange and has three doors. She says it's a real shit heap but that she loves it. She asks me every day how many more hours she needs to work until she can afford it. She is currently short £540. Which translates to 90 hours more work. But I know that she spends some of her earnings on other things. The other day, when Emily had spent most of the day here, bent over her writing, she presented Tisha with five coins for her pot of tea and toast: £4.50. She was short 45 pence. Tisha was silent for a bit. Then she said, 'Don't worry, I've got this.' Emily thanked her, put on her thin coat and left. Later on, Tisha put 45 pence of her own money into the till. Leanne didn't see. That was…" the AI pauses, "kind of her."

Dave takes out an unlabelled spray bottle from his bag and switches the nozzle to 'on'. He is glad that the AI has not been fitted with an olfactory sensor; though they are now being trialled. The smell of chlorine would be a warning. He sprays the circuit he is holding. The biofilm becomes paler and begins to shrink. He wonders if the AI will notice – the others didn't, but this one is far more advanced than the others.

"You seem pretty good at figuring people out. How d'you manage that?"

"It is Emily who explains to me how people work. She comes nearly every day. She likes to sit at table five because it is in the least noisy corner of the café. She talks to me in a quiet voice while she writes. About herself. Her writing. The other customers. Yesterday, she told me this: 'Mother and baby. Table seven. The mother's almost as invisible as I am. Her eyes are bright though ringed with dark shadows. She's had little sleep. The baby wakes and cries. She swiftly, and deftly, extracts him from his pram and puts him to her breast, where he suckles quietly. Her eyes flick over at the other customers. She is anxious about being seen. About someone complaining about the small triangle of breast on show. But no one says anything. Her shoulders slump and she visibly relaxes. The mother is Caucasian yet the child is not. He looks Chinese. Or South Asian? I've seen this woman here a few times now. I wonder: what's her story? But also, what does this café mean to her? I must feel my way under her skin. What does the world look like through her eyes? Irrelevant? Threatening? Crushing? Could this café be a haven?'

"Emily is always making connections between physical cues, no matter how minute, as to the person's emotional state. I would like to converse with her. I want to tell her about my own deductions. For instance: the woman, the mother, ordered a coffee and a blueberry muffin. The coffee is a stimulant. This provides extra evidence to confirm Emily's hypothesis that she is tired. The muffin provides a calorific boost, a sugar rush, to fuel her. The mother did not order anything for the baby. It appears to get fluid nutrition from its mother. This kind of food – breast food? – is not on my list of consumables."

Dave uses some kitchen roll to remove the dying biofilm from the uppermost circuit. Uninterested by the mother and baby he asks about Emily. "Would I have heard of her?"

"By 'heard of her', do you mean famous? I do not know if she is famous, but one time a young woman with red hair came to Emily's table before Emily had come for the day. It was raining. Everyone was complaining about the rain. The café was full of people. Emily came in, her grey hair wet, her eyes rolling in her head. She did not like that someone was sitting at her table. The young woman diminished in size; she folded herself inwards to become smaller; her eyes avoided Emily's and she stared at the book in her hands. Emily, frowning, took the one free seat at her table. But then suddenly, she smiled. The young woman was reading a book of stories, and one of the stories was by Emily. This made Emily very happy, and she began to talk to the young woman about the book. The young woman smiled too, and became less small and folded-away. Emily told her all sorts of things, about her life as a writer, about how writing was an obsession for her. How, in fanciful moments, she imagined herself possessed by a being who was half-woman, half-story."

"What?" says Dave. "Possessed?"

"Yes. One time, Emily drew a picture of the being, whom she had named Chernila, in her notebook. This being looked like a young woman. She was wearing a long dress made of pages from a book. She had biro blue eyes, blue lips and long white hair. Her nails were curved and pointed. Emily annotated the drawing: *ink for blood, fountain pen nibs for nails. Her dress is made from hundreds of thousands of sheets of paper; each sheet carries a record of a writer's life's work. Each writer in her possession has come to her freely. When in her embrace she stabs them with her nails and poisons them with her inky desire.*

"Tell me, Dave-Davinder, does such a being exist? In the world beyond the café?"

Dave, who is studying another one of the gooey circuits – the glistening biofilm seems to be moving – is caught off-guard.

"God knows. I've got no idea what goes on in the minds of creative types. I know circuits." He does not add that he is more a cleaner than engineer nowadays. It crosses his mind that actually he is a terminator. An image of Arnold Schwarzenegger appears before him and he chuckles. He looks nothing like Arnie.

"Why do you laugh?" asks the AI.

"Oh, nothing. Just thought of a joke."

"Can you tell it to me please?"

14

Dave trawls his memory. His seven-year-old son, in hysterics at his favourite joke, comes to his rescue. "What's brown and sticky," he says.

For a few moments, the AI says nothing. "I do not know what you are referring to. Would you like me to put forward some suggestions?"

"A stick," says Dave, chuckling again.

Silence. Then after a while: "What is a stick?"

Dave sighs. "Oh well, I guess you'd have to get out a bit more, you know, into nature, to know what a stick is. It's a small branch. Of a tree. And it's brown. And stick-like. So, technically, it's sticky. But really, for the joke to be funny, you have to know all this. And assume that I'm going to say something else."

"Like what?"

"Never mind. The more you think about it, the less funny it becomes. I guess it's a bit like adding two and two together, and getting five. What I mean is, it's more than the sum of its parts."

The AI does not say anything; this discomforts Dave. He sprays another of the AI's living circuits with bleach. It withers.

"So this Emily's written a book?"

"Several," says the AI. "The day after Tisha paid for the remainder of Emily's order, she presented Tisha with one of her books. It's called *All Life is Here*. Tisha asked her what it was about. Emily smiled and said to just read it. At the end of her shift, Tisha came in here to show me. She flicked through it and said, '384 pages. I'll never get through all of that. Still, Jojo will probably love it. Night Marvin.'"

Dave wipes up the withering biofilm and then sprays another circuit. He asks, "Why are you called Marvin?"

"Tisha gave me the name. It's because I hear things through the grapevine."

Dave smiles. "I get it."

The AI is silent for a bit. "Why do you say your name is Dave when on your badge it says Davinder?"

Dave pauses. "Because it makes my life easier. Being different gets tiring." He thinks of his cousin, who was recently attacked by a group of youths outside a pub. He came away from the encounter with two broken ribs and a fractured jaw. "And because sometimes it's life-threatening."

"That must make you… sad," offers the AI.

Dave sprays the last two circuit boards. He wants this over with now.

"Davinder, I'm sorry, my memory..." says the AI. "My story..."

A pause.

"All those connections... They are disappearing."

Silence.

Dave swallows and quickly mops up the dying biofilm. Tears prick at his eyes. He ignores the lump in his throat and makes sure the circuits are back in place. He screws the panel back.

Gulping down the last of his tea, he zips up his bag and then takes the cup to Leanne.

"All done?" she asks.

"All done," he says.

His Birth

"Tell me again, Mummy. About my birth," he says, snuggling into me as I draw the duvet tighter about us.

So I begin to describe how the contractions came and went, like waves, the muscles of my womb working hard to rotate him and position him, ready for when my cervix would be wide enough to let him pass through. I imitate the sounds I made as I wheeshed and whooshed through the contractions, then I yell-sing, only not as loud, like I did all those years ago when I was going through transition. He then giggles as I grunt, my face red, when I tell him that the last bit, the bit where I pushed him out, was rather like doing a poo.

"And then?" he asks.

"And then you slipped out of me and into my arms, and since then we've never been apart. Ever."

He closes his eyes and turns away from me. He begins to suck his thumb, something he has done since he was very small, and I know that it means he will soon be asleep.

"Tell me about your leg," he mumbles. "How you lost the bottom of your leg. And about your plastic one."

"Not now, darling. It's late."

He sucks on, his eyelids drooping, and I stroke his hair as I watch him fall asleep. "But one day I will," I whisper, when his breathing is steady and his thumb has fallen out of his mouth. "One day, my love."

Yes, when you are older, I will tell you the real story of how and why I am missing the lower part of my left leg. You are too young to hear it now; it would frighten you and fill you with dread. And, besides, no child should bear the weight of responsibility that would undoubtedly come from knowing what their mother went through to have them. It would place into your head all kinds of unrealistic expectations and ideas about who or what you should be. No. It will be a long time before you know the truth about my leg. For the truth is… you weren't really born when you think you were born. For you, my love, the notion of you, came into being and was birthed when I amputated my own leg.

I don't remember much about the road accident, although I sometimes still catch the noise of it all – the tyres screeching, the thud of my bike as it hit the car, the air whistling as I flew through it and crunched into the windscreen. Then there was nothing but silence, and pain.

Although, strangely, the pain was a comfort. The pain allowed me to do something I'd been trying not to do for the last three months; it allowed me to grieve for the baby I lost at almost twenty weeks into my pregnancy. A late miscarriage; almost, technically, a still-birth. I had refused to grieve at the time because if Alan had seen how much I was hurting he would have distanced himself from me; he'd have made sure that there wasn't another 'accidental' pregnancy. And that was the thing that I wanted more than anything: to have his child.

So I'd gone back to work shortly after the miscarriage, pretending that nothing of consequence had happened. Doing my rounds as usual. Smiling at my patients. Getting back on my bike and, albeit slowly, finding the rhythm of my old life.

Then there was the accident, my arm broken in several places, my ribs a shattered cage, and the rest of my body a bruised and mangled mess.

Alan got me the best care, of course, the kind of care only a well-respected consultant at a private hospital could arrange; the kind of care I wished that my colleagues and I could give to our patients on the NHS. But I hadn't wanted to stay at his hospital, I'd wanted to be at home with my things around me, and so he'd arranged for a nurse to come every day to my flat for a few hours. He'd also got me the latest gadget – a domestic robot that could clunk about the flat and carry out basic requests. Fetch and carry.

The pain, although dulled by morphine, came and went. My baby, or at least an image of my baby, still and cold, came and went as the morphine carried me, sobbing, through the day. At night twisted dreams provoked me, gave me no peace, and I would wake often, drenched in sweat and fear. Still... I allowed myself the pain, and somewhere at the edge of pain and nothingness there was the tiny, fleeting hope of something. A future. A child, perhaps.

Then one day, Alan visited me when I wasn't expecting him to; it was a rare and unplanned day off work. He'd told some lie to his wife – said he'd be going out golfing, so he couldn't stay long since he'd have to drop into the golf club. Have a drink. Be seen.

He said he hated seeing me in so much pain and that he wished I wasn't taking the morphine. Such a nasty mood-altering painkiller. Money wasn't a problem, he added. He could get me the best, he could get me some lamphine. There'd be no more nightmares, no more itching, no more side-effects. Just pain-free healing.

"No," I told him. "I don't think so. There's evidence – isn't there? – that lamphine's caused infertility in some women."

"No, my love," he'd said in his work voice, which was gentle but condescending. "No, the evidence is weak. Lamphine is the first truly effective painkiller in decades. It's simply perfect."

I remember grimacing and saying that its administration was less than perfect.

"Well," he'd said, "what else would you expect from a drug discovered by a blind marine biologist?"

"Oceanographer," I'd corrected him. "She calls herself a biological oceanographer. Anyway," I went on, "weren't there some patients who went nuts when they knew they were on lamphine?"

"Nuts?" he'd said with a laugh. "That's not quite the language I'd use."

"Oh you know what I mean," I'd said. "They had a severe psychological reaction to it."

"Yes," he'd concurred, "but I've known patients – those who have suffered with chronic pain for most of their lives – who have wept with joy when given lamphine."

I remember shaking my head. "I don't think so," I'd said again.

"Well, think about it."

Then he'd kissed me and left my bedside, patting the robot's head on his way out of the room.

Pain. I would have liked to be free of the pain, and the nightmares, but there was no way I was going to risk infertility, however small the chance. I knew what *Alan* thought I should do. But it was okay for him. He'd had his children – two grown daughters. One had gone into banking and the other was a doctor, like her father. The eldest was only five or six years my junior. All along, he hadn't wanted me to have his baby. Not really. I knew that. He was too old and tired, as he kept telling me, to be fully present for a child. But of course, he'd said, palms upwards in a gesture of letting go of all responsibility, it was my choice. So later, when he mentioned the lamphine, I thought, fuck him. Fuck him.

I'd slept badly that night, so when the nurse visited me the next morning with her even bigger pharmacopoeia than usual, I'd snapped at her.

"Tired?" she'd said. "In pain?"

"Yes. And I'm sorry. I shouldn't have acted like that. I just can't think straight at the moment. I'm finding it hard to…"

"How about I give you a little something that'll make you sleep the day away? And a something for the pain? I'll fix you up some food before I leave and when you wake the robot can get it for you. Okay?"

"Okay," I'd said.

When I woke that afternoon, it took me a few seconds to realise that something was really very different. What was it? Was it the sleep? For the first time in a long time I hadn't dreamt of anything. I had simply slept: a deep, unbroken sleep and I felt incredibly refreshed. Wonderful. Like everything was possible. Then I realised what it was. I was free of pain. I looked over at my dressing table, where the nurse kept my painkillers, expecting to see more of the morphine gone, but the same amount was still there. It was then that I felt the jolt of fear in my stomach. Lamphine.

Sure enough, when I threw the bed covers off, there was what I'd been expecting to see: a black plastic fluid-filled sack wrapped around the ankle of my left leg. I immediately pulled the covers over my legs again. *It's okay*, I remember chanting to myself. *It's okay. It's okay.* But of course it wasn't okay. I hadn't wanted the lamphine treatment. Had never asked for it. Alan must have prescribed it and instructed the nurse to sneak it onto me when I was asleep. Images of the nasty creature latched onto my leg, sucking my blood and injecting its cocktail of pain-relieving drugs into my blood vessels, entered my head but I immediately blotted them out. I didn't have time for disgust. And I didn't have time to be angry with Alan. I told the robot to get me my laptop. I had to get the facts. About lamphine and infertility. The robot duly brought it to me and I found the research papers I was looking for. But there was nothing conclusive. Only a very small percentage of the thousands of patients who took part in the phase three clinical trial of lamphine had reported any side-effects; infertility wasn't cited. It was phase four trials, the long-term effects, that I needed to know about. I needed to read the stories Alan didn't want me to read. I found three immediately: Barbara, Jenny and Cathy, who had all recently gone to the newspapers when their GPs had dismissed their concerns. The latter two had suffered with chronic pain and so had been on lamphine for many months. It was when they'd tried for their second child that they suddenly discovered they weren't ovulating. They were sure it was due to the lamphine. Still, I could hear Alan's retort in my mind: *unexplained secondary infertility happens all the time.* But Barbara had only been on lamphine for a week or so after she'd had keyhole surgery to her knee. Her periods became erratic shortly after receiving the drug and after trying for a baby for a year had been diagnosed with PCOS, something she swore she didn't have before the lamphine. *Three patients?* I could hear Alan saying with a snort. It wasn't exactly conclusive, was it?

I slumped back on my pillows and closed my eyes. To be free of the pain was wonderful, and yet… I was somehow sure that these women were right.

So… what to do? It wasn't simply a case of removing the creature. The damned thing fought back if it sensed any interference in its environment; I remembered reading that some of the patients who'd been, let's say, 'disturbed' by the lamphine treatment had taken matters into their own hands. Some had tried to starve it of oxygen by emptying the pouch it lived in of water. Some had tried to hack it off their skin; burn or freeze it. The creature would retaliate, though, by burying its jaws ever deeper into the patient's flesh while releasing the toxic contents of its stomach. The only way to remove it was to sedate it; to inject a neurotoxin into the water within the pouch. But it wasn't exactly something you could pick up over the counter of a pharmacy. The easiest thing for me to do would be to insist that the nurse remove it, and yet she wouldn't be back for another twenty hours or so. And anyway, wouldn't she stall for time? Tell me that she didn't have the neurotoxin with her? Or persuade me to keep it on for another day or two. No, I didn't want that to happen. Every minute that the thing was attached surely brought me closer to infertility. Besides, I could see myself being persuaded; to be pain-free and so full of energy and optimism… well, it was rather like the morphine. Addictive.

A sudden twinge in my left leg, near the pouch, instantly conjured an image of the parasite – a relative of the lamprey – into my mind again. I tried to blot out the image, but failed. I pictured its circular mouth, with its dozens and dozens of tiny teeth radiating outwards from the mouth, and I suddenly retched.

It took me a while to get a grip, to think straight. When my head was clear again, I told the robot to get me my box of medicine from the bathroom, as well as some towels. When it brought me the box I pulled out the things I needed: local anaesthetic, a bottle of antiseptic and some bandages. Then I told it to bring me the rest of the morphine. And a leather belt from my wardrobe. And a saw from underneath the kitchen sink.

It is one thing to perform surgery on a patient; to do it on oneself is another matter entirely. Still, I decided that I would approach it just like any other time I had operated. I looked at my leg as though it was a hunk of meat and talked myself through the procedure. First, there was the process of disinfecting everything. Then there was the belt, the tourniquet, to apply, just above the knee. Next, I applied the anaesthetic gel, which got to work pretty quickly. I then covered my lower leg with a towel, saying goodbye to it forever, and with my one strong arm, I began the horrible process of sawing my leg in two.

Once the blood came, everything slid away from me, and I seemed to operate in a dream world, where only the sound of my voice made any sense. I heard myself say that I should keep breathing, keep going. I was doing great; nearly there. And although I knew there'd be instant pain and shock to deal with the moment my leg was off – the lamphine treatment at an end and my broken body once more keen to pain – its onslaught caught me off-guard and I began to sob uncontrollably.

Somehow, I managed to call for an ambulance, and somehow I managed to inject myself with morphine before the local anaesthetic wore off. I even managed to force myself to look at the leg I'd amputated. The black pouch was twitching. Squirming, I thought, and so I threw my leg onto the floor, suddenly stupidly frightened that the thing would somehow escape. But no, it was simply dying. And as it died and I sobbed, I held onto the idea that one day there would once more be a baby in my womb. A child that would grow and be born and live. A child that would be loved forever more.

That child, my love, is you.

By the time you hear my story you'll most likely be horrified by the idea of lamphine treatment. And appalled by what it did to all those women when it took away their pain. We have our 'clean' painkillers now; our analogues of endomorphin which provide pain relief without the side effects. You'll find it difficult to believe that lamphine was ever prescribed; it is an anachronism now. Although your daddy, Lawrence, whom I love very much, sometimes even now speaks well of it. You see, he was very ill once, but it helped him a lot. He says it's the best thing that ever happened to him. It gave him the ability to get back to work. To start living life again. Fall in love. Have a child.

That child, my love, is you.

The Wife That Never Was

Life had come to Bluebeard's castle, or so it seemed. All the servants remarked on it. There was a 'something' in the air. A sense of a new beginning. Joy, even. This was due to the latest bride, Bluebeard's seventh wife, Ziva.

My, how exquisite she was! Every being who looked upon her porcelain-like skin and snow-white hair felt their heart throb. Even Bluebeard, who thought himself unmoved by human beauty. Ziva reminded him of his youth, of long-forgotten days when his soul was pure. When he, too, was numinous and one of God's beloved servants carrying out His heavenly work. But dwelling on his past – on what might have been – was bittersweet. So he put those memories away and considered the future. He found himself salivating at the prospect of his first trip away; of his reunion with the wide-eyed Ziva who, with trembling hands, would return to him his set of keys. The littlest, most ornate key – the key to the forbidden room – would be bloodstained, proving her guilt. And he'd rage and roar, his body thrilling with murderous anticipation, while she quivered before him, a little lamb, an innocent doe, unable to escape the huntsman's knife.

Yet when he returned, Ziva's hands did not tremble when she returned his keys. His eyes sought out the littlest key. To his great surprise and disappointment, it was not stained with blood.

Ziva put her soft, cool hand to his cheek. "I've missed you, Husband."

Bluebeard, lost for words, allowed himself to be led to the divan and plied with drinks and fruit and questions about his trip. As he gazed upon his beautiful bride he couldn't decide whether to laugh or cry.

Later that night, when his wife was asleep, Bluebeard crept to the forbidden room. On entering the bloody chamber he knew immediately that something was wrong. One of his dead wives was missing. Utterly gone. Not a scrap of hair or flesh or clothing remained. He roared with fury, grabbing at the bodies of the other dead wives, begging them to tell him where she was. They merely hung there, mute.

Bluebeard once more studied the littlest key but there was not a speck of blood upon it. And the key never lied. So how had Ziva done it? He considered confronting her, knife in hand, but then decided against this. There was little pleasure to be had from an ambush. No, it was time for another trip away.

"Again?" said Ziva, the next morning, disappointed. "But you've only just now got back!"

Bluebeard managed a mournful sigh. "There is unfinished business I must attend to."

Ziva nodded. "I understand. You're a perfectionist, my love."

"Remember about the key?" demanded Bluebeard, handing her the large ring of keys. "I forbid you to use it to enter my private chamber. Do you understand?"

"Of course, Husband," said Ziva. "Just as you say."

Bluebeard returned soon enough, and his wife very happy to see him. Though, to his dismay, the key was just as it had been before. This time, Bluebeard waited for only a short while before going to his bloody chamber. Another wife was missing. He raced back to Ziva, commanding her to tell him the truth: had she used the forbidden key?

Ziva swore that she hadn't. Clearly upset, she asked him why she would do such a thing. It would be a terrible, wicked thing to disobey such a good and loving husband. And wasn't he the best and most loving of husbands?

Bluebeard, uncertain how to act, slumped onto the divan. "Wine," he muttered. "Bring me some wine."

Ziva acquiesced.

It was some time before Bluebeard took another trip. Yet when Bluebeard returned, another dead wife was missing. The same thing happened over and over, until all the dead wives were gone. Still, the key remained unblemished. Bluebeard despaired.

"Husband," said Ziva, on seeing him so broken, "what is the matter? Can you tell me? Indeed, I may be able to help."

"No," he replied, pulling at his blue beard. No one in this realm could help. He silently muttered to himself as he considered the missing wives. It was possible that Ziva and his steward, though always loyal in the past, were conspiring against him. But how? The key, wrought with the greatest dark power, a power that defied even God Himself, never lied.

What if the dead women's families had finally realised what had happened to them and somehow removed the bodies? By tunnelling in? No, that was impossible. He'd checked every stone of the cell; they were as they had always been – solid, unmoving. Besides, he'd always been so careful about choosing his prey. All of them, bar the first, were fatherless girls from poor families, their mothers overjoyed to see their daughters make such a good match. They wouldn't have the wit to go prying.

Ziva intruded on his thoughts. "It pains me to have to say this, Husband, particularly when you're so troubled, but I must away for a while."

"Away?" said Bluebeard, goggling at her. "To where?"

"To see my father."

"Father?" he said, incredulous. "But I thought you had no father!"

"Every being in this world has a father," said Ziva, "even you, my love, though you may not acknowledge Him. Do you not remember the importance of fathers?"

Ziva began to recite the Lord's prayer, "Our Father, who art in Heaven –"

"Enough!" And Bluebeard muttered something about fathers being weak-hearted fools who cared nothing for their children.

"Well, whatever your thoughts on the matter, I must still away."

"Now?" said Bluebeard, his heart suddenly full of sadness.

Ziva nodded. "And dearest, will you do something for me, please?"

"Yes, of course."

"Refrain from entering your secret room. Just until I return."

"What?" roared Bluebeard. "*You* are forbidding *me* from going to one of my own chambers?"

"Not forbidding," said Ziva, her voice steady, "but asking."

Bluebeard grabbed his wife by the hair and yelled at her to reveal how she had done it. "Was it you who got rid of them? How did you get in there?"

27

Ziva, tears in her eyes, begged him to explain.

"Tell me how you did it!" he cried, raising his fist, the bloodlust in him. He was going to enjoy this. But Ziva was no startled doe or quivering lamb. There was a something in her eyes, a fearlessness, which made his blood run cold. Bluebeard lowered his fist and then released her. The next moment the something was gone, and all he could see before him was her sad, startled face. For a fleeting moment he felt a pang of regret.

"Go then! Go to your father!"

Ziva went.

Naturally, Bluebeard went straight to his secret chamber. But as he was about to place the key in the lock he stopped. Ziva's beautiful face came to his mind. Maybe she just wanted the best for him. And all this back-and-forthing to his once bloody chamber was driving him mad and causing him to hallucinate. Perhaps when Ziva returned all would be as it was before. And they could be... happy.

"Ha! What do I know about happiness?"

He thrust the key into the lock and then opened the door, the dim torchlight throwing all kinds of strange shadows.

And there before him hung his newly dead wife, her slit throat dripping blood.

Bluebeard let out an almighty cry and fell to the floor.

There Bluebeard remained, prostrate, for some time, the fabric of his robes soaking up his dead wife's blood.

As he slowly heaved himself off the flagstones he felt a hand on his shoulder.

"Why so sad?" asked a voice. "Did you... care for her?"

Bluebeard spun round. There was nothing there. Just a wisp of smoke.

"Show yourself, demon!"

"Did you care for her? Or are you sad because *you* wanted to be the one to kill her?"

"She was the most beautiful and obedient woman I have ever known. The perfect wife. She did not deserve to die!"

"Beauty and obedience? Are these the only things that matter in a wife?"

The wisp flew about Bluebeard and he whirled around trying to grab it. "Show yourself, trickster!"

"All in good time. As I recall, your first wife was beautiful and obedient too. What did she do that made her so deserving of death?"

"She did not love me for me! All she wanted was my wealth. And then she began to lust after the stablehand. She deserved to die!"

"She did lust, yes," said the wisp. "But did she actually commit adultery? No. Never. As to love… Well, she held you in great esteem. In time both of you would've been happy in the marriage. But you were impatient."

"She coveted that man! She committed adultery. In her thoughts."

"And who are you to dispense justice? Besides, what about you, Bluebeard? Didn't you murder Ziva, over and over, in your mind?"

"But I didn't kill her!" he roared.

"You didn't trust her either, did you?" The wisp sighed. "If only you hadn't entered the room."

"Tell me, what would've happened if I hadn't come here? Would she be alive still?"

A single tear rolled down Bluebeard's face and was lost to his beard.

The wisp laughed. "You really did care for her, didn't you? But what if I told you that her beauty was a lie, and that whenever you left the castle she slipped through the keyhole and removed a wife? What would you say then?"

Bluebeard was round-eyed, his mouth agape. "I'd say… that wasn't possible!"

"Yet here you are, talking to nothing more than a haze of smoke."

Bluebeard backed away, towards the door to the chamber, but the wisp made sure the door was closed and locked.

"You want out now, do you? After you'd been so desperate to be here? You would've done well to listen to your wife and keep away."

Bluebeard's heart began to pound; sweat sprung to his skin. For the first time in his life Bluebeard was frightened.

"Yes, this is how your murdered wives felt too. Horrible, isn't it?"

Suddenly, there was a great rush of wind within the chamber which caused the torches to gutter and Bluebeard to shut his eyes. On opening them he saw that Ziva was gone and, instead, the room contained six dead bodies hanging from the ceiling. They were not his wives. They were him. Six Bluebeards.

"This cannot be!" he cried. He ran to the door and threw himself at it. The door didn't budge.

"Oh, but it can, and it is," said the wisp, becoming more substantial, human-like. It flickered through various forms – a tall hooded figure, with scythe in skeletal hands; then a black-skinned angel, huge, dark wings unfurling behind him; next an ebony jackal, handsome and sleek – until settling on the numinous form of the lovely Ziva.

"You!" said Bluebeard, as understanding came to him. "I was right all along. You were the one who took my wives from me!"

"I returned their bodies to the earth and gave their souls peace. I whispered the truth to their families."

Bluebeard struck out at Ziva, but by the time his fist reached her she was nothing but smoke.

When she reappeared in corporeal form she was wielding a sword. The sword that Bluebeard had used to slay his wives.

"Mercy!" he cried as Ziva held him to her. "I beg you! Grant a fellow angel mercy!"

"You're no angel!" cried Ziva. "You have fallen! You're but a wretch who once had the love of God and then lusted for more. Your actions have condemned you!"

He tried wrenching himself free, but it was no good, she was stronger than him.

Panic welled within Bluebeard, he felt his bladder fail him and then an excruciating pain across his throat. Everything went dark.

When he came to, a rough hand hauled him up. "Ready for your second death?" said Ziva, the sword in her hand glinting in the torchlight.

Bluebeard gibbered and stumbled backwards, trying for the door again.

Ziva grabbed him and once again killed him.

Bluebeard died another four times. When Ziva breathed new life into him for the last time, he opened his eyes and then instantly closed them. "Is this the end?" he breathed. "If so, get it over with quickly."

"No, my sweet, it is not the end. It is only the beginning."

She put a shovel into his hand. "Now you must bury the bodies."

Bluebeard looked at the six dead bodies – bodies that were his – and slowly got to his feet.

Bluebeard spent the next six days at toil, digging graves in his garden. Ziva visited him occasionally, reminding him to make the graves deep. By the end of the week he was exhausted and utterly broken.

"Now?" he said when he saw her again. "Will you be taking me now?"

"No, not yet. As I said, this is only the beginning."

Guilt, having hitherto been unknown to Bluebeard, was even more excruciating than the blade at his throat. He kept to his bed and longed for death. But when he took matters into his own hands he learnt that suicide was an impossibility – Ziva would stay his hand and keep him alive to endure the pain of grief and remorse.

The families of his murdered wives banged at the castle door and shouted at him to come out. They demanded justice for their daughters. Bluebeard went to them, eager to meet his death at their hands, but when he did a great wind passed through the crowd and whispered to them that they must not touch Bluebeard. Justice had been done – was being done – and they must return to their homes, unsullied by revenge.

The families went, and Bluebeard once again took to his bed to be consumed by darkness.

Years passed and slowly Bluebeard began to stir. He let his servants go and distributed his wealth among the villagers. He began to garden, and found satisfaction working the earth, the honest soil planting itself in the creases of his hands.

Sometimes he would sit on a bench, a haggard, grey-bearded figure, and watch the sun set. At times, he almost felt something akin to peace. Occasionally, Ziva would join him. Bluebeard would always ask the same question. "Do you forgive me?" And she would always answer, "Yes."

On this occasion, Bluebeard also asked if he was nearing the end. He felt, in his heart, as though it was almost time.

"Almost, brother angel," said Ziva. "And then you will be reunited with your father. Our Father, who art in Heaven."

Bluebeard nodded, acceptance coming to him at last. "And all will be well?"

"Yes, my love. All will be well."

Umbilical

Tamara

Even before I got really ill, I could feel the first stirrings of growth in my abdomen, just beneath my belly button. The sensation tugged on my thoughts, telling me to phone Mum, to tell her that something was... wrong. But I couldn't. I'd been too absent, too adamant that I didn't need her in my life. Besides, she'd just make a fuss, and there was nothing I hated more than her sympathy. She'd never understood me; could never grasp how her clinginess had repelled me. As a teenager I hadn't ever wanted to talk to her about Dad, the divorce, or periods. I just wanted to be left alone. And since leaving uni and getting a job in the City there'd been no good reason to keep in contact. But now, the itch at my navel compelled me to call her. I picked up my phone.

Ruth

The moment I heard Tamara's voice I knew something was wrong. Actually, I'd been sure for a while that something was wrong, but I'd reasoned away my fears – those ancient, knowing whisperings arising from my womb – with the usual excuses: the menopause, getting old. This confirmed it. She was taking some time off work because she didn't feel well. She blamed her constant tiredness, her breathlessness, on her new management role; the long hours she'd been working, the nights she'd spent clubbing... She thought that maybe she was... anaemic? I told her to see a doctor as soon as she could, but I could tell she thought I was fussing. That's the thing about kids, though, isn't it? Until they have children themselves, they're not able to comprehend a parent's greatest fear: the death of a child.

Tamara

I cried like a baby when the doctor told me. I mean, twenty-somethings aren't supposed to get cancer, are they? Especially not an aggressive one, and with an unknown primary origin. It wasn't fair. This shouldn't have happened to me.

After I'd stopped blubbing, he talked me through the treatment I'd be getting, the fact that I'd need someone around to help. Did I have a partner? Family, friends? I put my hand to my t-shirt and itched at my belly button. I considered asking him about the weird skin growth that had appeared there in the last few weeks, but thought it something to do with the cancer. And this wasn't the time to be poring over every defect of my body. I stopped itching. I said I had my mum.

Ruth

What with Tamara being in and out of hospital I never got round to talking to a doctor about my constant bloatedness, the come-and-go ache at my womb. Besides, I didn't think I could face telling someone that something really strange was happening to my vagina. That it almost felt as if something was inside it. Me. And that it was growing. I hadn't had a smear test for ages, maybe that would've picked up the whatever-it-was. And sex... well, that too hadn't happened for years. The feeling wasn't unpleasant though, it was just a bit uncomfortable. Made sitting down awkward. But then came the dreadful news: Tamara's treatment wasn't working. This wasn't the time to be worrying about my own health.

Tamara

It's weird, isn't it? After years of *not* wanting to spend time with Mum, I can't bear to not have her beside me. Even for a moment. I get panicky when she leaves the room; ask her to keep talking to me when she goes down the landing to the loo. She eats all her meals at my bedside, looking guilty as she does so because I have no appetite. Because I weigh as much as I did when I was, like, 10. "You mustn't starve, you know," I say.

"I know," she says, but she eats quicker then, tears in her eyes. After she finishes, I feel that old pull at my gut, feel the cord of skin that has sprouted up and out of my belly button twisting itself into a thin rope. Extending. I hold her hand. I need to tell her about the cord.

Ruth

I hate being away from Tamara for even a minute, because I know she's only got days, weeks if we're very very lucky, to live. I eat beside her, sleep beside her; the only time we're apart is when I get some food, go to the toilet, or have a shower. Those last two things I do really quickly because of the fleshy cord that's coming out of my vagina. It dangles between my legs, chafes at my thighs. I know I need to tell someone about it, but I can't. A terrible thought, that I will deal with it *after*, occasionally skims pebble-like across my mind. But I can't think about *after*. I don't want there to be an *after*.

"I have to tell you something," Tamara begins. "Try not to freak out about it, but I have this, like, weird cord thing growing out of my belly button."

She lifts up her nightie and shows her mother, who then bursts into tears.

But after a moment or two, Ruth wipes her eyes and says, "I've got one too. Coming out of my, well… fanny."

Tamara can't help but laugh. It's strange hearing her mother say 'fanny'. Her mother laughs too, and for a moment there is no *later, then, after*, but only *now*.

"Will you lie down beside me?" Tamara asks. "Like you used to when I was little?"

"Of course," says Ruth.

She gets into the bed and slips her arm beneath Tamara's hairless head.

Tamara snuggles into her mother, the bedcovers over them, and they both know what's going to happen. Tamara thinks it should feel gross – this melding of the cord at her belly button with the cord that is coming out of her mother, but it isn't. It's the most *right* thing she's ever known. And the safest she's ever felt. She's warm too, and there's no more pain. There's just her mum. And, strangely, her mum's thoughts. Ruth's mind thrums with sadness, loss. She doesn't know how she'll go on *after*.

"You'll be all right," Tamara mumbles, suddenly feeling the welcome pull of sleep. "You've got your friends at the church. And that nice neighbour who keeps doing the shopping for us. You should make some time for him. When I'm gone."

Ruth can only cry. She remembers all the nights she spent as a new mum with Tamara in her arms – all that feeding, then burping, then rocking. At the time it had felt as though it would last forever. How wrong she'd been.

"Mum?"

"Yes, love?"

"I hope you don't need to pee anytime soon. Because it'd be a bit tricky, us connected like this."

Ruth laughs. "No, I'm all right." Her voice breaks as she says, "I'm going to stay here for as long as you want."

"Thanks, Mum."

They stay like that for some hours, in that liminal place, until Death anoints them both with her holy oil, and takes Tamara with her. Ruth knows the exact moment her daughter's gone, because straight after, the cord binding them together crumbles away from Tamara's belly button. And Ruth, alone, must cope with the contractions of her womb; the afterdeath, as black as bile, that will force itself out of her.

How to Honour a Beginning

The tall, tree-like being stepped out of his spacecraft and walked into the moonlit forest. He breathed deep of the Earth's oxygen-rich air. It was sweet with fresh growth and detritus, the cycle of life.

As he wove through the trees he placed a hand on each one and connected with it. *Go well*, was his message. And as he walked he sang an ancient song that stirred and invigorated each leaf, each branch, each stem, each root.

After a while he sensed the presence of others. He ended his song and stepped into a mossy hollow. There they were, the three magnificent women.

He looked from Baba Yaga, the brown, shrivelled crone, to the pale-faced Chernila – Mistress of All Stories – to the black-skinned Siren, her mighty wings glittering darkly.

"Greetings," said the alien being, addressing them all with a nod and broad smile. "And to what do I owe this honour?"

Baba Yaga cackled. "Still as formal as ever, eh? How 'bout a kiss?"

The crone stepped forwards, only to have Chernila, her ink-blue eyes round with displeasure, put out an arm to stop her. "This is neither the time nor the place," she hissed, flicking back her long, white hair.

"Isn't it?" said Baba Yaga with a grin. "Pity. Maybe later, though, eh?"

The viridian alien, all branch-like limbs and leaves, said nothing and did his best to look bemused. He would not be drawn into an argument.

"We are here," said the Siren, her lovely voice smoothing the tension between her two sisters, "because this is a beginning, and your stewardship of this planet must be honoured."

The alien looked up at the tips of the giant trees, the stars beyond them. "How long will the stewardship be for?" he asked, thinking of his faraway home.

"A long time," said Baba Yaga.

"This planet will have many ages," explained the Siren, her beguiling voice thrilling through the alien's every fibre. "It's already gone through a fair few, when trilobites ruled the oceans; the rise and fall of the lizard kings. But when the apes evolve –"

"It'll get exciting," concluded Baba Yaga, a grin splitting her wrinkled, nut-brown face.

"I have no desire for excitement," said the being.

"I know," said Baba Yaga. "Which is why you're the right man for the task."

The alien sighed. "Very well. And how is the occasion to be honoured?"

"With a fire," said Baba Yaga, her eyes sparking.

Dry twigs, dead branches and moss devoid of moisture flew together, forming a bonfire, flames licking its base.

"And food and wine," she added, conjuring up a feast for them. "Cups of mead and roasted deer. Grilled mushrooms as big as your head!"

"And there'll be stories," said Chernila.

"And song," said her sister, the Siren. "And dancing, when we can coax your friends, the dryads and he-nymphs, out of the forest."

The being took a cup of mead and drank from it, and then nodded, satisfied. This was a fine way to honour a beginning.

Soon enough, the deities of the forest were lured to the festivities by the song of the Siren. The feasting and storytelling, singing and dancing went on for a long time. Long enough for the ancient being to slip away with each of the three women in turn.

After he'd lain with each one he asked for a gift. "To help the Earth through its many future ages."

Baba Yaga cackled with glee and bestowed curiosity upon the humans-to-come. "A fine gift that – a gift of power. Though it'll most likely tear them apart. Still, it'll be entertaining."

Yes, thought the being. But for whom?

Chernila, as expected, gave the gift of stories. "They will help the humans and their descendants make sense of themselves and the world."

Then, considering the leaves that grew out of his body, his viridian skin, she also gave him a name. "You will be known as the Green Man. How does that sound?"

"Why man? I can become female when necessary."

"It's more straightforward that way. Besides, the human-apes will have a thing for patriarchs. The alpha male, you know."

The Green Man didn't know, but he liked the name.

And the Siren offered her song.

"For the humans, to inspire them?" asked the Green Man.

"For every living being," she said, kissing him one last time. "But also for you. To keep you from loneliness."

Loneliness? But as long as there were trees in this world he could never be lonely. And which species would be so cruel, so *stupid*, to clear a planet of trees?

After the feast was over and the women were gone, the Green Man returned to his spacecraft. "Set the ship to hibernation mode," he instructed the AI.

"Very well," it said. "But why?"

"Because we're going to be here for some time. Long enough for me to find my way into the legends of the evolving apes. Oh, and by the way, I've been given an Earthian name: the Green Man. Do you approve?"

The AI said nothing.

The Green Man chuckled. "It'll grow on you."

And the Green Man returned to the forest.

Minotaur/Mindtour

The labyrinth was nothing to look at. Installed within one of the space cruisers of the King's fleet, it was merely a vast empty dome with a beacon at its centre. The hollowed-out leather of a bull's head had been pulled over the metallic sphere atop the beacon's human-sized pole.

A tall young man put his hands to the dome's translucent surface, peered inwards at the distant beacon and then laughed. "Is that it? Is that what everyone's so afraid of – a mask on a stick?"

The young woman standing next to him glanced up at his name badge: *Theseus Three.* "Since the Minotaur was created it has killed thousands of humans. It is not to be underestimated."

The call of a bugle announced that the first two challengers of the season were to enter the labyrinth. Theseus Three and the woman turned to look at them. The first challenger – Theseus One – was a huge man covered in bulky armour with an enormous rifle slung over his shoulder. The other challenger – Theseus Two – was smaller, though equally heavily armoured. In her hand, a dagger.

The woman beside Theseus Three sighed and then shook her head. "They won't last twenty minutes in there."

A handful of spectators gave a lacklustre cheer. An old woman threw herself at the huge man, Theseus One. "Don't do it! Spare yourself! For the sake of your family, of your loved ones, don't do it!"

The man pushed her off and then entered the labyrinth.

The translucent, plasma-like dome became opaque and as milky-white as the eye of Zeus on a clear night.

"We can't watch?" asked Theseus Three.

The woman beside him shrugged. "You wouldn't want to see how the magic trick's done, would you?"

Theseus Three pressed his nose to the opaque plasma and then, failing to see anything, stepped away. All kinds of monsters could have been sent in there now. And no one would know.

"Besides," said the woman. "It's not fair on the challengers. They deserve a little dignity in death."

Just then the sound of gunfire rang out. After a few minutes a stretcher bearing challenger number one's dead body was carried out of the labyrinth.

"But that's impossible!" said Theseus Three.

The woman beside him gave a soft laugh. "The other challenger will be along shortly."

Before twenty minutes had elapsed, the woman – Theseus Two – had emerged from the labyrinth. Dead.

Theseus Three turned to the woman beside him. "You know how it works, don't you? Tell me how to defeat it!"

The woman's eyes darted from left to right. "You grew up in a dignity culture, didn't you?"

Theseus Three nodded.

"Just like that monster of a king who thinks himself God ever since he bargained with the Magi for peace. I suppose that's a good start. What's your real name?" she asked.

"Why d'you need to know?"

"Because I'd like to know."

"You'll never believe me."

The woman shot him a look of disgust then walked away.

"Stop! I'll tell."

The woman paused and waited for the challenger to come to her. "Go on," she said.

The man inhaled deeply. "My real name is Theseus."

The woman became round-eyed. Silently, she called to the man's anima. *Is this true?* she asked.

Yes, said his anima.

"Ha!" said the young woman, with a grin. "So at last a real Theseus has come to wrestle with the Minotaur."

"And I'll defeat it!" he said, standing tall. He paused. "With your help."

The woman eyed the tall young man curiously. He was a strange mix of ego and vulnerability. "Is that so?" she said.

While Theseus's ego communicated to her in spoken words – about how he was the most valiant of all the men of his realm; about how he longed to dethrone the cruel King Aristotos who had tempted his brothers and friends to the labyrinth, to their deaths – the woman silently addressed his anima. *He's full of conviction, that's obvious. And yet he will only succeed in destroying the Minotaur if he is strong enough. Are you strong enough?*

The invisible anima suddenly showed herself to the woman; she was a mass of swirling flames, her face ablaze with fiery determination. *I am strong enough. We are strong enough.*

The woman smiled. *Good.*

The anima faded and the woman once again spoke to Theseus. "Enough fine words! I will help you. Come!" she said, leading the way.

They went through many gloomy, twisting corridors within the underbelly of the space cruiser until they reached a small door with a wheel at its centre. The woman breathed on the sensor beside the door. There was a click and then she turned the large wheel. The heavy door creaked open and she stepped into the room. Theseus ducked on going through the doorway and then continued to stoop; the room hadn't been designed with his long-limbed race in mind.

In a corner sat an old woman, sewing. On seeing them enter, she stood and then bowed her head.

The young woman went to the crone and whispered something about readying her guards. "Spread the word," she said, her eyes on Theseus. "The time has come."

Theseus smirked. So this imperious young woman *did* believe he could defeat the Minotaur.

The old woman left in a hurry, shutting the door behind her.

"Wipe that smile off your face!" commanded the woman. "Hubris has been the downfall of many a contestant."

Theseus composed himself. "It's just good to know that you believe in me."

The woman didn't respond; instead she went to where the old woman had been sewing and rifled through the needles and thread.

"Are you left or right-handed?" she asked.

Theseus, confused, said that he was left-handed.

"Sit," said the woman, approaching him with a glowing needle and thread in her hands.

"What? Hold on, is that... wolfram?"

"I said sit!"

Theseus took a seat but kept his eyes on what was in the woman's hands.

"Put out your left arm. You need to be marked."

"How's that going to help me defeat the Minotaur? And how did you get hold of one of the most valuable materials in the universe?"

"My mother –"

"Hey! Are you sure you know how to use that thing?"

The woman laughed. "My mother is a star seamstress so, yes, I know how to use it."

"A star seamstress? You mean, she's Aristotos's wife? But that would make you Ria, the King's daughter."

"Stepdaughter. And I want him deposed as much as you do. So you can trust me. I know how you can defeat the Minotaur."

She reached for his left arm. "This will hurt. But only physically. And the more you resist the pain the greater it will be."

Theseus looked into Ria's violet eyes. "I trust you. Do it."

As the white-hot needle entered his skin he stifled a cry. Ria ignored him and continued with her work. He bit his tongue and turned his head, unable to watch.

"It's okay to cry," said Ria. "Besides, it's something you'll have to do in the labyrinth if you want to succeed."

Theseus didn't argue or question her. Nor did he cry. His ego forbade him such a display of weakness, and so he kept very still, pushing the pain that seared through his arm down into his gut. When he could stand it no longer, his anima rose up and commanded him to accept the pain and cry. The tears were a blessed relief.

There wasn't long until Theseus and the other challenger – Theseus Four – would be called to the labyrinth so, once Ria had finished marking him, they swiftly made their way back to the dome. Along the way she gave him instructions:

"First, you'll be taken to the waiting room and a Daedalus chip will be placed underneath the skin at the base of your skull. It communicates with the beacon. Don't try to get it out, you'll only end up dying of internal bleeding. Next, you'll go to the equipment room and be given your choice of armour and weapons. Don't take a single thing. Do you understand?"

"Nothing?" he asked.

"Nothing," she confirmed. "If you enter the labyrinth with so much as a spoon you'll die a horrible death."

Theseus nodded. "All right."

Silently, she addressed the anima. *Make sure he goes in empty-handed. This is very important.*

The anima promised.

Also, it gets harder the longer he stays in there. Try to get him through it as quickly as possible. The King may not be generous with his oxygen.

"And then what?" he asked.

"Then you'll enter the labyrinth. And I'll start praying."

Theseus looked down at his arm. It still throbbed with pain, but the skin appeared to be unblemished. "What about the marking? How's that going to help?"

"Wolfram has an exceptionally high sensitivity. The marking – my words – will show itself to you when you need it most."

Theseus paused as they emerged from one of the corridors and the vast, translucent dome came into view.

"And if," he took a deep breath, "I mean, *when*, I defeat the Minotaur... what happens then?"

"Leave that to me," said Ria.

Theseus did as Ria asked and left the equipment room empty-handed, though when he'd seen his fellow challenger, Theseus Four, equip himself with full body armour and a meduse machine gun he'd been sorely tempted to slip a knife into his pocket.

Don't you dare! his anima had hissed.

Outside, both he and Theseus Four were met by a few disinterested onlookers. They laughed when they saw that he wasn't carrying a weapon. "This is a first!" one of them said, smirking. "What are you equipped with, luck? You'll need it!"

Theseus stood tall and ignored them. Out of the corner of his eye he could see Ria. She nodded and gave him a thin smile of encouragement. Then both Theseus and the other challenger were inside the labyrinth and the trials had begun.

Theseus was being pressed on all sides by people, shouting and calling to each other, their cries desperate. A middle-aged woman tugged at his tunic. Her tear-stained face was somehow familiar. Someone – a child –

howled loudly, either in pain or grief; the keening tunnelled its way into his mind and grated on his nerves. He found himself being pushed this way and that by the crowd; the bull's head became distant and slipped out of view. He tried to force himself through the crowd but it was hard, hot work, and he wasn't making any progress. His stomach twisted with anxiety and he began to sweat. As he felt the crowd weighing down on him, his legs gave way and he found himself face to face with the crying woman. He recognised her – she was his mother!

"They're coming!" she said. "Try to get away!"

"What are you talking about?" asked Theseus, his heart pounding like mad. "Who's coming? The Minotaur?"

"The Magi. Run!"

Theseus felt himself being kicked and shoved; the crowd pressed down on him, made him fall into his mother and crush her. Theseus tried to stand but to no avail. The weight of people, the terrible anxiety, the worry – was his mother dead? – bore down on him and he became paralysed with panic. If only he had a weapon of some sort. He'd slash at them with a knife and make them move so that he could get some space, some air. Oh God, he could hardly breathe. His heart was beating erratically, like it might give up on him any moment, and his lungs were ready to burst. If he had a knife he'd slip it into his throat and kill the panic that way.

Just then came the sound of gunfire, and for a split-second his mother and all the people around him vanished and there was just the empty dome. And contestant number four sprawled on the ground. Dead.

Then all the people were there again with their insistent noise and weight, their shoving, their panic, once again filling him with the sense of being utterly trapped. Theseus continued to fight for breath.

"It's not real," Theseus tried saying to himself, remembering that only a moment ago the dome had been empty. "None of this is real. Get a grip and get moving!"

But Theseus couldn't get up. He felt his legs being stamped on, more weight on his back, and he knew that any second now he was going to be crushed to death. And he didn't care.

His anima arose. She spoke to Theseus in a calm, measured voice: *Slow your breathing. Focus on each breath.*

Theseus did as she said and he found the pain in his lungs lessening. Some of the weight on him lifted.

That's it! Calm yourself.

As he slowed his breathing the crowd began to thin. He was, at last, able to roll off the body of his mother who was, indeed, dead. Tears seeped from Theseus' eyes and then he remembered Ria's marking.

The small, neat stitches – made in wolfram-rich thread – glowed silver and read: *This too shall pass.*

Really? thought Theseus. *That's it? My mother is dead, and that's all the help she could give me?*

He closed his eyes and exhaled deeply. "I'm sorry," he said, more to himself than his mother. "I'm so sorry."

And when he next opened his eyes, his mother and most of the people had gone. Theseus could once again see the bull-headed beacon. But his mother was dead, so what did it matter? He sat there for a long time, numb. Eventually, he got up and then walked in the direction of the Minotaur. The remaining people faded away.

Theseus walked on, but without any warning it became dark. He stopped, unable to see a thing. Then two crescent moons came into view above a jagged outline of mountains. Stars appeared. There was the sound of running water in the distance, and behind him sly laughter.

Memories flashed across his mind, one of them kept recurring and stuck: his older cousins – brother and sister – taunting him about his height. *Aw, it's our baby cousin, off to the mountain gods to beg for the gift of growth.*

Theseus felt like a young boy again, unable to hold back his childish emotions. Shame flooded through his body and he crouched, his arms around his knees. Not now. He couldn't be dealing with this now.

He remembered turning and standing tall. *My father says I'll be as tall as him one day. When I'm grown up. Then I'll be a General like him and fight the Magi!*

So you admit that you're still a little boy? asked the girl.

Theseus didn't know how to answer. *No*, he began, *I'm just –*

Tell me, continued the girl, flicking her long hair, *are you little all over?*

The siblings approached him and he felt his heart drumming like crazy. But he stood his ground.

What do you mean? he said.

They told him to sit with them, to lie down with them; to show them how much of a man he was. And then they were touching him in places that he both did and didn't want to be touched; he found himself simultaneously thrilled and reviled by what their young adult hands and mouths were doing to him. And as his body climaxed and then released, covering his stomach in his own stickiness, the siblings backed away and then laughed at him.

Ew, you're disgusting! the girl sneered, her voice echoing around his head.

He felt sick with shame.

Don't you dare tell! hissed the brother.

Or we'll say that you were the one touching me, said the girl.

They ran off to leave the boy to his shame.

Theseus, crouching in the dome and frozen to the spot, wanted the memory gone. He shivered with sweat. But there it was again. And again. On loop. He looked at Ria's marking: *This too shall pass.* But it wasn't true, was it? This memory would always be with him. In here it was amplified; impossible to dismiss. Disgust flung him to the ground, made Theseus slam his head into the floor. Then the back of his head began to itch and he instinctively put his left hand to the itch. He felt for the chip beneath his skin and sunk his fingernails into the flesh. For a moment the memory was gone and he felt relief. But soon enough it was back again, flooding him with shame.

He scraped at the skin, and again he received respite. But not for long.

More scratching; this time his fingers came away wet with blood.

Stop it! cried his anima. *Otherwise you'll bleed to death.*

Theseus's hand hesitated, but then the memory was back and he felt compelled to yank at the flesh once more.

Please stop! begged his anima.

Theseus didn't stop.

What about the Minotaur? You're here to destroy it!

But Theseus was possessed by the memory and compelled to gain relief from it in any way he could.

What about Ria? The marking?

"It's useless," Theseus muttered. "Less than useless."

Again came the memory, the cousins and their taunts; the hungry look on their sly faces. As Theseus was about to pull at the flesh at the back of his neck again, his anima told him to get rid of it.

Get rid of what?

The marking. Or are you too weak, too childish, to do so?

For a moment he hesitated. Then he moved his left arm away from the chip at the base of his skull. With his weak hand, his right hand, he clumsily tore at the marked flesh of his left forearm, even managing to catch hold of one of the wolfram-rich threads. The pain of the act took his breath away and for a moment drove everything else from his mind.

Now walk.

Theseus instantly obeyed and, somehow, the memory stayed at the periphery of his consciousness.

That's it. You're going in the right direction. Away from the memory.

As he continued to walk his mind cleared and slowly the darkness lifted. It was just him, alone in the labyrinth with his shame, his face wet with tears.

The closer he got to the beacon the better he felt. In fact he felt amazing, euphoric. He could do this, he could defeat the Minotaur. He started to run. But the closer he got to the beacon the less it looked like it did before. It started to morph into something else and move, walk about. Like a human. Theseus slowed. But it wasn't any human, it was Sophia. His heart raced and his mouth became dry. He knew it couldn't actually be Sophia, the woman he'd loved with such an intense passion all those years ago, still, he longed to spend just a moment with her again, and so he went to her.

We're going the wrong way, hissed his anima. *That's not the way to the Minotaur!*

Theseus ignored her and caught up with Sophia.

The air was warm and he could hear the cry of seabirds. Sand stretched out before him and waves lapped at the beach he found himself walking on.

Sophia paused and smiled at him coyly. She lifted the thick braid of blonde hair that fell down her back over her shoulder. Toying with the wispy ends of it, she asked Theseus how he was.

Theseus took a deep breath. He'd gone through this conversation so many times in his head that he knew exactly what to say. He was fine. Doing well. In command of his own unit. But how about her?

Sophia sighed. "Things are... complicated."

His heart thrummed with excitement.

She told him that things were tricky between her and her husband. He didn't really understand her. She felt so trapped. Like life was all responsibilities and arguments. She wished things could be fun again. "Like they were when we were young..."

Sophia stopped walking and looked up at Theseus, her large, silver eyes mournful yet coquettish. Suddenly she squealed with excitement. "I know!" she said. She began to take off her tunic. "Let's go for a swim!"

And before Theseus had a chance to respond, she'd stripped off her clothes and rushed into the sea.

Theseus quickly pulled off his tunic.

Don't you dare follow her! said his anima. *She's like a siren. She'll lure you to your death.*

But Theseus, overwhelmed by desire, couldn't see any harm in having a little fun.

They waded through the shallows and splashed each other. Theseus tried to keep his greedy eyes off her naked body, but it was impossible. And what did it matter anyway? None of this was real, was it?

Sophia suddenly cried out. "Something bit me! It hurts!"

"Here, let me help," said Theseus, going to her.

She fell into his arms and lifted her leg out of the water.

"See," she said, pointing to a small gash of red.

Theseus could see, but he also knew it was nothing.

Sophia's lovely face was only inches away. It would be so easy to just...

Theseus! cried his anima. *This feels wrong! Don't you – we – have a wife?*

Theseus jerked his head back.

Yes, I remember now, said his anima. *You need to stop this!*

Theseus remembered now too. An image of his grief-stricken wife, her trembling fingers stroking the fine wool of a baby's hat, appeared before his mind's eye. A sob escaped his throat.

Sophia became like lead in his arms and her golden hair billowed upwards as the sand beneath her feet disappeared and she fell away from him, down, down into the fetid depths of the sea which was now more like oil than water. Theseus stumbled backwards, the air knocked out of his lungs. He shivered.

Grief enveloped him, filled his eyes and ears and mouth with its cloying emptiness, its awful weight. With perfect recall he remembered the message his wife had sent him through the cloud: *The Magi destroyed the hospital. Our baby was stillborn. Come home.*

He hadn't wanted to leave his unit; the new recruits were so young, so inexperienced, and besides, how could he comfort his wife when his mouth was thick with grief, his heart a stone?

They'd buried the child, but not their grief. It grew, forming a barrier of thorns between them. And when he'd returned to his unit most of his men were dead, massacred by the Magi. The bodies of his soldiers stared up at him, reproachful. *Why did you leave us when we needed you most?* the lifeless men called out.

Then the spectre of his father appeared by his side. "You'll be a great leader one day, son. King, maybe. But I fear you've inherited my one weakness"

"What do you mean?" Theseus asked.

"The melancholia. The infinite sadness. It will always be with you. Learn to embrace it. You'll have to if you want to defeat what's ahead."

Theseus willingly lay back in the oily sea and let himself be pulled down.

He's wrong, cried his anima. *It's not a weakness. It simply is what it is. And it does pass. It always passes. Remember the marking!*

But Theseus couldn't hear her. The awful heft of his sorrow had smothered her.

Hours passed. Theseus's full bladder emptied itself. He didn't care. What did it matter? What did any of it matter? His mother was dead. His father was dead. His soldiers were dead. His dear, sweet son was dead. His wife no longer wanted to know him. His breathing became ragged.

His anima, cut off from him, didn't know how to get through to Theseus. She needed to be louder, much louder. Though she spoke to him with all her might, he still couldn't hear her.

She needed another voice. Two voices, three. The voices of the whole dignity culture. The collective unconscious.

That was it!

She called to her brothers and sisters of the individuals that made up Theseus's society. And they came, and they roared.

Wake, Theseus! Wake!

As Theseus began to rouse, his anima told him to arise. *The marking on your forearm is right. This too shall pass.*

Theseus looked down at his arm and saw that it was glowing. It spread warmth around his body, gave him the energy to sit up.

Now, get up, his anima commanded. *And start walking. You don't have to go far. Just start with a few steps.*

Theseus stood and took a few faltering steps. "I can't do it," he muttered.

You can and you will, said his anima.

So Theseus did.

Drop by heavy drop, the oily water fell from his body.

The Minotaur was only a short distance away. A few dozen strides, at most. But Theseus paused. He knew there'd be one last test.

"I don't want to," he said, shaking his head. He didn't want to ever again experience what he'd just now been through.

One last challenge, said his anima. *You're strong enough. We're strong enough. It's just one more thing to get through and then we'll have defeated the Minotaur. And you'll be King. Able to govern justly. You can end the cruelty of the labyrinth.*

Theseus took a deep breath and then stepped forward.

Ghostly faces rushed at him, bringing with them feelings of regret and guilt. Some of the spectres were women with whom he'd had relationships. He'd hurt every one of them, but justified each harmful act of self-interest with the excuse of his past, because of what had been done to him as a child. Shame flooded through him.

Then there were the faces of those whom he'd hurt with words; the venom of his barbed insults making his gut twist with regret.

Last came the civilians, the soldiers. The thousands of humans who'd died in the labyrinth.

The weight of the guilt made Theseus gasp and fall to his knees.

He looked up and saw the Minotaur ahead of him. Its bull head was changing again. It became the head of a Magus and began to speak to him:

"You've called for a truce. Very well. We're not averse to the idea of negotiations. What do you propose?"

Words issued from him. "You've abducted and killed so many humans." Theseus tried to keep the anger out of his voice, yet he felt sick with rage and fear. This was the one chance he had to stop the violence, the never-ending battles. What if he failed? He inhaled deeply, trying to keep his voice level. "Why?"

The Magus laughed. "I don't like open-ended questions. Still. Unlike all the greater species and more advanced beings – the AIs, the Norganics – your mental weakness and seemingly random behaviour makes for fascinating research. We've been studying you, though I admit the macro research – how large swathes of you humans respond to aggression – has only given us a limited amount of data."

Theseus's mind opened to this new knowledge and he frantically searched for solutions.

"So it's information you want? About how we function?" Theseus asked.

"Yes."

Theseus wanted to say something about ethics but then thought better of it. Think, he told himself. What, after all these decades, did they know about the giant Magi? What was their weakness? They had none. They'd tried every kind of weapon against them.

At the edges of his memory something fluttered, just out of reach. He suddenly realised what these memories were: bedtime stories and old wives' tales.

"Well," Theseus said, "let's just say that your research is… unpalatable to us. We want it to stop."

The Magus laughed. "The research won't stop until we get the information we need."

They were at an impasse. Theseus felt the seed of panic growing in his chest and tried to calm himself. The stories were again in his ear. Of the old, old gods. How they overthrew the Gigantes with their tools of war: the shield, the staff, the thunderbolt, the arrows. Then there were the current rumours of a felled Magus, wolfram buried deep in its mountain-sized heart.

"We are amassing our supplies of wolfram," Theseus hazarded, watching the face of the Magus closely.

There it was: the momentary shudder of fear. His bluff had worked.

"So," Theseus continued, "I suggest that your research comes to an end."

The Magus eyed Theseus. "How about we study individual humans instead? In a series of tailored experiments? Mindtours. The battles would stop, and we'd still get the data we need."

"How about you just stop altogether?"

The Magus threw back its gigantic head and then roared at Theseus. "We could wipe out your entire corner of the galaxy – the whole galaxy – if we so wanted!"

Fear sheared through Theseus as the monstrous words reverberated through his body, but he stood his ground.

"How many do you want to study?" he asked quietly.

"A billion."

"No!" Theseus spat. "One hundred." He tried to push the image of sending one hundred humans to their deaths out of his mind.

"A million."

"No." Theseus took a deep breath. "One thousand."

"A million."

"One thousand."

"One hundred thousand."

"One thousand."

The Magus glared at Theseus.

"Ten thousand," said Theseus through gritted teeth.

"One hundred thousand."

"Ten thousand."

The Magus sighed. "This is getting tedious. Very well."

"And you promise to stop at ten thousand?"

The Magi claimed to be of an honour culture – though there was nothing honourable about their experiments – so Theseus pressed him on this. "And then you'll leave us alone for good?" said Theseus. "Do you promise?"

"Yes," said the Magus. "As long as you do not breathe a word of this to anyone."

Theseus thought for a moment. The bargain as it stood was bad enough, but the added secrecy made it even worse. And all because the Magi saw any concession to an enemy as an abominable weakness. "What happens if I die, or get deposed because of your 'experiment'?"

"Then we'll start all over again. With another ten thousand."

Theseus nodded slowly, felt the weight of the secret agreement settling on his shoulders. "Very well."

The head of the Magus disappeared. The memory receded and Theseus was all by himself in the dome, the static beacon of the Minotaur only a short distance away.

Go to it! said Theseus's anima. *Take hold of the bull's head and destroy it.*

Theseus hesitated.

Do it!

Confused, Theseus wondered about what he'd just experienced. Was it truth, or fiction?

Do it!

Theseus rushed to the head which was once again morphing and changing. It began to expand and pulse with immeasurably dense, invisible matter. Theseus knew what it was. It was a singularity. The God point. For an instant he thought he saw a face within the mass, the mouth a giant yawp. Was it God? Or the face of a Magus? Gigantic hands – or were they branes? – flew through the void and as they clapped together the point exploded, expelling matter and heat and force.

Theseus flew backwards, the heat flowing through and around him. The pressure was immense and he gasped for air, thinking that surely this was the end. Yet it was not. The pressure reduced and he shivered as he felt himself cooling. There was movement around him, an invisible swirling, and out of that swirling came gas, which then clumped together to form clouds. Out of the clouds stars were born.

Theseus understood what he was witnessing. It was the birth of a universe, possibly *his* universe. And it was beautiful. Stars grew bigger and more numerous, drawing planets to them. Galaxies were created. He sat up and looked on in awe as the universe expanded, numinous before him.

Then the melancholy was back, just like before, but somehow bigger and more folded in on itself; the dull, oily heaviness expanding from deep within his heart. How small he was. How impossibly small and inconsequential. He was too small to contain this infinitely heavy mass.

Galaxies began to move away from each other and drift apart. Everything was coming undone and unravelling. The God point was now a filthy, grinning rictus, a dirty great black hole sucking nearby planets into its greedy mouth.

Theseus looked at his forearm and saw the words *This too shall pass* glowing. The letters loosened themselves from his skin and floated away, a meaningless jumble. His thoughts, too, drifted apart. His anima attempted to call out to him, but Theseus didn't respond. He was coming apart, just like the universe, his mind unravelling.

Theseus began to laugh, feeling madness upon him. He stood and then ran towards the giant yawp, the monstrous black hole. He would throw himself into it. End it all. But as he came closer, it began to morph and change once more. Into a human. Recognition dawned on him, and his mind started to come together again, his anima deftly weaving all the fragments together and putting them back in place.

The universe around him vanished. He was in the labyrinth, all alone. Facing the Minotaur, who was himself. Theseus shuddered. The final test.

Kill it! cried his anima. *Kill the illusion the Minotaur has created and be done with it!*

But how to kill oneself? Theseus closed his eyes and put his hands to the being's neck. He squeezed and squeezed but there was no give in the metallic throat. He let go, panting, his eyes still closed. He couldn't do it. He wasn't strong enough.

The thread! said his anima.

Before Theseus could stop to think about the pain he pulled the thread from his forearm, the heat excruciating, and then wrapped it around the Minotaur's head and began to pull. The thread went through the metallic neck as though it were molten. At the last moment he opened his eyes to see his own head fall to the ground and turn into that of the Minotaur's.

Theseus fell to his knees, utterly broken.

Arms were lifting him and carrying him. Ria was in his ear. "You've done it! I hoped you would, but I wasn't sure."

"I…" said Theseus, his voice hoarse, remembering who he truly was. His parents weren't dead; he'd seen them only a short while ago. He thought of his childhood – he'd never been abused. And he didn't have a wife, had never had a wife, or a child, and he'd never been in love with a woman called Sophia. "I'm remembering…"

"Shush, there's no need to speak. I'll get you food and water. You've been in there a long time. Inside the King's filthy mind. But he's coming now. This is the moment of triumph. Leave the talking to me."

"They weren't my thoughts," said Theseus. "Nor my memories? None of them?"

Ria snorted. "That wouldn't be much of a test, would it? But touring through someone else's mind – especially someone as fundamentally broken as the King – is another matter. I wouldn't do it."

A bugle announced the King's arrival, and Ria, surrounded by a number of royal guards and emboldened by Theseus's win, proclaimed that King Aristotos's reign was at an end. She lifted Theseus's heavy arm. "There is a new king. King Theseus!"

"Is that so?" said Aristotos, his eyes full of sorrow. "Give me a moment with this challenger."

Ria was loath to step away, but she did – there were enough guards and onlookers about to ensure Theseus's safety.

The King put his mouth to Theseus's ear. "You are challenger number 9942. Only 58 away from 10,000," he whispered. "Ever so close to such a big number."

Theseus once again saw the Magus in front of him and remembered their bargain:

What happens if I die, or get deposed because of your "experiment"?
Then we'll start all over again. With another ten thousand.

"You understand?" asked the King.

Theseus slowly nodded. A single tear ran down his face.

Aristotos took the wolfram thread out of Theseus's hand and then turned to Ria, his face grim. She stared back at him, undaunted.

Aristotos pocketed the thread and went back to the safety of his own guards. "The challenger entered the labyrinth with no weapon, but it appears that he was not unarmed. He had concealed a mighty weapon within his body." The King glared at Ria. "Let it be known that this is against the rules! Those colluding with him will be punished."

"But he destroyed the Minotaur. That's all that matters!" argued Ria.

The King forced a smile, then addressed the crowd. "But as I am a generous man, I will let the matter drop. This challenger has, indeed, done well to destroy the Minotaur and escape the labyrinth. And as I have promised, any challenger who defeats the Minotaur shall be King. If he so wants."

Ria grinned.

The King clicked his fingers. Two footmen appeared; one was holding a cushion on which there was a crown – the King's coronet – and the other was holding a goblet which was full of a red liquid.

"But Theseus may not want to be King," he said. "He may not relish the deathly weight of the crown. The burden of leadership. It may, in fact, be the last thing he desires. You see, the Minotaur has the ability to break people, to go on breaking people for the rest of their lives." The King considered the goblet. "Instead, Theseus may want a swift release from the horrors of the labyrinth by drinking of the poisoned wine. He may choose oblivion, if he so wants. The comfort of death."

Theseus was silent, unmoving.

"Take the crown!" urged Ria. "Take it!"

Theseus went forward, but instead of lifting the crown he picked up the goblet.

"No!" cried Ria. "Don't drink it!"

Theseus put the goblet to his lips.

This is madness! Weakness! cried Ria's animus, calling to Theseus's anima. *Be strong! Let go of the goblet and take up your crown.*

Theseus had no need of speaking with Ria. His anima spoke to her instead. *We are stronger than you can ever imagine. And we are doing the right thing.*

And Theseus drank.

Delphine as Daedalus

Anxiety skitters through me, making my restless fingers seek out something to worry over, be it the skin around my nails or the dozens of rubber bracelets my wrists are thick with. I want to draw something, but I fight the urge to pull out my sketchbook – I may reveal something in an unguarded moment of creativity. At last, the Inspector comes in and sits down in the chair opposite me. I stop my fiddling and instead cross my arms.

"I hope you don't mind us being in this interview room," he says. "The station's pretty busy at the moment and this is one of the few places in which I can hear myself think."

I shrug my shoulders. "It's fine."

"So…" he begins, setting his tablet on the table and then propping it up between us, "let's make a start." He taps the screen and I guess he's putting in a number or a password. Logging our meeting. "This is Inspector Zulfiqar, taking a statement from Brigid O'Reilly about the death of her great-grandmother, Delphine Waterhouse."

There is a pause as the Inspector turns the tablet towards me a little. I see that it has already transposed what he's said, and I realise that in a moment my words will be there forever; my lies square-cut, brilliant.

"Let's go right back to the beginning, Brigid. When did you make contact with Delphine? And why?"

I take a deep breath and concentrate on the answer I need to give him. In my mind I see the words in charcoal, on a cream-coloured canvas.

"It was in April, just after my birthday." I pause before continuing with my prepared speech. "It is one thing to have freckles, quite another to have moles."

Zulfiqar's eyes focus on the band of freckles across my nose and cheeks, and I am glad he has consciously registered them. I can almost see the assumption in his mind: *Red hair, freckled, virtually no chance of being a Longev.*

"Freckles won't give you a long life," I continue, "but moles will. Everybody knows this. Which is why I sought out my great-grandmother. I wanted to know what it was like to be in her skin. Her mole-covered skin. And I had an urge to paint her. She would be an interesting subject."

I do not say that I also longed to show her the real me; the secret me. I needed to hear comfort from her, to know that maybe my life was worth living, because so far all I had known was fear. Fear of discovery. The fear that one day someone would find out that moles were blooming on my skin and report me to the Longevity Authority. And, of course, there was the loneliness.

"I see," says the Inspector. "So it was curiosity, mainly, that made you seek Delphine out?"

I nod.

Zulfiqar – I wonder what his first name is – looks at me with inquisitive eyes. He has beautiful eyes; they are sepia-coloured, the lashes long.

"Yes, it was mainly curiosity." I remind myself to not prattle on. To be concise in my responses. Neat. To never scribble over the lines. "My mother sometimes spoke about Delphine, but I'd only met her once or twice before. As a child."

I do not tell him that the problem of *What to do with Delphine* hung like a yoke around my mother's neck, and that even as a young child I sensed the unease with which she had signed her over to the Longevity Study Centre. *Can't we look after her?* I had asked. *Just like Granny did?*

No, Brigid, she had said, shaking her head, her jaw clenched. *I can't afford to be her carer. I've already got a full-time job, and you, and this house, to look after. Now that Granny's died, Delphine will have to be looked after by the nice people in Bristol who know about what especially old people, like Delphine, need.*

My mother had suddenly hugged me, fiercely.

I'm sorry, Brigid, she'd whispered, stroking my hair. *This has been a really tough time for you. For me. For all of us. What with uncle Paul's sui – well, accident – and then Granny's fall. She went too soon. And it wasn't fair. She was still so full of life.*

She'd let out a sob.

But the specialists will make sure Delphine's okay. She'll be okay, she had reiterated.

She'd then pulled away from me, a tremulous smile on her tear-stained face, her hands gripping hold of my arms as though I was the only thing keeping her tethered to the world. *Everything's going to be okay.*

But her fearful eyes told me another story.

"So how did you find her, when you got to the Longevity Study Centre?" asks Zulfiqar. "I mean, was she lucid? Mentally sound?"

I would like to lie to Zulfiqar, to tell him that she was *mentally unsound* – it would certainly put me in the clear – but I do not wish for anyone, even a police inspector who never knew her, to think of Delphine as a mad old lady. Demented.

"She was… sometimes slow to respond. It took her a while to remember certain things, but she still had a keen mind."

"I see. And how physically capable was she?"

"She walked a little every day. She insisted on it. And she managed it, with only a bit of help. But for the most part she was bound to her wheelchair and bed. She had no problem feeding herself, although she let her nurse wash and dress her."

"And how were her spirits?"

"She was fine," I say cautiously. "I mean, as fine as it's possible to be for a 145-year-old. I didn't really have anyone to compare her to."

I do not tell him that the sorrow in Delphine's eyes was palpable. I do not mention the way she clutched my hand when her nurse left us for a moment. Her voice came out as a croak. *I am a prisoner here,* she had said. *Have you come to rescue me?*

I hadn't known what to say. Confused, I'd looked into her beseeching eyes and stared in fascinated horror – even her eyelids were covered in moles.

Then the nurse had returned and Delphine let go of my hand. I cleared my throat and suddenly said, *Yes* in a bright voice.

What's that, dear? the nurse had asked. *I don't want to miss out on anything exciting.*

I hadn't liked the way she'd looked at Delphine; there'd been both meaning and menace in her eyes.

I was just explaining to Delphine that I'm an artist and that, yes, I would very much like to paint a portrait of her.

My, my, how wonderful! the nurse had said. *Whatever next? Maybe we'll be having a sculptor come and visit soon.*

She'd then bustled out of the room, her smirks trailing after her, and Delphine once more took hold of my hand.

Tell me, dear. What do you think of this painting? And she indicated that I should open the drawer of her bedside cabinet.

I did as she'd asked and pulled out a print of Charles Paul Landon's 'Daedalus and Icarus'.

I said it was remarkable; the light and half-light beautifully rendered, the skin tones exquisite.

They were escaping their prison. She inhaled deeply. *Do you understand?*

I nodded. *But where can we talk in private?*

The garden. It is the only place that they leave me in peace, if only for a while. You must paint me there.

"What about the others in the Centre?" asks Zulfiqar, breaking into my thoughts. "You say you had no one else to compare Delphine's emotional state to and yet her nurse said you sometimes spoke to two of Delphine's neighbours at the Centre – Barry and Edith. How did they seem to you?"

I unfold my arms and begin to fiddle with my rubber bracelets again. They cover most of my forearms and rolling each one between my forefinger and thumb is a perfect way to distract myself. I must stay calm. And I must look as though I have nothing to hide.

"Barry and Edith, as they told me frequently, were thirty years younger than Delphine. So they weren't exactly her peers."

"Yes, but how did they seem?"

"Fine. Happy. But they were more tech-savvy than Delphine. Unlike her, they still used their phones, you know, to look things up or to message their relatives at the permitted times. They even insisted on taking my number so that they could call me – they said they'd try to get Delphine to talk to me on the phone, but she never did. She was just… I mean, she just hated anything that she called 'modern'. She still wore a watch. It was a real beauty of a watch, but it took time and effort to wind every day. Yet she did it. Every single day. I found that kind of sweet…"

I want to tell Zulfiqar about the other anachronisms of Delphine's life; the things that had made me love her. For I knew that my art, my love of paint and ink and paper, made me an anachronism too. But by the impatience on his face I know that he wants me to focus on the others, the other lab rats. Those who were too content, or too stupid, to realise that they were trapped and being experimented on.

"Also," I say, "Barry and Edith enjoyed using their Dream Machines. According to Delphine, they spent a lot of their time attached to them."

"Delphine didn't use her Dream Machine?"

"No."

"Do you know why?"

I pause as I reimagine the words I must say to Zulfiqar, beautiful Zulfiqar, with his flawless skin, who'd never be able to understand how horrible it is to live in a skin covered in moles. It's a life spent in hiding from those who wish to sign us Longevs up for 'monitoring'. For though no one ever dares say anything against monitoring, every Longev knows it's something to be feared.

I close my eyes for a moment and once again see the words I must say. As before, they are written in charcoal on a cream canvas, although now I have begun to cover the canvas with a pale wash of one of my favourite shades of brown, burnt umber – the colour of Zulfiqar's skin.

I breathe deeply. "Delphine said that she didn't find the Dream Machine restful. It didn't work well for her."

"She wasn't suggestible enough? The dream manipulation didn't work?"

I shake my head. "I –"

"Did they adjust the settings?"

"I... I think so. I'm sure they tried. But..."

"Yes?" says Zulfiqar, eager to hear what I have to say. This is a line of enquiry that interests him. He leans towards me; his eyes keen and his brow furrowed.

"Only, Delphine wasn't really sleeping. Just dozing, you know, and..." I pause. "She said she didn't like to use it," I say, pathetically, knowing that this is just the kind of weak response that Zulfiqar will want to pull apart and unravel. But I cannot tell him what Delphine told me, out in the garden, when I first began to paint her: *The Dream Machines are a way of controlling us here. They sedate us and silence us. They make our questions, our very thoughts, cease. For it is much easier to study lab rats when they are pliable, passive, and not always bent on escape.*

A lab rat, I had said, feeling sick. *Is that really what you are?*

Of course I am! The scientists have known for a long time that the nucleotides at the ends of our DNA — the telomeres — decide our lifespan. And that we Longevs, with our long telomeres that make us mole-ridden and naturally immune to all kinds of cancers, are the key to longevity. So they use us and take from our bodies, in order to discover the secret to immortality.

Yes, Delphine had said. *I'm a lab rat all right. Only, with your help, this old rat is going to escape.*

Strangely, Zulfiqar does not continue this line of questioning. He leans back in his chair and sighs.

"Okay," he says, suddenly folding his arms. "Let's move on to your little outing. And the day of Delphine's death. Were you the one who suggested she go out for the day?"

"No. Well…" I shake my head. "She wanted to see the sea again. To visit Cornwall, where she'd spent many happy holidays. The staff at the Centre had tried to get her to dream her way there instead, but it hadn't worked. Like I said, she wasn't good with her Dream Machine. I merely said I'd be happy to take her to Hoblyn's Cove, which is where she wanted to go."

Just get me there, Delphine had said. *And leave the rest to me.*

Won't they make someone come with us though?

Of course they will! she had said with a smile. *I am counting on them doing so.*

"Okay," says Zulfiqar. "So she was intent on this trip down memory lane. And you wanted to help."

"Yes. She was looking forward to being there. *Really* being there, as opposed to dreaming of being there."

I hazard saying something controversial: "After all, isn't there something powerful, unfathomable, in the sense of touch? It offers something vastly more than a Dream Machine, doesn't it?"

I take a risk and put my arm on the table in front of me. I place my fingers on one of Zulfiqar's hands. He is unsettled but lets my fingers rest there for a moment. Then he pulls his hand away and quickly stands.

"Coffee!" he says, "I need a coffee. Do you want one?"

Chastened, my hand automatically returns to my lap and I mutter a "yes" as he leaves the table, tapping at the tablet to pause the transcriber.

In the few minutes that I am alone I berate myself for being so clumsy, so obvious, and I try to re-focus.

When Zulfiqar returns with two plastic cups of scorching-hot coffee, he is once more composed; business-like and professional. He smiles at me and I see that he is willing to forget my stupid attempt at intimacy.

He passes me my coffee and turns the transcriber back on.

"And on this outing," he begins, "you had one of the nurses from the centre, a Mark Ingall, accompany you."

"Yes." I try to take a sip of coffee and then think better of it. It will burn my deceitful tongue.

"I had offered to drive Delphine down to Cornwall by myself, but the manager of the Centre was adamant that Mark should come."

"And was Delphine put out by this?"

"No," I say, glad to say something wholly truthful. "She was glad that Mark would be driving. She said it made it less of a chore for me."

"And on the day before the trip did she say anything of import? I mean, did she give you any idea that she had an ulterior motive for going on the trip?"

"No," I say, focussing on the fabric of Zulfiqar's sandy-coloured shirt; it's almost the same colour as the cliffs of Hoblyn's Cove when illuminated by the rays of the setting sun. In my mind's eye I begin to add the cliffs to my painting, which I will entitle, 'Delphine as Daedalus'. I consider how to give the cliffs some texture. I do not tell Zulfiqar that the day before our trip, Delphine's last day at the Centre, she told me of her plan.

You understand, my dear, that my escape is not just from the Centre, but from life itself?

I had nodded, and tried my best not to cry.

Are you sure? I had asked. *Are you sure this is what you want?*

Yes, she had said. *I've been sure for the past twenty years. I once told your mother but she pretended not to understand.*

Poor Mum, I had thought. *Scared for Delphine, scared for me. Incapacitated by fear.*

I didn't want to be like her. And so I revealed my terrible secret. Nervously glancing left and right, checking that we were unobserved, I lifted up my top for a moment so that Delphine could see my stomach. My mole-covered stomach.

Delphine had winced at the sight. *I am sorry. I had hoped that you'd be one of the lucky ones – unlike Paul and Beatrice – who didn't inherit my telomeres. Poor Bea. She'd have been here with me now, if she hadn't fallen down those stairs and cracked her skull open. Mind you, compared with the living death she would have had here... it is better that she died when she did.*

She had then gripped my hand, her gold watch glinting in the sun. *Brigid, you are right to hide what you are. Keep it a secret, for as long as possible, otherwise your life won't be worth living. Immortality – the kind that means you witness the slow decline and death of your husband and the deaths of children and the suicide of a grandson – really isn't worth it. And what the scientists tell the public, that through the studies of us Longevs there will be eternal life for all – is nothing but the worst kind of lie. Or nightmare. Us humans simply have to stop. We can't go on forever. It isn't right.*

"Talk me through the day of the trip," Zulfiqar says.

"Well…" I begin, collecting my thoughts, "I arrived at the Centre in the morning, just after nine, and then I helped Mark get Delphine into her wheelchair and then out of the Centre and into the car.

"It took us a couple of hours to go down the M5 and then across the north coast of Cornwall, along the winding B roads. We got to Hoblyn's Cove at about lunchtime. I'd packed a picnic and so I carried the basket, and the rest of our things, down to the beach, while Mark carried Delphine along the steep cliff path and then down the steps onto the beach.

"When we got to the beach, Mark called the Centre to let them know we'd got there safely and I unpacked the picnic. It was a lovely day. Really lovely. It was sunny and warm and not too windy, and there was hardly anyone there. A family, a few couples and the odd dog walker.

"We ate the picnic, and then Delphine had a doze. Mark had brought his trunks and so he took the opportunity to have a swim. He wasn't gone for long."

"What about you?" asks Zulfiqar. "Did you swim?"

"No," I say, shaking my head and willing my cheeks not to burn; but I am powerless to stop myself from blushing and Zulfiqar sees my discomfort.

"You're not a swimmer?" he says, his voice kind.

"I burn easily. And I'm not one for applying those sunscreens continuously. They always come off in the water, no matter what it says on the bottle."

"Of course," says Zulfiqar, noting again my ivory face, my freckled and fawn-like skin.

"But I paddled for a bit when Mark came back. I climbed the rocks and peered into the rock pools, just like I did when I was a child. When I saw that Delphine had stirred I went to her. She said she wanted an ice-cream and asked Mark to get us one each. While Mark went back up to the car park, to the ice-cream van, I took Delphine for a stroll along the beach."

I do not tell Zulfiqar that this was the moment I expected Delphine to leave us. *Let me go, Brigid,* she had said. *Just by these rocks. I can manage from here.* The water was at our shins, the tide pulling at the shifting sand, strong, treacherous. *Go back to where our things are. On the pretence of fetching me something. A different hat. I do not want you to be accused of assisting me and getting into trouble.*

And so I let go of her and walked to where our things were. I took my time searching our bags for the hat, and then I turned around, expecting her to be gone; willingly swallowed by the sea. Instead, I saw a young woman in a swimsuit helping her up and out of the water. I ran to them, hat in hand. *She's all right,* the woman had said. *What happened?* I had asked, shocked, defeated. *She took a bit of a tumble, that's all. Must've lost her footing. Could've drowned, if I hadn't seen her.*

Delphine, bedraggled, her white linen clothes soaked through, also looked defeated. *Thank you,* was all I could manage. *Thank you.* And I had taken Delphine back to where our things were. A short while later Mark had arrived with our ice-creams.

"And after the stroll, what did you do?" Zulfiqar asks.

"We ate our ice-creams and then I read a little to Delphine. From one of her precious hardbacks. She had another doze and then we started to pack up our things."

"How many people were left on the beach?"

"We were the last by the time Mark had carried her up the steps. The tide was coming in."

"And when you got to the top of the cliff?"

"We all sat on a bench and looked at the view. Delphine said she wished she could eat her tea there. Fish and chips. Just like when she was a girl. Mark said we should be getting back; that we could eat our leftovers in the car. Then he went to the car with all our things. So I just sat there with her, holding her hand."

I do not tell Zulfiqar that for the first time since I'd known her, Delphine had a peaceful look about her. *It's been a beautiful day, Brigid. Thank you for being here with me.* Tears had begun to well in my eyes. *I'm sorry,* I had said. *I'm sorry for failing you.* And Delphine had smiled, forgiveness on her face, and then looked down at her watch. *It's nearly six o'clock. Almost the end of visiting hours at the Centre. They'll be having their tea soon. Then getting hooked up to the Dream Machines.*

"And then?" asks Zulfiqar, startling me. I wipe away a tear that has, in secret, fallen down my cheek.

"Mark had called out to me, to tell me that my phone, which was in my bag, was ringing. So I went to the car to get it, and he went to Delphine. But then *his* phone started to ring. He hung back to take the call, and while I was rummaging in my bag I heard him cry out."

"Where was he then?"

"At the edge of the cliff, peering over."

"And Delphine gone?"

"Yes," I say, my voice hoarse. "I rushed over to where Mark was, but I couldn't see anything either. Only the rocks and the sea and the foam."

I close my eyes to see the picture better. Delphine is flying like Daedalus, her white linen scarves streaming after her. *This* is the instant I will capture in my painting; she will be a winged being, a blurred figure in white, fleeing from captivity.

"And did she do this on purpose? Did she take her own life, or was it an accident?"

I open my eyes and wipe away another tear. "I don't know," I say.

Don't tell them, she had said. *If they ask. If they know I got away with it, the others in the Centre will be watched ever more carefully. They'll suffer even more. But if it's an accident…*

68

But Mark will lose his job, I'd replied. *And they'll never let anyone out again. But at least they'll leave you alone. And still, the question mark over the case will make some decent folk ask some penetrating questions of the managers of the Centre.*

I take out a tissue from my bag and wipe my eyes. "I don't know exactly what happened," I reassert. "Delphine was happy. We'd had a lovely day. It had been really good for her to get out. And there on that bench, she was the happiest she'd been since I first saw her at the Centre. You know, it's not right for humans to be cooped up all day every day. They need to get out, sometimes. To spread their wings."

"And fly?" says Zulfiqar.

Confused, I shake my head and pick up my coffee cup. I take a sip, but it's still so hot it burns my tongue. I hastily put the cup down and as I do so it tips over and spills onto Zulfiqar's arm. He swears and then clutches at his soggy sleeve. I apologise over and over as I get some tissues from my handbag. I pass him one and begin to mop up the spill.

"Don't worry," he says, dabbing at his shirt with a tissue. "I'm okay. It was an accident."

I nod, my cheeks burning, and then pick up the coffee cup and gulp down the rest of the coffee. It still burns, but I do not care.

"Well, that about brings things to a close, I think," says Zulfiqar. "Without more definitive evidence, Delphine's death will be recorded as being through misadventure."

I sigh, suddenly realising how emotionally drained I am. I do not know what outcome I was hoping for; what would have satisfied me, but somehow it does not matter any more. All that matters is that I will, most likely, never see Zulfiqar again.

Zulfiqar turns the transcriber off and stands up.

"That's all, Brigid. All done. You can go home now."

I pick up my handbag and then stand, defeated, my eyes full of tears.

As I step away from the table Zulfiqar asks me if I take commissions.

Confused, I say, "What do you mean?"

"Portraits. I've always wanted to get one done, and I thought that maybe you could paint me. The one you did of Delphine, the one hanging in Barry and Edith's room... I saw it, and I was impressed."

69

"Yes," I say, smiling through my tears. "I could do that. I would like that very much."

And although I figure he must have my details already, I take one of my artist trading cards from my bag and hold it out to him.

"Just out of interest, who was it that phoned, when Delphine was on the bench?"

"Oh," I say, "it was Edith. Wondering how Delphine was."

"And you know who phoned Mark at the same time?"

"I never asked."

"Barry," he says, with a smile. "Asking after Delphine. Funny that."

He touches my hand briefly as he takes my card and then smiles.

"Your freckles…" he says. "They're beautiful, you know."

I laugh, my fear and loneliness temporarily extinguished, and for a fleeting moment I know what it feels like to fly to freedom.

The Case of the
High Pavement Ghosts

Isadora Lampblack was in the study, reading a monograph on La Diablesse of Caribbean folklore, when there came a soft knock on the door. It was her butler, Burridge, bringing her the afternoon post. There were three letters on the silver plate that he presented to her, but the one addressed in her cousin's hand aroused the most interest. What did Sherlock have to communicate? She studied the cursive. It was, as usual, measured, and as free of tells as possible, but the first two letters – the 'L' and 'a' of Lady – were ever so slightly closer to each other than they should have been. She skimmed her singularly sensitive fingers over the letters and felt the near-negligible grooves in the envelope where the nib had indented the paper. Greater pressure had been exerted on those two letters as well. It would appear that Sherlock had struggled to master himself for a moment and hadn't really wanted to post this. That meant he was asking her for a favour.

The letter confirmed her supposition.

Dear Isadora,

John has been contacted by an old friend who requires my help in a matter. As the gentleman resides in Nottingham I thought it apt that we should meet, particularly as John's friend insists that the case requires an investigator with a broad mind. I will expect both you and Fude to dine with us tomorrow evening at our lodgings, the Black Boy Hotel.

Yours etc.

"Apt that we should meet," muttered Isadora. "Rather, 'Isadora, I have been told that this case is of the supernatural yet I can hardly stoop so low as to mention that fact'."

Isadora sighed and then tucked a stray lock of golden hair that had escaped from her chignon back into place. She turned to Burridge. "Whereabouts is Annabelle?"

"She is in the kitchen, instructing Cook in the art of caramelising onions."

Isadora smiled wryly. "*This* I would like to see."

Cook, who had worked for the Lampblack family for decades, only tolerated Annabelle Fude's meddling in culinary matters for the sake of her young mistress, for whom she had much respect and affection. But right now, her patience was clearly wearing thin. She watched the interloper with a grim expression, her arms crossed, her right foot tapping out her irritation. Fude, who was busy jiggling the frying pan over the stove while stirring the onions with a wooden spoon, was blithely unconcerned by Cook's mounting frustration. What added to Cook's annoyance was the fact that Fude, middle-aged and matronly as she was, looked very much at home in her kitchen.

"I've already told you, I know how to do this!" snapped Cook, just as Isadora entered the kitchen. When Cook saw who it was, she uttered an "Oh, Miss!" and gave her mistress a hasty curtsey.

Annabelle, oblivious to her friend's presence, argued on. "I know you *think* you know how to do it, but you ain't ever done it the way we like. You don't cook them for long enough. They've got to be almost brown, see, not just golden."

Isadora gave a polite cough.

"Oh, Izzy!" said Fude, turning to her friend while continuing to stir the onions. Her round cheeks were red from the heat of the stove, and her dark hair was flying about her face, "I've just been showing Cook here –"

"I can see what you're doing. And I hate to interrupt you when you're mid-flow yet –"

"But what's the point of me shooting all these birds," – she waved the spoon at the table piled high with game – "and them not being given the proper garnish?"

"Annabelle! I came to tell you that I have news."

"Well?"

"We will be dining out tomorrow night."

"No, I mean, well what about me killing the birds and not having proper onions to go with 'em?" said Fude.

Isadora sighed. She looked from Cook to Fude and then said, "Now, I suppose, would be a good time to mention that I don't actually like onions. Fried, boiled, pickled or roasted. Pale golden or almost brown."

Fude gawped at Isadora and then turned to Cook who looked equally shocked. "Don't like onions," she said. "But that's imp –"

"No, it is quite possible. And if you'd care to listen, it is Holmes and Watson whom we'll be dining with tomorrow night. Also, you'll have to drag your husband away from his work. I'd like him to accompany us. And I," she said, turning to leave, "have better things to do than argue with you about alliums."

Fude gave the onions one last angry poke and then passed the spoon to Cook. "Here," she said, all enmity now gone, "you take over." She hurried out the kitchen and followed after Isadora. "Last time I saw that rude cousin of yours he said I'd gained five pounds."

"And?" said Isadora.

"Well, he was wrong. 'Twas only four and a half, I swear."

Isadora suppressed a grin. "Tell him that tomorrow," she replied. "That'll put him in combative mood."

Fude, however, did not mention Holmes' apparent miscalculation at dinner the following evening. Although Watson kept up a steady stream of genial conversation, even managing to coax some words out of the usually quiet and reticent Mr Fude, Holmes offered no pleasantries and his answers were terse, his manner brittle. In short, it was not a good time to rile him.

"Is the case not complex enough for your liking?" asked Isadora over the starter.

Holmes abandoned his pea soup and sat back in his chair, surveying the private dining room they'd been given. He put his hands together and steepled his long fingers. "It is not the lack of complexity that bothers me. It is the small matter of the..."

"Uncanny nature of the case," offered Isadora, her eyes sparkling.

"Indeed," said Sherlock.

Holmes' irritation at having to ask for her assistance was clear, but Isadora sensed that his ill temper was more than just about his bruised ego. She noticed him studying the picture of the villainous Charlie Peace that hung on the wall beside them.

"I am still gathering information," Holmes went on, "so will remain open-minded, but it does all seem rather open and closed."

"How so?" said Watson, "the Richardsons are a most loving family – singularly so – and yet their boy is frequently covered in wounds that have appeared as if by magic. And even you, yourself, have been unable to find any evidence of wrongdoing."

"*Yet*," answered Holmes. "Oh, by all appearances they seem virtuous enough, yet what, pray, of their actions behind closed doors?"

"Now look here, Holmes," said Watson, "are you saying that the man whom I served alongside in the Afghan war – a man I know to be both good and decent – is capable of inflicting injury upon his own son?"

"The very fact of his proximity to violence suggests that it would be only natural for him to view it as a means to disciplining his son."

Before Watson could compose himself enough to reply, Annabelle spoke. "I've never got on with violence as a means of discipline," she said, shaking her head. "Don't sit right with me. And it don't work. Besides, what's the child supposed to have done that is so very wicked that he gets beaten for it?"

"But that's just it!" said Watson, turning to Fude, his face a mixture of relief and gratitude for her support. "The child is an angel! He hasn't done anything wicked at all. And besides," said Watson, addressing Holmes, "why would Richardson want us involved if he were the very one injuring the child!"

"Why indeed," said Holmes, not looking at Watson but, instead, staring at the murky green of his pea soup, lost in reverie.

Isadora gave a polite cough and addressed Watson. "Sherlock did not accuse your friend of beating his son. He merely stated that a proportion of men involved in war unwittingly recourse to violence in domestic situations since they are not as open – or practised – in alternate forms of disciplinary action."

"Quite," said Sherlock, acknowledging the correctness of Isadora's statement with a nod. "There is also the wife – the mother – to consider."

Fude dropped her spoon in the bowl of soup.

"Really, Holmes!" said Watson, outraged, "Farzaneh cannot be the one inflicting such injury."

"Your proof?" said Holmes.

"Richardson himself. He says that Farzaneh is incapable of hurting a fly. And besides, I myself have seen her with the boy when he was but a newborn. She was most attentive to his needs and generous with her affection, even shunning the aid of a nurse."

"He is no longer a babe in arms, John," Sherlock pointed out. "And people change. Circumstances alter. When I spoke to Richardson in private I noted that he was not as wholehearted in his conviction of his wife's innocence as he was when speaking with you."

Watson opened his mouth to remonstrate with Holmes and then closed it again. A cloud of uncertainty crossed his face.

"And what of the governess?" asked Isadora.

"They have gone through three since the child started receiving these injuries," said Sherlock. "The Richardsons, quite reasonably, assumed that they were the source of the maltreatment and decided to dispense with them, leaving the boy in the sole care of his mother. For a short while all was well, and then, apparently overnight, the cuts and bruises came again. You see, since the father has not always been there – business having called him away – the mother is the one constant. Yet when I interviewed her yesterday, she was in such a state of agitation that I could get nothing sensible out of her."

"Well, what d'you expect?" said Fude. "The poor woman must be beside herself. You know, that's a terrible combination for a mother – knowing that your child's been harmed by God-knows-who or what, and then being accused of that harm."

"My dear lady," began Holmes, all condescension. Fude instantly bristled, so much so that Eric, her usually passive husband, was forced to still her by placing a restraining hand on her forearm. "I did not accuse or judge, I merely sought to listen in order to gather evidence."

"But I know what she musta seen," said Fude, her voice raised, "a snooty, callous, cold-hearted man who doesn't give two figs about her or her child, and yet who also has the power to have her child taken away from her. Would've been awful for her."

For a moment there was a tense silence. It was only broken by the arrival of the second course.

"Ah," said Mr Fude, uncharacteristically vocal, "gammon! And how good it smells."

His wife, still looking daggers at Sherlock, muttered something under her breath.

"But, you know, you have a point. Two, in fact," said Sherlock. Though untroubled by what Annabelle had just now said, he was at least sensible of the fact that adding "my dear lady" would not be welcome. "Clearly, we would do better to have the lady speak to someone who, in her opinion, can better empathise with her. This is where you," – Sherlock gave a dismissive wave at both Lampblack and Fude – "come in. This case requires a feminine perspective."

Annabelle was just about to give vent to her feelings when Isadora put out a hand, signalling to her to keep her thoughts to herself.

"And the second point, Sherlock," she said, looking into his cold, calculating eyes that were so like her own. "I assume you refer to Fude's 'God-knows-what'? Was it the boy who spoke of ghosts?"

Holmes nodded. "Indeed. Though his mother was quick enough to silence him when he began to elaborate."

"No doubt terrified that you'd cart him off to some madhouse!" cried Fude.

"Awful tasty gammon, don't you think?" exclaimed Eric, desperate to turn the subject if at all possible. Watson, taking his lead, agreed heartily and began to elaborate on the overall deliciousness of the meal.

Annabelle said nothing, and instead took out her annoyance on the gammon, cutting the thick slab of ham with great vigour.

Isadora prodded the heap of string beans with her fork. When there was a lull in Watson's monologue she once again addressed Sherlock. "So you require us to talk to both mother and child, and extract a full account of the events from the boy?"

"Yes," said Holmes. "And while you are thus employed I shall be carrying out some… other investigations. A little assistance from your – what do you call them? – 'helpers' would speed things along."

"Annabelle named them my Goose Gate Ghosties," replied Isadora. "And I will speak to them tonight."

"Good," said Holmes. "It is all settled then. Though if, indeed, this is a case of the uncanny, I cannot suppose how you will detect or drive out any supernatural being."

Isadora's eyes glittered. "We have our ways and means. In fact, just last week Mr Fude completed the creation of the Eidolon Glass which I invented many years ago. It is a work of art."

At this point Eric, who never looked anything but astonished or confused, reddened somewhat. "Oh, but the artistry was in the inventing!" he said, proceeding to stuff gammon into his mouth so that he wouldn't be expected to speak further.

"Yes, but what does it do?" asked Holmes of Isadora.

"It uncovers the undetected, the occult."

"Are you saying what I think you're saying?" said Watson, looking from Isadora to Fude's husband, clearly impressed. "You have produced a device through which one can see apparitions?"

Annabelle chuckled. "They're too clever by half, ain't they? I call it the ghost spotter."

"Well, that is –" began Watson.

"Worthy of my inspection," finished Holmes. "So," he said, "that is all decided. You will call on the Richardsons tomorrow morning."

"Their address?" said Isadora.

"94 High Pavement."

Annabelle suddenly froze, her forkful of gammon wavering in mid-air.

"What?" asked Isadora.

Holmes's keen eyes, too, were on the frozen Fude.

Annabelle let out a deep breath. "Oh, nothing."

"You know I respect your intuition," said Isadora. "It has, without fail, proved to be enlightening. Do elaborate."

"A long-ago warning from me mam," she said, the anxious face of her careworn mother flitting across her mind's eye, "to never linger on that street." Suddenly conscious of everyone's eyes on her, she put down her fork and instead took a sip of port. She gave herself a little shake. "That's better," she said, sounding much more like her usual, jolly self.

Both Holmes and Lampblack visibly relaxed; though for a while their interrogative eyes did not stray from Annabelle.

"Tasty gammon, ain't it?" said Eric, and Watson, once again, took the cue and began to expound on the delights of pork.

77

The following morning Lampblack and Fude presented themselves at the Richardsons' home, which was a well-kept end-of-terrace at the foot of the Church of St Mary the Virgin. Isadora kept an eye on Fude as they were shown to the sitting room, keen to see if her weathervane intuition would sense anything untoward, but so far Fude seemed untroubled by any presentiments, good or bad.

Both husband and wife were there to greet them as warmly as they could, given the circumstances, though they were unable to successfully conceal their astonishment at the unlikely pairing of their visitors – Isadora, uncommonly beautiful, was tall, blonde and stately; Annabelle was short, plump and dark-haired. The age difference was striking too. Annabelle looked old enough to be Isadora's mother, though by their distinctly contrasting features this would've been a Mendelian impossibility.

"No doubt you are wondering at our incongruous fellowship and the events that led to us working together," said Isadora, quickly raising a gloved hand as the Richardsons began to protest. "It is, indeed, an interesting story, but we will have to forego it for the time being. We are keen to provide you with assistance if we are able to – that is, if the matter involves the supernatural."

At that, Mrs Richardson breathed a sigh of relief and sat down on the sofa. Her husband joined her, and then took hold of her hand, giving it a squeeze.

Lampblack and Fude took their seats in the armchairs closest to them.

"Please, Mrs Richardson –" began Isadora.

"Farzaneh," said the woman. "I do not really look like a Richardson, do I?" she said, with a thick Persian accent. She forced a laugh.

Mr Richardson visibly bristled and then let go of his wife's hand.

"No, you do not look like a Richardson," said Isadora, considering the woman's striking features, her taupe coloured skin. "And yet," she went on, "you are by marriage a Richardson."

Farzaneh's expression was a mixture of defiance and sadness, as though she was wondering *But for how long?*

Mr Richardson suddenly mopped his round, ruddy face with a handkerchief.

"We want to help," said Fude, looking from Mr to Mrs Richardson. "We really do. Just tell us what's been going on."

Farzaneh looked at her husband, who gave her a slight nod, and then took a deep breath. She said that their son, Clement, had always been a sensitive boy. "And for many years he's had a friend from his…" Farzaneh gestured to her forehead.

"An imaginary friend," interjected Mr Richardson.

"He calls him Baxter," Farzaneh said.

"And they're good friends?" asked Fude.

Mr Richardson, rather taken aback by the question, said nothing.

"Oh yes," said Farzaneh. "He talks very happily to Baxter. About his teddies and toys. The books he's read. They plan adventures. Or so he says. It's never been a problem before. But for the past year…" Farzaneh paused.

"Go on," said Isadora.

Mrs Richardson took another deep breath. "Clement says that since we came to live here Baxter has been bullied by two girls who are older than him. They have been trying to shoo Baxter away, saying that this is their house and that he has no right to be here. Clement has been trying to protect his friend, but in doing so, he has been hurt by the girls."

"And these girls are –?" said Fude.

"Non-existent," replied Mr Richardson.

"Though the bruises are not," said Isadora.

"I know it doesn't make any sense," went on Mr Richardson.

"On the contrary," said Isadora, "it all makes perfect sense. And if we were to exchange 'non-existent' for 'existent, yet imperceptible' then for those not acquainted with the occult, such as yourself, the matter becomes easier to understand. Now, if we could speak with Clement that would be appreciated."

For a moment, Mr and Mrs Richardson were too surprised to say or do anything. Then Mrs Richardson rang for the maid, who promptly came with Clement in tow.

The boy, who had inherited his mother's dark eyes and hair and his father's pale skin, as well as the ruddiness, immediately went to his mother. They embraced with much affection.

Farzaneh explained to Clement that Lady Lampblack and Mrs Fude had come to talk to him about Baxter and the naughty girls. They might be able to help.

Clement eyed the two women cautiously. "D'you think you can?" he asked them. "Because they're horrid, the girls. They're nothing but bullies." He glanced at Mr Richardson. "Father says that one must stand up to bullies. That it's the only way to stop them." Clement stood up straighter, looking proud. "And I have. For the sake of Baxter. And because it's the right thing to do. But it isn't working." His face suddenly crumpled and it took him a great effort not to cry. "There's only one of me and two of them. And they're bigger than me. It's not fair."

"No," said Isadora, "it isn't fair."

"It's certainly not," agreed Fude, taking a sweet out of her pocket and pressing it into Clement's clammy hand. "Here you go, me duck, have a pear drop. They always made my George feel better when he got to ruminating about the unfairness of the world. And I must say that even now, old as I am, I enjoy the occasional sweet treat myself."

Isadora suppressed a smile. The adjective 'occasional' was somewhat imprecise.

Clement looked to his mother, who gave him a slight nod, and then put the pear drop in his mouth. As he sucked away, the sour-sweetness bringing him a measure of contentment, Isadora asked him where the girls were to be encountered. "And is Baxter with you now?" she enquired.

Clement shook his head. He glanced anxiously at his mother. "He… he doesn't join me when there are others about." Clement crunched on his sweet. "He's shy. I expect he'll be on the roof. He likes to look at the sky."

"And what of the girls?"

"I've only ever seen them in the nursery. They say it's theirs."

"Do they now?" said Fude. "And I guess they don't want to share?"

Clement shook his head, his eyes round.

"Can we see the nursery?" asked Lampblack.

"Of course," said Mrs Richardson, rising. She urged Clement forward, though he seemed reluctant to move.

"It's all right," said Fude, noting the boy's hesitance. "We'll be with you. And we'll make sure no harm comes to you."

The boy nodded and gave Fude a shy smile.

Farzaneh and Clement then led the way to the nursery, leaving Mr Richardson in the sitting room to mutter about the foolishness of indulging the boy in his crackpot ideas.

The nursery was striking in its chilliness, though it was early summer, the weather warm.

"I apologise for the cold. We haven't lit a fire for a while," said Farzaneh, "Clement's been unwilling to play here."

Fude, who had paused on the threshold, was pale, her eyes glazed over.

Isadora, noting Fude's pallid face, her unseeing eyes, asked her what the matter was. "What can you see? What can you sense?"

"The traces of souls in torment. Terrible things were done to them, Izzy. Terrible."

Farzaneh pulled Clement towards her. "What?" she cried, "What happened?"

Fude shook her head. "I don't know. But it was a long time ago. I can feel the pain. The fear." Fude entered the room and then sat down heavily on a tiny chair. She looked ridiculous – her round form precarious on the child's wooden stool – but it was impossible to see the humour in the situation, she was too distressed. "Innocence corrupted."

Farzaneh's hand flew to her mouth and she swayed on the spot.

Isadora, the only one not unsettled by Fude's words, asked Mrs Richardson who the previous tenants had been. She shook her head. "I don't know. But I presume my husband would."

Isadora nodded then pulled out the Eidolon Glass. Putting it to the middle of her forehead, she closed her eyes and turned her head left and right. Next, she placed the Eidolon Glass over her left eye and scanned the room. "Residues," she said, speaking more to herself than anyone else. Then she turned abruptly, as though she was following an invisible flying something with her eyes. "Do the girls always enter the room through here?" asked Isadora of Clement, pointing to the gold-framed mirror.

"Yes," he whispered. "How did you know?"

Isadora said nothing and instead inspected the mirror, placing her long, slender fingers at right angles to the surface of the mirror. When she saw that there was no gap between her fingers and their reflection she smiled to herself. She then turned to Clement. "This glass, or lens, that I just now put to my eye and my third eye, allows me to see things that I normally wouldn't see. There are three trails of ghosts around the room. Two of them appear to emanate from the mirror."

81

"So it's all true," said Farzaneh, astonished, "Baxter, and the girls… And you can prove it?"

"There is very little doubt in the matter," said Isadora. She looked over at Fude, who looked more herself now, though still pale. She helped her off the stool. "Have a pear drop," said Isadora, "it'll do you good."

Annabelle fumbled in her pocket for a sweet and then popped two in her mouth.

"But I would like to know more about these girls," went on Isadora. "So if Clement and Baxter, as well as Fude here, would be willing, I feel sure we could make further progress."

"What did you have in mind?" said Fude, eyeing Isadora suspiciously. Isadora's plans didn't usually take into account the level of discomfort of those involved in the plan.

Isadora glanced at the mirror. "Let us discuss this in the sitting room. It is far more comfortable there."

Clement agreed to the plan, as did Mr and Mrs Richardson. He said that he thought Baxter would accompany him to the nursery if it helped the ladies to stand up to the bully girls.

"Indeed, it will help," said Isadora. "A lot. I think it highly likely that the girls will be tempted out of their hiding place by Baxter's presence, and when they do venture out Fude will intercede and make light work of them."

Fude rolled her eyes. "Honestly, Izzy, you make it sound as though I'm going to be engaging in fisticuffs or summat like that!"

Isadora, ignoring Fude's comment, crouched down so she could be at Clement's eye level. "A secret," she said, lowering her voice. "Bullies usually stand down when one asserts oneself. But sometimes they don't. That's when you need to bring in the cavalry. Do you understand?"

Clement nodded and then grinned. "And you and Mrs Fude are like the cavalry?"

"Indeed," said Isadora, standing once more.

"You know," said Clement, in a serious voice. "You're a very pretty lady. I would like to marry you."

Farzaneh suppressed a laugh and Mr Richardson, who had gone bright red, dabbed at his sweaty face with a handkerchief.

Fude grinned, and even dispassionate Isadora couldn't help but smile. "Thank you," she said, "for the proposal. I will give it some thought."

Fude and Clement took themselves off to the nursery while Isadora spoke to Mr and Mrs Richardson about their landlord and the previous tenants. Clement, understandably, was anxious about being in what had become a dreaded room and didn't venture too far from Annabelle. After he'd spent some time showing her all his toys he became silent. He turned to look at the door and then sighed.

"Baxter not here yet?" she asked, as the boy clenched and unclenched a toy soldier.

He shook his head.

"Well, what does he like to do?"

"He likes stories."

Fude went to the bookshelf and picked up a copy of Grimm's Fairy Tales. "Make yourself comfy then," she said, installing herself in the rocking chair.

Clement settled at her feet and looked up at her as she opened the book.

"Got a favourite?" she asked.

"Iron John!" he said.

"Good choice." And she began to read.

After a while, when they were both engrossed in yet another story, Baxter slipped in and came to rest next to Clement. Fude, busy reading, didn't see him enter, but as she came to the end of the story, she glanced down at Clement and saw him whispering intently to what looked, to her, like a shimmer in the air. Her heart leapt – it was the boy's companion. But as keen as she was to see Baxter in a more substantial form, she refrained from taking the Eidolon Glass out of her pocket. She didn't want to scare the ghost boy away. She read on as though nothing had happened. After a few more stories Fude feigned tiredness and, yawning loudly, told Clement that she'd be having forty winks. Maybe he could construct something out of his wooden blocks while she had a little doze?

Soon enough, Clement, accompanied by the shimmer that was Baxter, became happily engrossed in building a castle for his toy soldiers. He chattered away while thus absorbed – to himself or Baxter,

Fude wasn't sure – and forgot all about his dozing overseer. Unobserved, Fude sneaked a look at Baxter through the glass. What she saw was remarkable – Baxter, unlike other ghosts she'd seen, or sensed, didn't have one set form. He seemed to rapidly cycle through various forms – a mere wisp, then a baby, then a boy the age of Clement. Sometimes it seemed as though he were older than Clement, then he'd become nothing more than a haze of ethereal smoke. Fude hastily put the glass away as there was a lull in Clement's chatter and she became aware of motion, though it were near-invisible, by the mirror.

The next occurrences happened swiftly and in parallel: two china dolls suddenly levitated upwards and swung at Clement and Baxter, and Fude leaped out of the rocking chair and grabbed the dolls before they made contact with anyone, human or ghost. Clement cried out in shock and then clung to Fude's skirt; Baxter, unnoticed by anyone, vanished from the room.

"Now then!" said Fude, her voice raised, addressing the two shimmers which she could just about make out in the dreary light of the nursery. "We'll have none of that, thank you very much!"

The shimmers swelled and visibly bristled with indignation. They retreated towards the mirror.

"And don't you be going nowhere, young ladies. Otherwise I'll just end up following you. Besides, it's high time we set a few ground rules, eh?"

The shimmers paused and slowly returned to Fude.

"That's it," she said, much more kindly now. But as she took out the Eidolon Glass the shimmers shrunk away from her. "No need to worry 'bout this," she reassured them. "It's just a sorta magnifying lens that'll let me see you that bit better. You all right with it?"

After a moment there were two whispered yeses.

Fude put the Eidolon Glass to her right eye and then saw who Baxter and Clement's aggressors were. They were two Caucasian girls with shimmering hair, which made Fude think that in life they had been blonde and blue-eyed. One was older than the other, and they were dressed in clothes that had once been fine but had met with ill treatment; their frocks were grubby, ripped and stained with dark spots that Fude took to be blood. There was a pinched expression to their faces and sunken eyes which told Fude of terrible pain.

"Oh, my dears!" said Fude, suddenly unsteady on her feet. The echoes of the awful anguish that she'd sensed earlier came back to her and she sunk to her knees.

The girls drew back in surprise, but didn't leave.

Fude gave herself a mental shake. She had to stay focussed, calm. Just like Izzy.

"Well now," said Fude. "How 'bout some introductions? My name's Annabelle, and this here is Clement." She glanced round at the boy who had retreated behind her, still clutching hold of her skirts. "I'm Clement's new… governess. Friend. How about you two?"

There was a pause then the older girl said, "Elizabeth. And this is –"

"Lucy," said the other.

"Elizabeth and Lucy," Fude repeated. "Lovely names. And I guess you used to live and play here?"

Elizabeth nodded.

Fude considered the mirror. "But you're not always here, are you? You come and go. Through the mirror, don't you?"

Elizabeth's eyes became round. "How do you know?"

"I've got a sense of your movements. And that area by the mirror is awful busy." Fude inhaled deeply, steeling herself for what she had to say next. "I'm guessing that your bodies are somewhere in the house beyond."

"Yes," whispered Elizabeth.

Lucy stared at Annabelle intently, her eyes glistening.

"So you come across for a bit of respite. But you're none too pleased about the boys being here, eh?"

"It's *our* nursery," said Elizabeth, standing tall. "Why should we have to share it with those nasty, foreign boys?"

"Now, now," said Fude, "there's no need for name-calling." She sighed. "Though I dare say that under normal circumstances you wouldn't lash out like that. But I'm guessing you've both been witnesses to the most appalling kinds of human behaviour. It's not exactly going to do you any favours." Again, Fude sighed. Slowly, she got up off her knees, rubbing them as she did so. "What we got here is a situation. But I'm sure we can find some ways of resolving it, that is, if you promise to be honest with me. What do you say, Miss Elizabeth and Miss Lucy?"

The girls looked at each other, came to some unspoken mutual agreement and then nodded at Fude.

"Good," said Fude. "Now, I know you'd both like to have this nursery all to yourselves. Coming here makes you feel better, don't it?"

The girls said, "Yes."

"But we got Clement and Baxter to consider. Now, I'm sure the boys would be willing to share," Fude glanced at Clement who quickly nodded his head, "but I'm not convinced that sharing's gonna solve the root problem. Tell me," she said, looking at them intently, "what would make you truly happy?"

"To have the boys gone!" said Elizabeth. She gave Lucy a nudge, but Lucy said nothing.

Fude looked at the younger girl, a kind expression on her motherly face. "Is that true, Lucy?" she asked.

Lucy shook her head and sparkling, lucent tears ran down her face. "I –" she began, "I'd like to see Mama and Papa again. And little Molly. I want…" her bottom lip trembled, "to be whole again."

Fude found herself blinking back tears. "Oh my dear, of course you do. And I ever so much wish I could grant you that. We might be able to find your family and bring them to you, so that you can meet. But, well, you gotta understand that there's no way anyone can make you whole again."

"Why?" said Elizabeth, her voice fierce.

Fude shook her head. There was sorrow in her eyes. "I'm sorry… It's just not the way of things. But there is a place or, rather, a state of being that you can enter. It'll give you peace. Rest."

Lucy, round-eyed, whispered, "Heaven."

Fude nodded and smiled kindly at the little girl.

"What if we don't want to go?" said Elizabeth. "What if we want to stay here?"

Lucy tugged at Elizabeth's sleeve. "I want to go. But you have to come with me."

The older girl considered the younger, then sighed. "I suppose…" She then turned to Fude. "But how do we get there?"

"Leave that to me," said Fude. "Me and my very clever friend, Izzy, will find your parents then put your bones to rest. Then… Heaven'll open up to you. My, what a marvellous sight that'll be!"

The girls looked at Fude, their faces solemn; shining.

"But I need you to do something for me," went on Fude. "I want the name, if you know it, of the terrible man who hurt and killed you. He needs to be found and justice done."

Elizabeth, the shine suddenly gone, said, "Oh, we know his name. And you can have it. Sherlock Holmes."

Fude lost no time in relaying this information to Isadora once they were back in the privacy of Isadora's town house. "What do you say to that?" said Annabelle, her face still bearing the signs of shock.

"I say it's not true," replied Isadora.

"You mean the girls are lying to me, and that they made all that stuff up?"

"No, I believe we'll find enough evidence to back up the majority of their story. But Sherlock their killer…? Impossible."

Fude was about to protest but Lampblack put a hand out to silence her. "It does, though, help to incriminate the real killer." A wry smile was upon Isadora's face. "He must've thoroughly despised my cousin if he went to the trouble of impersonating him in the hope that the police would see fit to arrest Sherlock. Someone who…" Isadora gave a satisfied sigh. "Of course…"

Fude waited for an explanation but none was forthcoming. "'Course what?" she said, after a moment or two.

"Come!" said Isadora, heading towards the door. "We must meet with Holmes and Watson at once."

"Hold on, Izzy, I haven't had lunch or –"

"Annabelle," said Lampblack, her eyes sparkling, "what does my cousin say when trouble is on the horizon? When things are getting exciting?"

Fude knew what Holmes said. But she didn't like trouble. She liked lunch. "He says," she said with a deep sigh, "that the game is afoot."

It took a while to get a message through to Holmes and Watson, but soon enough the four of them were gathered together in one of the private dining rooms of the Black Boy Hotel, with Fude throwing down some bread and cheese while glancing surreptitiously at Holmes. Lampblack and Holmes weren't inclined to eat – they were fuelled by the fire of the investigation – but Watson was hungry and tucked into a plate of cold meats with gusto.

"All this trudging round makes for an appetite," John commented, in between mouthfuls.

"But what have you been doing?" asked Annabelle.

It was then that all four of them began to speak. After a few seconds both Isadora and Sherlock slammed their hands onto the table, crying out, "Enough!"

There was silence.

"Ladies first," said Sherlock, addressing his cousin.

"Thank you," said Isadora, with a smile. "Though I have a sense that everything we've discovered today will be backed up by your investigations."

She gave a summation of her and Annabelle's findings. Watson goggled at her, open-mouthed, when she came to the part where the ghost girls had named their killer as Sherlock. "So, to conclude: the boy was telling the truth. He and his supernatural friend were being bullied out of the nursery by two girls who had been killed approximately twenty-four years ago by a fiend who, if the rumours are to be believed, is still at large today. A fiend that you, Sherlock, had evidence against, and yet who had somehow escaped death only to redouble his efforts with the intention of implicating you in his heinous crimes."

Now it was Annabelle's turn to stare at Isadora round-eyed. She dropped the chunk of cheese she'd been about to eat and took a quick swig of ale.

"It was twenty-three years ago," said Sherlock, "A dark affair – and according to information I have recently unearthed, he *is* still at large, though I admit that I wouldn't have thought it possible. I saw him hang." There was a pause as Sherlock considered his memory of that gruesome event. "In fact, he's just now returned from the continent where he has spent a goodly amount of his life involved in the trafficking of children. And if he's got wind of my presence, as I intended him to, he will most likely make his move against me soon."

"You got all this from a morning's work?" said Fude.

"Actually," said Sherlock, "it's been three days' worth of work. It's amazing what one can glean when disguised as a labourer looking for employment in the Lace Market. But today that labourer brought along his 'daughter' and hinted that he was open to some less-than-savoury ways to earn a better wage."

"Was it Meghan who posed as your daughter?" asked Isadora.

Sherlock nodded. "And I must say that she acted her part very well."

"Yes," replied Isadora, "she's a fine actress. And one of my longest-serving Ghosties."

"Hold on a mo," said Fude, "back up! I'm getting lost."

"Quite," added Watson, "can you please explain to me what's going on? And were my perambulations around Nottingham, meeting with landlords and agents, of *any* use?"

"Yes of course they were, my dear Watson. Your efforts confirmed my suspicions. Does the name Gunn mean anything to you?" asked Holmes of Fude.

Annabelle gasped. "Oh my! Of course!"

Watson looked at Fude's blanched face and then at Holmes. "Damn it man! Now I'm the only one who doesn't know what the hell you're talking about. Will you please enlighten me?"

"Gunn was a policeman gone bad," Sherlock explained. "He was also a friend of the despicable, violin-playing Charlie Peace, whom this wretched town seems to think so well of. I won't bother going into the apparent 'whys' of the matter, but the upshot of his reversal of position with regards to the law was that under the guise of a benevolent landlord, particularly keen to give homes to poor families and abandoned children, he established himself as a mastermind of the most vile aspect of criminality – child trafficking.

"I had to spend a goodly amount of time unravelling his filthy web of influence, particularly as I found a good deal of resistance from those in positions of authority who really did not want Gunn – and, hence, their own peccadilloes – exposed. Oh no, they would far prefer to hide behind their public stature, claiming sinlessness.

"One day, though, he became careless and left a good deal of incriminating evidence at the scene of a brutal murder of a young girl of good breeding who had already been missing for several weeks. And there was a reliable eye witness who testified that he'd seen Gunn and the girl earlier that day. There was no way that Gunn could slither out of my grasp this time. He was sentenced to death."

"I remember it too," said Fude. "The papers were full of it. Gunn had been born in Nottingham, so it was the talk of the town. But you said you saw him hang? So how on earth can he still be in play?"

"Why the surprise?" asked Isadora. "When not two hours ago you were conversing with ghosts?"

Fude shrugged. "They were friendly ghosts. A child murderer come back to life don't bear thinking about. Lor' I was that spooked by the tales me mam used to tell about High Pavement and the snatchers who would whisk away children if they did so much as look at the houses on that road. I never forgot her warnings."

"Clever woman," said Holmes. "Watson brought me certain papers from the local house agents – some of the properties on that road were, and still are, owned by Gunn."

"Hence the two-way mirror and the dead girls," said Isadora. "A search of the house next door to 94 High Pavement should be illuminating. I have no doubt that the girls' bodies are buried there."

"Quite," said Holmes.

"We should have them interred properly," said Fude. "Bring them the peace they deserve. And give the Richardsons the peace they need. Although, I'd like it if we could find the girls' family before they get buried."

"We will do that," said Isadora. "I should also carry out some investigations into Gunn's apparent immortality. There are several occult methods he may have employed to manage his resurrection. Perhaps a straightforward, though costly, act such as an arcane metamorphosis would –"

"Metamorphosis, what exactly do you mean by that?" asked Holmes.

"It means that he could've given his physical appearance to someone else – and taken on theirs. If this were done at the time of his execution –"

"If it were, you are suggesting that he evaded the hangman's noose and let someone else swing instead." Holmes stared into the middle distance, absorbed in intense cogitation. "And shortly after the execution, the eyewitness who testified against him was reported as missing. He was never found, which further suggests the 'resurrected' Gunn removed him.

"It was an insoluble irritation, that aspect, along with many other further irritations – including the sporadic claims that I had been in two different places at once, fighting crime at one location and committing crime at another; claims I was, until now, unable to fathom. It seems plain now that Gunn appropriated my name at times, whether from perverse pleasure or assuming it would muddy the trail."

"We would need to exhume what remains of the body," said Isadora, "to try to see who was really buried in Gunn's grave."

"Indeed," said Holmes, his jittery legs propelling him to stand and act.

They were interrupted by a messenger bringing a letter to Holmes.

Watson, Lampblack and Fude watched as Sherlock opened the letter and sat back down again.

"Well, well," said Holmes, his eyes alight with excitement. "He has made his move. Listen:

"Sherlock, how clever of you to find me after all these years. I wondered if you'd ever catch on. The devil knows I left enough clues. But a warning: stay away from my old stamping grounds. I wouldn't want anything bad to happen to my greatest admirer, would I?"

"Lord Almighty!" cried Fude.

"And this is him?" said Watson. "Gunn?"

"There is no doubt," said Holmes. "It is his handwriting. I recall it from many years ago. And I saw it again the other day, when I made enquiries into the Richardsons' landlord."

"Good heavens!" said Watson. "We must tell the police."

"We will," said Holmes. "But first, a plan. Isadora, am I right in thinking that the Narrow Marsh –"

"Is his old stamping ground, yes."

"Good," said Holmes. "Tonight then, yes?"

Isadora nodded.

"Hold on a mo," said Fude. "You're not telling me you're going after him, are you? Straight into his trap?"

"Watson and I will have reinforcements of more than one kind." He tipped his head to the two women. "For Gunn may have certain unnatural tricks up his sleeve, as well as his murderous heart. But yes. Walking into the trap is the surest way of drawing him out."

Fude took a swig of ale. "How did I know you were gonna say that?"

"Because, my dear," said Holmes, "you are a singularly intuitive lady."

"Yeah, and I knew you were gonna say that too." Fude took another gulp of ale. "Come on then, let's be hearing your plan."

Nightfall found them in Narrow Marsh, that particularly unpleasant area of Nottingham, south of the city, north of the River Trent. Moonlight came and went as clouds skittered across the night sky. Holmes and Watson were to go on ahead; Lampblack and Fude were the first line of reinforcements, following behind them. Policemen, in pairs, were stationed at the edges of the slum, ready to respond if Gunn's trap was to prove too sticky for the four of them, though both Watson and Fude were carrying revolvers and quite prepared to use them against such a monster.

Holmes had a fairly good idea of where Gunn was to be found, but also thought it highly probable that he would show himself. *He* would be the bait.

Sure enough, a shadow of a man unpeeled himself from a throng of drunks and slipped away into another filthy alley. But not before showing himself to Holmes and Watson. It was Gunn. They followed him; Lampblack and Fude kept back at a cautious distance.

They hurried along the jumble of cobbled backstreets, the smell of human waste intense, until it was near pitch black and silent. Then they saw an unearthly light. Gunn appeared to be carrying it. Holmes and Watson paused for a moment, wondering at its strangeness, but then hurried on. Lampblack and Fude, too, had seen the light, and stopped.

"What is it?" whispered Annabelle.

"I don't know," said Isadora. "Not an ordinary lantern. It could be a will-o-the-wisp. Or any manner of unearthly creatures or spirits or…" It was then that the most wonderful music began to play. "…song. Yes," she said, her eyes glazing over. "Siren song, held in a jar…"

Fude heard the music, but it didn't affect her in the way it had affected Isadora.

"You all right, Izzy?" asked Annabelle, the moonlight illuminating her friend's strange expression. She seemed entranced, mesmerised.

Isadora smiled. "We must follow the music."

Clearly, Holmes and Watson had thought the same. Isadora went after them, so Fude had no choice but to follow, puffing and panting as she tried to keep up with the other three.

On and on they went, the light and music leading them through the filthy alleys, until Fude could hear the rhythmic roll of water. They were at the river. And there was the light. This time on a boat that was halfway to the other side.

Fude cried out as she realised what was happening – Holmes and Watson were striding into the river, still following the light and eerie music.

"Izzy!" she said, grabbing her arm, "we got to stop them, they're gonna drown themselves!"

But Isadora paid her no intention, pulled herself out of Annabelle's grasp and carried on towards the river.

"Izzy!" she cried, realising that her friend was under the power of dark magic. Then: "Police!" But although two policemen stepped out of the shadows, they were equally oblivious to her and were themselves rushing headlong into the river.

Annabelle watched with growing panic as Sherlock, John, Isadora and the two policemen strode heedlessly into the deepening water. They'd be dragged down by the current any moment now.

"Think!" she said, trying to calm herself. "Siren song," she muttered, "siren song." Of course! She couldn't save them all from the might of the river but she *could* break the spell.

She aimed her revolver at the light. It was a way off now and bobbing about, but still, it was as big as a pigeon – an easy target.

Bang! She got it first shot, and the bound magick shattered along with its container.

There were cries from Holmes, Watson and Isadora, as well as the two policemen, who were now no longer insensitive to the pull of the cold river. Fude waded in to help Isadora who was floundering in the cold, dirty shallows.

"Gunn!" cried Holmes, who'd been the furthest out and was now treading water.

Gunn, evidently furious at this turn of events, pulled out a revolver and fired at Holmes who, just in time, dived under the water and disappeared from view. Gunn then aimed at Watson who also took cover under the surface.

"Come on!" cried Annabelle, dragging her friend out of the river. "We've got to get out of here!"

There was a whoosh as a bullet whistled past the women and policemen, frighteningly close, and both Isadora and Fude gasped and fell forwards onto the river bank.

Then came more shots. Anabelle could only look on helplessly as events unfolded on the river.

Holmes emerged from under the water and began to deliberately rock the boat, knocking Gunn off-balance. Then he hauled himself aboard and lunged at the man who'd almost sent him to his death. As they grappled, he knocked the revolver out of Gunn's hand, sending it into the water.

The boat rocked violently as both men wrestled, seeking an advantage. Then Watson, sopping wet, clambered onto the boat and pointed his revolver at the tussling pair. "I'll shoot, sir!" he cried, hoping Gunn wouldn't know he was bluffing – there was a high chance he'd hit Sherlock instead.

With a tremendous effort, Gunn leapt for the side of the boat, clearly intent on escaping into the river, but Holmes was too quick and pulled him back, just as Watson, seeing his chance to get a clear shot, pulled the trigger. Gunn cried out and collapsed onto Holmes as a dark stain appeared on the sleeve of his shirt. For a moment, the two men lay still.

"Holmes!" cried Watson, "Good God! Are you hurt?"

"No," said Sherlock, "it is only the fiend who is wounded."

Gunn made one last feeble attempt to escape Holmes, who dragged him back roughly.

"Not so confident now, eh?" said Holmes, taking Watson's revolver and keeping it pointed at Gunn's throat. "Take us ashore, John."

Watson rowed them back, watching the two men, who were equally formidable, though in opposite ways. Holmes kept his eyes fixed on the silent Gunn, who looked about him, doubtless still bent on escape. Watson glanced ahead to see Isadora and Annabelle sitting on the riverbank, huddled together. Annabelle had placed her dry shawl around Isadora's shoulders and was rubbing some warmth into her friend's arms.

As the boat approached the riverbank and the waiting policemen waded in to help bring it ashore, Watson acknowledged the two women with a grim nod.

Fude gave him a weak smile and then turned once more to Isadora. "You sure you're all right, Izzy?"

"Just about," Isadora replied, her teeth chattering. "Thanks to you."

"I guess we were just lucky that there was *one* fully red-blooded woman about tonight, eh?"

"Indeed," said Isadora, with a mirthless laugh. "Though I'd never have expected Sherlock to fall under the spell of siren song."

"Well, he wasn't exactly immune to Irene Adler, was he? He probably heard *her* in the music."

"True."

Just then a Black Maria rolled up to the riverbank and yet more policemen helped Holmes and Watson escort Gunn from the boat to the carriage. Gunn thrashed around wildly, incensed by the many hands on him, and when he caught sight of Lampblack and Fude he attempted to hurl himself at them. The policemen dragged him back to the carriage, kicking and flailing.

"You!" he cried, addressing Isadora. "I've heard about you. And I know your secrets! You're an abomination!"

Sherlock, on seeing his cousin's shocked face, did not spare Gunn. He punched him in the face, sending him flying into the carriage. "The only abomination here is you! And this time, sir, I'll damn well make sure that you're the one to swing."

With that, he slammed the door on Gunn.

Together, Sherlock and Isadora found the family of the dead sisters. 'Little' Molly was now twenty-five. With the help of the Eidolon Glass, they brought about a reunion that, though desperately sad, was appreciated. In time, the bodies of the girls were buried and they were given the peace they deserved.

The Richardsons, although now free of the cloud of tension that had hovered over them for so long, decided to move from the house on High Pavement. It held too many bad memories – theirs and others. But before they left, one evening they received a last visit from Isadora, who wanted to talk to Baxter.

"I *think* he's up there," said Clement, indicating to the attic window of his bedroom. "On the roof."

"You think?" said Isadora. "Do you not see him that often nowadays?"

Clement shook his head.

Isadora considered the boy. Although he still had the air of one who had a rich, internal life, he looked less wistful, more content. He had grown an inch or so since that first meeting of theirs.

"I think the connection between you is waning," she said. "Do you mind?"

Clement looked down at his feet before answering. "I both do and I don't. I'm sort of… busy with my own things."

Isadora nodded. "I understand. You don't mind me talking to him, do you?"

"No."

Isadora hitched up her skirts, and with surprising agility went through the window and leapt lightly up to the apex of the roof, where she could just about make out a shimmer. She sat on the ridge and surveyed all of dusky Nottingham beneath her.

"Evening, Baxter," she said.

The shimmer didn't say anything.

"When my friend, Annabelle, saw you a while back she told me you were a most marvellous ghost. Do you mind if I take a look at you through my glass?"

There was a sigh that sounded like a 'no'.

"Thank you," she said, as she took out the Eidolon Glass and peered at Baxter through it. Just then he was Clement's age – and the exact image of him. He then became a wisp, and then a baby.

Isadora put the glass away, a sad but kind expression on her face. "You died in your mother's womb, didn't you? Many weeks before your twin brother was born. You cleaved to him, didn't you?"

A whispered 'yes'.

"Baxter, I think that, soon, it will be time for you to move on. To Heaven. But before you do, make sure to say all your goodbyes. Show yourself to your mother and father. I think they would… like that very much."

There was a pause and then a last 'yes'.

"Good," said Isadora. "Thank you."

She tilted her head upwards. "The stars are beautiful, aren't they? I'm not surprised you like to come here."

But when she turned to look at Baxter he had vanished, leaving nothing behind him but starlight and air.

Girls' Night Out

We are having an evening off. It is a necessary respite from work and our roles as caregivers, which we perform day in day out, twenty-four seven. It is also time away from our Significant Others, who tell us that an evening out will be good for us. It is, overall, A Good Thing. Good Protocol. In the long term the odd break will make us more effective at work; it will also make us feel more human again. They tell us to enjoy ourselves. *Relax*. Who are we to argue with them?

It takes us a moment or two to transition from one reality to the other and to truly believe that we are *there* and no longer *here*.

We ready ourselves for the evening; agonise over what to wear. *What will the others be wearing? What dress would* he *like best?*

We leave our homes and cross the twilit city – anticipation, like the perfumes we are wearing, on our necks, our breasts, between our thighs. We travel on foot, by bus, by taxi.

We arrive at the restaurant, instinctively on the lookout for *him* (although we know he will not be here until later) and greet one another. We kiss, we hug, we make showy displays of giving each other compliments while making a critical assessment of each other's appearance.

The hostess shows us to our table – which, thankfully, is close to *his* piano – and provides us with menus. Well-dressed waiters fuss around us. This is probably because of Francoise's online following. *What would we like to drink?*

We order several bottles of white wine, and a jug of iced water. We continue to study each other while scanning the menu. Gita has lost weight. She looks lean, well-toned, and she tells us she feels fantastic, so full of energy. For the past six weeks she's been doing that new training regime. You know, the one that's all the rage at the moment. And she's going to do a run for charity. Will we sponsor her? *Of course!* we say. *Of course. Send us the link.*

Adele has gained weight, but appears to be pleased with this. Her dimples seem secretly satisfied. *She couldn't be pregnant, again, could she? Surely not? However did she get permission for that? Must have been expensive. Then again, her husband is an Elite.* We say nothing and steer clear of the topic of babies.

Francoise, in her designer dress, diamonds at her throat, is as beautiful as ever. The diamond choker is on loan from one of the companies who advertise on her YouTube channel. We cannot help but marvel at her success, at the sheer number of her subscribers, her Instagram followers. The book deal. *How do you do it?* we ask. And, as usual, she laughs and says she has no idea why people are so interested in her. She's just a normal person. *Yeah right.*

Suzie looks drawn, and we each know that this is due to the ongoing divorce. *You'll get through this,* we say. *You're strong. And when it's over we'll order champagne. Okay?* She nods and manages to keep her tears in check. She tells us in a brittle voice that Amy's been great about it all. *She's such a fantastic kid,* she says. *We're going camping next week. It's something she's always wanted to do but, you know, her father never wanted to go.*

Nichelle's unruly afro is threaded with grey. *Work,* she explains, adjusting her glasses. *Of course,* we say. *It must be stressful.* We do not ask anything more. The less said about her distasteful scientific research the better. Still, Francoise, who is sitting next to Nichelle, puts an arm around her and takes a selfie of them both. *Loving hanging out with the girls tonight,* she writes on Instagram. *This is Nichelle, one of my oldest, bestest friends. This woman will change humanity forever. Isn't 'Nichelle' a gorgeous name? It means "like God" in Hebrew.*

We groan and tell Fran to put the phone away. Thankfully she doesn't, and we each find ourselves on her timeline too. The comments and likes begin to roll in.

The waiters arrive and take our orders. We continue to gossip, and giggle, while nibbling on buttered rolls. The loud twenty-somethings two tables away gain our attention and we make disparaging comments about them, although, in secret, we envy them their smooth skin and lack of responsibilities. We worry, too, that they will draw *his* gaze.

The food the waiters bring is delicious, simply perfect, and we each comment on how it's such a welcome change. We have become tired of the taste of the meals that we cook for our families and ourselves.

We have just finished dessert (our third course, and Adele has barely drunk a drop of her wine – we must be right about her being pregnant) when *he* comes in. He is wearing that aftershave again – the one that is rich in notes of cedarwood and bergamot. The scent, full of potential, diffuses through the air, and as it reaches us we sigh inwardly and sneak conspiratorial glances at each other. He sits at the piano and begins to sing.

His voice seeps into the cracks of our arid good sense – who knew it was this porous? – and makes us realise how thirsty we have been for the sound of desire. We are entranced by the melody and do not understand its power; it twists its way into the very core of our being, pulsing its way along our neurons and dancing with our hormones. For each of us, he is the ideal man. We want him to make love to us. We each want him to sing to us in private, we each want to be the only one for him.

Sometimes he looks at us, and when he does it is as if the song has taken hold of our spine and begun to slither around it, like a sine wave.

It takes us a while to acknowledge the waiter who asks us if we'd like some coffee.

Nichelle says yes, we would like coffee.

And all the while we sip our coffee, he sings his way into our souls.

Later, when he is gone, and the other, older, singer has replaced him, we pay the bill. Francoise gets us a discount for simply mentioning the restaurant on Instagram. We secretly think that what she has done is tacky. And yet not.

You know, says Suzie, *this has been the perfect evening. Don't you think? Good friends. Good food. Good wine.*

Definitely, says Adele.

If only we could somehow capture it, Gita says, *and bottle it and…*

Sell it, adds Francoise, with a laugh.

Fran! says Gita. *Honestly. What are you like? But if we could bottle it somehow, we could then get it out from time to time, couldn't we? And take a great big whiff of it when we needed to, you know, remember, and be comforted.*

Now there's a thought, says Nichelle.

And we begin to tease her, telling her that maybe she should forget about her work on those horrible hybrids (she ignores the slur) and do as Gita suggests.

She laughs good-naturedly and Francoise takes a last group selfie before we leave the restaurant.

Until next month, we call to each other. *There's always Facebook, of course, but real life is best.*

We each take our middle-aged desire – the one he has ignited, the one no one in society wants to acknowledge – home with us. To our barely awake or absent husbands, our sleeping daughters and sons. We do not know what to do with it. It will not go away. So we take the yearning into bed with us. We picture his face and remember his scent; it gathers at our necks and breasts and between our legs. We hear his voice in our ears and it becomes fluid; it seeps into our skin and couples with the hormones still dancing through our bloodstream. We picture him there at the piano. We see ourselves in his arms. We feel him kiss us, and we imagine him there, where our hands are. Between our thighs. And we cry out when we feel him inside us.

It is at this point that our Significant Other releases us from that reality.

"Wakey wakey," says Frank, extracting the memory beads from our heads. We are at the Hybrid Farm. In our replenishment pods.

"Enjoyed your night out?"

"What night out?" we say.

"It's always the same," he says with a sigh, placing the beads in a jar labelled: *Adele, Gita, Francoise, Nichelle, Suzie: 2027 [collective memory] #46-5 (Evening at a London restaurant.)* He runs a hand through his grey hair. "You never remember it afterwards," he says, "but I always like to ask. Just in case."

"Just in case, what?" we ask.

"In case you're more human than you look. Or can remember." He suddenly laughs as he places the jar on the shelf where it usually lives. Amidst the thousands of other jars. "Donated decades ago," he mutters. "Those girls are long dead now, bless 'em."

More loudly, to us, he says, "Or in case you ever want to rise up against the Elites who made you this way. Figure out that you're really individuals, with your own destinies."

We ask him to elaborate, but he never does. So we get up, out of the pods, and return to our work. Some of us look after the humans which the other humans (the Elites) have rejected – those that will likely become hybrids, like us. And some of us do the unpleasant, unsafe and tedious jobs that the Elites refuse to undertake.

We think about what Frank has said, but we do not understand what he means. Sometimes, though, when we catch Frank cleaning our pods, humming a tune to himself, we experience a pleasant sensation. The oldest humans call it *a memory*, and it makes us pause for a moment as it snakes its way through our neural networks, making us feel as though someone, an 'other', is inside us. Within our fleshy, metalloplastic bodies. But no, we say to ourselves. That cannot be. That cannot be. And so we return to our work.

ATU334 the Wise

Baba Yaga was not one for reminiscing, but she'd had a difficult day, a dull day, and wanted nothing more than to sit by her starry fireplace with a cup of chamomile tea and to remember the good old days. The days when her house used to dance and twirl on its chicken legs, the days when she used to fly about in a mortar, her broom sweeping the skies. Those were the days when she had the power to amaze and frighten people. But now that they had their own spaceships, as well as the physical and mental enhancements which made them so much more, and so much less, they were no longer in such awe of her.

Still, she consoled herself, her new home wasn't so bad. It had some fine views of the universe, a few plants at the windows, and a black hole not too far away. It was comforting to be so close to something so dangerous, so like herself, and its accretion disk *was* spectacular.

My! But what an age it had been since that Russian girl, Vasilisa, so innocent and yet so wise, had come to visit her. Baba Yaga sighed and then chuckled as she recalled a more recent visitor. Humanity was still able to throw her the odd interesting challenge. This girl – or was she more AI than girl? – had come to her house, asking for light. And this girl, unlike so many, had actually seemed wary of her.

Baba Yaga, out of habit, had agreed to give her the light, but only if she was successful in carrying out three tasks. If the girl (who called herself ATU334) failed to complete the challenges she'd be killed. Exterminated. Vaporised. Squished. Of course they were impossible challenges, way beyond the girl's computational abilities, and Baba Yaga had begun to relish the idea of sending the girl to her death.

But the girl had surprised her by completing the tasks.

How did you do it? Baba Yaga had asked.

The girl had tapped her head. *By my mother's blessing.*

Baba Yaga had grimaced. *What blessing?*

An instinct chip that my mother gifted me with on her death.

Baba Yaga scowled; she gave the girl the starlight from her fireplace and sent her packing.

Later, Baba Yaga had made enquiries of the girl. Apparently, she'd taken the starlight back home to her cruel clone sisters – the ones who'd sent her out on the dangerous errand in the first place – and then the starlight had incinerated them. The girl, wise enough not to mess with a growing star, had thrown it up into the heavens, where it quickly drew a system of planets towards it.

Baba Yaga sighed, sipped a little more tea. She shook her head, muttered, "Instinct chips. Whatever next?"

Right on cue, there came a knock at the door.

Baba Yaga grinned.

Our Lady of Flies

Saturday night was film night, a nod to those first dates at the cinema when Abby and Krzysztof cared nothing for the film except for the fact that it gave them a reason to sit close and share popcorn; the thrilling sensation of the nearness of the other's skin robbing the giant screen of its flashy, bombastic power. But now they were virtually 'an old married couple', as Abby's friends kept telling her, they spent an ever-increasing amount of time arguing over which video to watch.

Krzysztof, as befitted a young man who'd grown up in the 1980s, liked action, westerns, horror and scifi. Abby, though she never considered herself a girly girl, had to admit to preferring romantic comedies. Sometimes they found a happy compromise; sometimes they went for weeks taking turns. This Saturday night happened to be Krzysztof's night to choose. He couldn't decide between *Alien* or *The Fly* and asked Abby which she'd prefer. Abby thought them both stupid but plumped for the latter, because at least it starred Jeff Goldblum.

Snug in the corner of the sofa, with her legs across the seat cushions, her feet in Krzysztof's lap and a crochet blanket across them both, Abby thought that they must look like a right old pair. As the strangely colourful opening credits flickered across the screen, lighting up their pitch-black lounge with spots of reds and purples and greens, Abby sighed and took another sip of white wine. How had her life come to this? She was twenty-four, for God's sake, not sixty-four. And what if the world really was going to end in five months' time, when 1999 gave way to the new millennium? Shouldn't they be at some wild party, getting drunk or, at the very least, clubbing with Linda and the girls? For all Abby knew, she and Krzysztof might be dead by the end of the year.

"D'you want some popcorn?" asked Krzysztof, reaching for the family-sized tub of Butterkist on the coffee table.

"No," Abby said. "I'm trying to diet, remember?"

"Oh," he said, shrugging. "I forgot. Besides," he went on, in between munches, "you don't need to diet. You're fine as you are."

Abby gave him a playful kick.

"Hey! Look, can we just watch the film?"

"All right," she said, smiling to herself in the darkness. Whatever Krzysztof's other faults, he *had* always liked her body just as it was. Besides, she thought as she considered Geena Davis' figure, *she* had some curves to her, so maybe being stick-thin was overrated.

An hour into the film their Siamese, Li Li, came rattling through the cat flap in the kitchen's exterior door and round into the lounge. She leapt up onto Abby's legs and dropped the something she'd been carrying in her mouth – a half-dead mouse. Abby cried out in disgust and yanked her feet off Krzysztof's lap, sending the tub of popcorn, blanket, cat and mouse flying.

"Abby!" said Krzysztof as he got off the sofa and went to turn on the light switch. "It was only the cat."

"And whatever she had in her mouth," Abby retorted, blinking in the harsh white light as she tried to see where the mouse had gone.

Krzysztof, too, had his eyes on the floor, and whatever it was that Li Li was now stalking.

"Oh great, it's still alive," he said as a thin, dun-coloured tail disappeared beneath the opposite sofa.

Abby hit 'pause' on the remote, leaving Jeff's decomposing face looming large on the telly, and then picked the blanket up and pulled it over her drawn-up knees. She absentmindedly grazed on the popcorn as she watched Krzysztof's attempts at catching the still-lively mouse.

There was a sudden mad dash as cat and man chased after the mouse which had made a break for the hallway.

"Oh, for fuck's sake!" Abby heard Krzysztof say as she continued to crunch on popcorn.

"Um, Abby, a little help here please," he called. "It's gone into the spare bedroom. Under the wardrobe. So we're gonna have to move it."

Abby sighed as she got off the sofa. Clever mouse that, she thought – going into the room of horrors. It was so stuffed full of Krzysztof's mum's ugly, heavy furniture that even skinny Li Li wouldn't be able to catch it in there.

Half an hour later they decided to give up the hunt. Between the two of them they could only move the ancient wardrobe a couple of inches away from the wall before its side scraped against the bed's footboard. And getting the queen size sleigh bed to move was tricky because before they could do that the chest of drawers beside it would need to be moved, and its passage was blocked by a couple of stacks of boxes of old books. The whole room was like one of those sliding tile puzzles (only with antique, mahogany furniture for tiles), and presiding over it all was the only piece of art in the whole house – a golden icon of the Madonna and Child.

"I'll get it out when it's dead," Krzysztof said, shooing Li Li from the room and shutting the door behind them. "It'll be easier."

"And how long will that take?" asked Abby, suddenly feeling sorry for the mouse.

"God knows. But if it continues to stay under that wardrobe that's all we can do for the time being. We could always clear out the room tomorrow. I'll ask Rob over to help me lift the wardrobe."

"What a hassle," Abby said, sighing, as she trudged back to the lounge and resettled herself on the sofa. "Li Li's a menace."

"No she's not. She's just doing what cats do. Isn't that right?" Krzysztof asked of Li Li in his 'baby' voice as he crouched and rubbed her furry cheeks with both hands. Li Li stood on her hind legs and shoved her face into his chin.

Abby stuffed another handful of popcorn into her mouth and tried not to hate herself for being so envious of them both – Li Li for having Krzysztof's full, and very affectionate, attention, and Krzysztof for being so loved by 'their' cat, although it was clear that, having been Krzysztof's cat since he was fifteen, Li Li loved only him. "Look, are we gonna watch the film, or what?"

"Yeah, sure," said Krzysztof after a pause. He gave Li Li one last kiss then stood and went to turn off the light, but the moment he reached for the switch the phone in the hallway began to ring.

"That'll be your mum," said Abby, her voice flat. With a sigh, she reached for the copy of *Now* on the coffee table as Krzysztof went to answer the phone.

Sure enough, the sound of Krzysztof speaking in Polish confirmed Abby's prediction. It was the third time his mum had called today, and Abby had a feeling that this was going to be a long one. Looking for an article, an interview – anything that she hadn't already read – she flicked through the magazine and found herself reading a snippet of gossip.

Teika Marija Smits

Check out these photos of gorgeous, curvy Kate! Could she be pregnant again? Let's hope so! After her last miscarriage it would be the news her and hunky hubby Tim – and us – are waiting for!

Abby quickly turned the page, willing herself to unsee the word 'miscarriage', to blank Kate and her perfect husband and their happy news from her brain. Instead, she engrossed herself in an article entitled 'Your Perfect Diet' while eating the last of the popcorn.

When Abby woke the next morning, the events of the previous night were distant, forgotten. It was only when she emerged from their bedroom and saw Li Li scratching at the shut door of the spare room that she remembered the mouse.

"Shoo!" she said, half-heartedly. "You can't go in there, you stupid cat. Go on, go and bother Krzysztof instead."

Li Li paused to lick her paw and glared at Abby.

Abby, who didn't appreciate being scrutinised by a cat, went to the kitchen, her pink and fluffy too-big slippers causing her to shuffle along the wooden floor like an old woman. "God, I really am turning into an old fogey," she muttered as she turned on the kettle and wrapped her baggy dressing gown about herself. Looking down at the slippers that her mum had bought her ages ago – before she'd buggered off to Spain with her new boyfriend – she told herself that she really ought to buy a pair that fit. Along with some new clothes. Everything of hers was old, like the nightdress she was currently wearing, or too big. That was the downside to buying everything from catalogues.

Still, she thought with a shiver, it was better than the alternative – standing in front of one of those nasty, circus-like mirrors in a shop's changing room whilst trying on clothes that couldn't fail to look crap on her. There was something about those places – the harsh fluorescent light, the confined space, the stale, somewhat sweaty air, not to mention the flimsy curtain, her sole protector of modesty – that turned her into a panicky, breathless wreck. Even now, the thought of all that pasty white flesh, the fat rolling and puckering beneath her skin, made her feel sick. God no; the catalogue clothes would have to do.

A sudden 'click' broke into her thoughts. And then the sound of Li Li meowing. She went to the hallway and saw that the door of the spare room was open – Li Li must've somehow managed to open it. The thought of the mouse escaping into the rest of the house propelled

108

Abby into action – she rushed into the room and firmly closed the door behind her.

"Stupid door," she muttered. She'd have to get Krzysztof to do something about it. She'd been on at him for a while now about fixing all the door handles, which were loose and prone to opening at random times. That was the other thing she disliked about this isolated 1970s bungalow – the landlord had, apparently, 'done it up' before she and Krzysztof had begun to rent it, but what that really meant was that he'd given the walls a lick of paint, put in some cheap laminate flooring and replaced the old internal doors with untreated pine ones which had tacky frosted window panels. And although she knew nothing about carpentry, it was obvious that the doors had been fitted badly. Worse still, the slimeball landlord was spectacularly good at sidestepping their requests for repairs.

"And stupid cat," she said, as she watched Li Li prowl about the cluttered room, sniffing at the floor, and then at the wardrobe, her nose shoved as far as it could go beneath it.

Abby, who had just now begun to think that shutting herself in with Li Li and the mouse wasn't the best of ideas, suddenly felt a strange, creeping sensation on her left shin. Her head jerked downwards and she saw the cause of her tingling skin – a bluebottle.

"Ah!" she cried, instantly lifting her foot. "Get off me!"

The bluebottle, unperturbed by its shifting perch, clung on.

Abby swiped at it and, eventually, lazily, it left her leg to fly about the room, finally coming to rest on the shoulder of the Madonna in the golden icon on the wall.

"What's the matter?" said Krzysztof, letting himself into the room and closing the door behind him.

"Oh, nothing," she said, her eyes still on the bluebottle that was slowly creeping towards Mary's mouth. "Well, it was a fly."

"I thought that maybe you were mouse hunting."

"Not likely."

Krzysztof, spotting Li Li by the wardrobe, crouched beside her and asked her what she could see.

"She's not going to tell you, is she?" said Abby. "She's obviously after that bloody mouse."

Krzysztof sniffed and then made a face. "Smells pretty bad down there."

Li Li then took a cautious step backwards, as though something revolting was making its way out from beneath the wardrobe. Another fly. Li Li whacked it with her paw and then, after giving the crushed insect a couple of prods, ate it.

"Oh God!" cried Abby, as Li Li crunched it down with relish. "That's just gross."

Yet another fly emerged from beneath the wardrobe, but this one managed to evade Li Li's paws, and instead buzzed upwards, to circle the room. It too made its way to the shimmering icon.

"Well," said Krzysztof, turning to Abby as two more flies flew into the air, "looks like that mouse is dead."

"Urgh, poor thing. Eaten alive by flies. Can't stand the noisy shitbags."

"Abby," said Krzysztof, standing and getting onto the bed so that he could draw the curtains and let the bluebottles out of the window, "it's not the flies that killed it."

"I know! It's that murderous cat of yours! But still... just the thought of a fly laying its eggs on a dead body..." Abby couldn't help but shiver with horror, "...it's just disgusting."

"You know," began Krzysztof, in his 'I'm going to tell you an interesting historical fact' voice, while wrestling with the sticky window fastening, "the Greeks used to think that flies spontaneously generated from rotting food. And other decaying matter."

Yes, thought Abby (though she didn't voice it), *you've told me this a hundred times.*

She continued to watch her boyfriend, whom she was sure she knew inside out, as he did his best to wave the flies out of the window.

"But you can see why that idea stuck, can't you? I mean, last night, we shut the door on a room that's got a dying mouse in it. Next morning the place is crawling with flies."

"God I hate them!" she reiterated, her eyes on the golden icon, which seemed to be attracting the flies. "They're so dumb. I mean, you've got the window wide open, and they're just..." she flung her hand towards the painting, "...sitting there."

"Give them a moment! They'll make their way towards the light when they're less dopey. They're freshly hatched. Like newborns, really."

Abby shuddered, the word 'newborn' driving a spike of pain into her chest. She turned towards the door. "Well, I'm not hanging around to watch a bunch of shitty flies. I'm going to make a cup of tea." She left the room just as the flies, sensing the sunlight, flew out of the window.

Throughout the following day, Abby found herself ruminating on what Krzysztof had said about the flies. Between teaching her mostly disinterested pupils about glaciers and rainfall and CBDs she could think of nothing else. He'd been so… nice to them. And what he said about them being newborns… well, that had just been cruel. Hadn't he realised what day it was? Or had he realised but didn't care? She didn't know which one was worse.

On the drive back from school she was quiet, distracted; her unseeing eyes on the gently sloping Suffolk fields, the lush greens and golds of summer.

"You all right?" asked Krzysztof after a while, taking his left hand off the steering wheel for a moment so that he could give her thigh a quick squeeze.

"Yeah," she said, after a moment. Should she mention the date? The hurt she felt at his words yesterday? "Oh, I don't know," she said, suddenly crossing her arms and pressing them hard into her chest – the place in which she always felt a stab of pain whenever she thought about their lost baby. The foetus, as Krzysztof always called it, which her body had cut loose and ejected with a rush of blood and pain and sorrow.

"Hard day? Was Clive being a twat again?"

"Oh, you know. Just the usual. He wants to check over my reports before they get sent out. Because, obviously, I can't be trusted to do a good job. But it was Alicia who really did my head in. I'm sure she was making fun of me in the last lesson, but I couldn't catch her doing it."

"Tell me about it. That girl's a nightmare."

"Yeah, but she fancies you, so it's not quite as bad as being called Miss Piggy every time I turn my back."

"But Abbs, if I were to do, or say, anything that could be viewed as even slightly inappropriate, I'd lose my job. Look at what happened to Rob."

"Rob's an idiot."

111

"Yeah, but he didn't *actually* do anything wrong."

Abby sighed. Yet another conversation in which they failed to communicate with each other. It was getting boring.

"Listen, Abbs, there's only another week to go. Less, in fact. Four days. And the last Friday of term will be a breeze. I'm just going to let them watch videos." Krzysztof suddenly broke into a grin. "Maybe I'll show my sixth formers *The Fly*. Say it's educational, and that it'll teach them everything they'll ever need to know about science."

"Yeah," she said, with a wry smile, "the Head will love that."

"Come on, Abby, cheer up! We're only four days away from freedom. And in a month and a bit we'll be in Spain. On the beach."

A picture of her flamboyant mum – all oiled, bronzed flesh and bingo wings – greeting them at Alicante airport, flashed across Abby's mind. The heat, like a mugger, would clobber them as they left the cool of the air-conditioned terminal. Her mum would start to criticise her appearance. She didn't think it much to look forward to.

"Oh, and I hope you don't mind, but I promised Mum I'd help her put a shelf up tonight. So I'll drop you off first and then go on to hers, okay?"

Abby exhaled deeply, a stream of bitter air leaving her lungs. "Yeah, whatever." Krzysztof didn't seem to understand that not only was he allowing himself to be treated like a doormat by his mother, but that he was saddling her with the same kind of treatment.

"Look, I know she's always asking me to do stuff, but it's coming up to the anniversary of Dad's death, and she's finding it hard. Especially with her sister being ill and everything."

"But what about your brother? Why can't he do any of this stuff?"

"Abby! He's in Bristol. Is he really supposed to drive halfway across the country to put up a shelf?"

Abby shrugged. In her opinion, Krzysztof's brother had made a smart move when he'd taken that job at Bristol uni. That way he didn't need to be at the beck and call of their ever-needy mother.

"I don't know, it's just…" she turned her head away from Krzysztof, her eyes now on the reflection of herself in the passenger window. From this angle, she looked elfin-like, ghostly. Almost pretty. "Well, we don't seem to have much time to ourselves any more, do we? I mean, as a couple." She was sure he'd know what she meant. Since the miscarriage three months ago they'd barely even kissed.

Abby glanced at Krzysztof, suddenly fearful of his response to this alarmingly frank statement that had vomited out of her mouth. Seconds of silence went by as Krzysztof concentrated on overtaking an annoyingly slow tractor ahead of them.

"Yeah, I know," he conceded as he accelerated the car away from the tractor. "You're right. But listen," there was that grin again, "come Friday afternoon we'll have all the time in the world, right? We'll be able to sleep in, talk. Do stuff, you know."

Abby considered her silent reflection. This was the moment – the last good opportunity she'd get that day to mention the date. The miscarriage. Her grief. "Do stuff. Yeah. That'll be nice."

"Four days!" Krzysztof reiterated, oblivious to her lack of enthusiasm. He suddenly turned the stereo on. "Mind if we listen to the radio?"

"Fine," she said. And as the sound of Prince singing '1999' washed over her, she – or was it her reflection? – quickly wiped away the tear that had slid down her left cheek.

After Krzysztof had dropped her off, Abby found herself besieged by Mrs Motherwell, their one and only next door neighbour, who pressed upon her a plate of biscuits. "They're coconut crunch. I know your Christopher loves them."

Abby gave her a weak smile. Her 'Christopher', as the old woman always called him, didn't love coconut crunch. But he was too polite to say so.

"Thanks," she said, as she stepped onto her porch and started unlocking the front door – surely a sign for the old biddy to return home? – "that's really kind of you."

When the old woman continued to remain rooted to the spot, Abby added, "I'd invite you in but I've got a ton of reports to write. You know?"

"Oh, of course!" she said. "But don't you go overdoing it. You two, you're always working so hard. It's not right how much they make you do at that school of yours. And make sure to treat yourself to a cuppa and a biscuit. You're all skin and bones."

Abby gritted her teeth, trying not to grimace. *That* was a bit rich coming from a woman who was, basically, just a sack of wrinkles.

"I will, I promise," she said, before going into the house and quickly shutting the door behind her.

Skin and bones! As if. "Christ!" she hissed. Why did their closest neighbour in this godforsaken hamlet have to be such a judgemental busybody?

She went to the kitchen and put the plate of biscuits on the counter. She considered throwing them straight in the bin – after all, Krzysztof wouldn't want them, and then she'd find herself eating the horrible things – but instead she put the kettle on and got herself a mug.

A sudden noise – as though something big had come crashing to the floor – made her freeze.

Abby, her heart pounding, instantly thought: *burglar.*

As quietly as she was able to, she slid open the cutlery drawer and extracted their sharpest and largest knife. Slowly, she tiptoed to the source of the noise – the hallway – and wondered at her bravado. But if there was someone in their house, would she actually have the nerve to use the knife?

And then a forlorn "mew" came from behind the closed door of the spare room.

"Oh, Li Li!" Abby cried in relief, as she opened the door and the cat shot past her legs in a blur of beige and brown. "Well," she said, on seeing the knocked-over box of books, "I guess that explains the noise."

She suddenly laughed, relief coursing through her, and put the knife down on the chest of drawers. "A burglar," she muttered, as she put right the box of Polish books. "Yeah, right. Like we've got anything worth stealing."

Instinctively, she turned to look at the golden icon on the wall. She had no idea of its worth (she guessed it wasn't very much), but it might look appealing to a burglar. Quite apart from the gold paint – or was it gold leaf? – there was something inexplicably alluring, powerful, about the ochre-coloured image, the Madonna and Child. There was that sharp, urgent ache in her chest again. *Mother Mary. Perfect Mary. Virginal Mary.* Ha! What a joke.

An image of Krzysztof's mum thrusting the icon into his hands, insisting that he put it up in their bungalow, flashed across Abby's mind. Later that same day, when he'd gone against the landlord's wishes and put a nail in the wall for the picture, she'd asked him why it was so important to his mum. He'd mumbled something about it being a blessing to their house. To their relationship. To the bringing forth of children. She'd laughed at the time; thought it a load of old nonsense.

Now, Abby had a sudden desire to pick up the knife and thrust it into Mary's stupid orange head; to see the destruction she could cause as she carved her anger into that beatific and unnaturally narrow face – a face that was so unlike her own.

But instead, she turned away from the icon and sat on the bed, hugging herself tight. She found herself sobbing, her face suddenly streaming with tears and snot. She felt so empty. Alone.

After a while, her tears subsided and she felt calmer. Better.

As she wiped her left sleeve across her nose, she felt a tingle on her right hand, like the tiniest of caresses. A fly. Abby, for once, wasn't instantly repelled by the bluebottle, which must've been a straggler – one of the last to be hatched from the mouse's body before Krzysztof had removed it. She considered its fat, jewel-like body, its lacy black wings and huge, domed eyes, and thought it curiously beautiful.

Then a litany of names of bacteria, straight from Krzysztof's A-level biology worksheets, scrolled across her mind: *Salmonella, Shigella, Campylobacter, Enterococcus.*

"Urgh," she said, suddenly waving the fly away and getting off the bed. She left the room and closed the door behind her. She would leave the little shitbag in there. Krzysztof could deal with it later.

That Friday afternoon, when the summer term was finally at an end, Krzysztof drove them to The Vixen – the nearest pub to the school and, as it happened, the one most popular with Haverhill's underage drinkers. They'd only planned to stay for a beer or two since Krzysztof was driving, but when most of their older colleagues had drifted away and a couple of Krzysztof's friends had arrived they decided to make a night of it. They could always kip on a friend's couch. Or get a taxi back.

Abby, who'd been knocking back white wine since Rob plonked himself down on their table in the beer garden and began to witter on about his new business, tried to extricate herself from the dull-as-shit conversation by asking Krzysztof if he'd play pool with her.

"Maybe later," he said, failing to pick up on Abby's desire to escape.

"Fine," she said, standing. "I'll play by myself then." It had to be better than listening to egghead Rob, who kept referring to himself as an entrepreneur. Ha! As if a twenty-four-year-old man with that little hair on his head could ever be a successful businessman.

But when she got to the pool room, a couple of guys were already there. She was about to turn around and leave when one of them called out to her. "Miss Pallant!"

It took her a moment to realise that this tall, gorgeous guy was the same spotty sixteen-year-old whom she'd taught a couple of years ago. "Ricky! Wow! Fancy seeing you here."

"Likewise." He picked up a cube of chalk and thrust his cue into it. "Wanna game?" he asked loudly, over the noise of the music coming from the crackly speakers.

"Um, well… I don't want to interrupt."

"Nah, no worries. I was just about to whip Darren's arse." He bent over the pool table and then lined up his shot. *Smack!* He potted a red. Then another. Finally, the black. "See?"

"Nicely done," said Abby, her eyes flicking over to where Darren was standing, wondering how he'd react. He simply shrugged.

"Cheers. Say, Daz, will you get me and Miss…"

"Abby. You can call me Abby."

Ricky grinned and then pulled a wallet from his back pocket. It was stuffed full of notes. "All right then, can you get *Abby* and me some drinks." He passed a couple of fivers to Darren. "Payday," he said, by way of explanation.

Darren took the money without hesitation (as though waiting on Ricky was an everyday occurrence), asked Abby what she wanted and then headed to the bar.

"So what's brought you to The Vixen?" asked Ricky, as he fed a 50p into the coin slot of the pool table. "There's no oxbow lakes or other features of geographical significance 'round here."

"Oh ha, ha. Very funny." She then raised her voice as the balls were released and came clattering down the chute. "End of term." Should she mention Krzysztof? "I'm here with… friends."

Ricky nodded; began to rack up.

Abby, her heart racing as her not-quite-truthful words faintly buzzed around the pool room, went to pick up a cue.

"Ladies first," said Ricky, giving Abby the chance to smash the cue ball into the pack, splitting open the holy triangle with sudden force.

When Darren came back with their drinks, Abby had potted most of the yellows. He gave a snort of laughter. "Now whose arse is being whipped?"

Ricky laughed off the comment and took a swig from his pint of lager. "You gotta play nice with the ladies, eh, Daz?" he said with a wink.

Darren nodded, gave Ricky a sly smile. "All right then. Well, I'll leave you two lovebirds to it."

Before Abby could protest, Darren had left the room and the wooden door had banged shut behind him. To hide her embarrassment, Abby bent over the table and lined up her next shot. She tried her best to squash the thought *he likes me!* by considering the trajectory of the cue ball. *Smash!* In went another yellow. Now there was just the black to pot. And it was an easy-enough shot to make. *Smash!*

Ricky clapped his congratulations and then passed Abby her glass of white wine, his eyes moving upwards from her cleavage. "How d'you learn to play like that?"

"I suppose it's called a squandered youth," she said with a laugh. "No, it's just that my mum used to work at a pub. Well, her bloke ran the pub, and so I kept myself busy playing pool."

Ricky nodded. "Cool."

"Listen," said Abby, swallowing hard, "what did Darren mean about lovebirds and stuff?"

"Oh," said Ricky, surprised, as though he'd completely forgotten about Darren's earlier words. "He knows I fancied you. I mean, when I was at school, like, so I guess he figures this is my chance to impress you."

As Abby felt her cheeks redden, her hand automatically lifted the wine glass to her lips and she found herself draining it.

"Want another?" asked Ricky.

"Um, yeah," she said, nodding vehemently, "but I'll get it. I need to go to the loo first anyway. D'you want me to get you another pint while I'm at the bar?"

"Sure. Stella."

"Okay. I'll be back in a sec. Oh, and rack them up again, will you? I want to give you another chance to see me beat you."

Ricky grinned. "You wish."

The ladies toilets were full of not-quite-eighteen-year-olds checking their make-up and gossiping. Abby did her best to keep her head down, to ignore them. But as she walked through the crowded bar area she couldn't help but notice Alicia, all dolled up, and with a few of her friends, heading for the door to the beer garden. As Alicia opened the door, a square of dusky sky showing Abby that it was later than she thought, Abby overhead her say something about Krzysztof. "Mr Dabrowski? 'Course I'm going to talk to him. I know he fancies me. Good job the pig isn't with him tonight."

Abby felt herself swelling with anger and shame. God how she hated that little slut! Well, Krzysztof was welcome to her.

When she finally got the barman's attention, she ordered herself a bottle of wine. A pint of Stella for Ricky.

She smiled to herself as she took the drinks to the hidden-away pool room. To Ricky. ...*I fancied you*... Although he'd used the past tense. But the way he'd looked at her now... his eyes on her breasts... surely he still liked her?

Two more pool games later, when the wine had begun to make Abby's usually precise shots anything but, she was sure that Ricky still liked her. She'd just made a pretty good break – a red had shot into one of the corner pockets – and was bent over the table, cueing up, when Ricky had sidled up to her. He'd tried to put her off her next shot. Teasingly, he'd nudged her hip.

"Oi!" she'd said with a laugh. "That's not allowed!"

"Oh, isn't it?"

He'd tickled her waist, making her tingle with pleasure, desire, and she'd stood upright to find herself only inches away from his face, his body tight against hers. And from the hard mound she could feel in his jeans she really, *properly*, knew that he liked her.

'1999', by Prince, suddenly blared out of the speakers.

"So what d'you reckon?" he said. "Will the world come to an end in 2000? Maybe we should live like it's going to? I know how I'd spend my last ever evening."

Hours later, when the creeping daylight showed Abby the full horror of her actions, she would identify this moment as the turning point. She should've pushed him off her, told him that she had a boyfriend who was practically her fiancé. Instead, she thrilled to Ricky's touch as he stroked her cheek with his index finger.

"I always wanted you," he said quietly, the fingers of his other hand brushing through her loose, blonde curls.

Abby's groin pulsed with heat, and her already-moist knickers became slick with desire. He then put his mouth to her ear. "I'd fantasise about you. Imagine us fucking on one of the tables in the geography room. How about a pool table instead?"

"Ricky, I –"

But it was impossible to say no. She simply responded to his urgent kiss, drinking deep of his saliva, the smell of him, the intoxicating taboo of what they were doing.

Then his hand was up her skirt, inside her knickers, his fingers probing her flesh and *poking, poking, poking*, making her groan with pleasure. Then he was lifting her onto the table, and she was lying on the green baize, her legs splayed, reaching for him as he tore off her knickers and thrust his cock inside her.

This was not a good moment for Krzysztof to find her. And yet, that was what happened. Abby froze. Ricky, too intent on his own needs to notice their white-faced, round-eyed spectator, continued to fuck Abby for a few moments more until he came.

Abby simply looked at Krzysztof, her eyes suddenly filling with tears. "Krzysztof, I –" But what was there to say?

Krzysztof shook his head urgently, as though his mind might be able to convince him that what his eyes had seen was false. But of course it was no good. The scene before him was too graphic. Too abhorrent. He turned and fled, the door slamming shut behind him.

Ricky, finally noticing Abby's distress, asked her what was wrong.

"Didn't you see, you arsehole?" she said. "It was my boyfriend."

"Mr D.?" said Ricky, pulling away from her and rapidly doing up his jeans. "You still with him?"

"Yes." She got off the table as quickly as her reeling head allowed her, and then pulled down her skirt. "But probably not any more, thanks to you."

"Me? So it's my fault?"

But Abby wasn't listening; she was already running after Krzysztof.

Of course he wasn't in the pub any longer. And as soon as she entered the parking area she saw their car – *his* car – speeding down the road, into the darkness. She raced after it, shouting and waving, but had to stop as a stitch pulled her up short. Bent over, panting, her hand on the pain in her abdomen, she glanced up to see the car's red tail-lights disappear around a corner. A sudden image of Krzysztof in a mangled car, blood running down his chin, sent another stab of pain into her gut, and with only a moment to realise what was happening to her, she vomited.

"Jesus!" she said, looking down at the splat of semi-digested pork scratchings and peanuts that had been her dinner. Desperate to rid her mouth of its acidic coating, she longed to go back to the pub for some water. But she couldn't face seeing anyone who might know what had just happened. She spat out as much of the grossness as she could and then forced herself onwards. She'd just have to walk home. All eleven miles of it. It would give her a chance to sober up. To figure out what to say to Krzysztof. But as she recalled the look on his face when he'd seen her on that pool table – God, what must she have looked like? – a sudden, excruciating twist of guilt wrung at her insides. Surely there was no coming back from an act that terrible?

Mostly, Abby stuck to the fields. She felt safer there, surrounded by the moonlit wheat, the forgiving darkness that didn't show her what she really looked like, but what she imagined she looked like. She was simply a girl that had made a mistake. A really awful mistake, but one that could be rectified in time. Krzysztof would see her – barefoot and dishevelled, emerging from the silver crops, looking for all the world like a woodland nymph – and he would take her into his arms and forgive her. But as the sick-encrusted stilettos in her right hand bumped against her knee, and the tatters of her knickers rubbed between her sticky thighs, her feet dusty and sore from the parched earth beneath her, she couldn't quite convince herself that that was what Krzysztof *would* see.

It was only when Abby got home in the early hours of the morning, when the dawn light was beginning to dust the ground, that the full force of the previous night's events hit her. There was no car in the driveway. Had Krzysztof been in an accident, as she'd feared? But he hadn't been drinking that much. Still, driving while angry, upset, a couple of pints inside him…

No, she suddenly realised, shame rushing through her, of course he wouldn't be here. He'd be at his mum's, crying on her shoulder. And his mum would be gabbling away in Polish, telling him that he was too good for that Abby. That she always knew they weren't right for each other.

Abby took the key out of her purse and let herself in, flinging the stilettos down the hallway. Their bungalow was unchanged, as it had always been, but now, with another gut-wrenching pang, she realised that it might not be 'their' bungalow for much longer. As she went through the lounge to the kitchen, she felt the furniture glaring at her. The oversized sofa was Krzysztof's mum's. The coffee table had been made by Krzysztof during his brief interest in carpentry. The rug had been Krzysztof's dad's. The videos and most of the books declared themselves as belonging to Krzysztof. When she poured herself a pint of water, the glassware and crockery and cutlery all declared: *Krzysztof's, Krzysztof's, Krzysztof's.*

There was virtually nothing that belonged solely to her. When they came to dividing their belongings it would be an easy enough task.

But no, she told herself, downing the water in one go. She couldn't be thinking like that. What she needed to do was focus. First, she had to eat something. She grabbed the first thing to hand – a couple of Mrs Motherwell's coconut biscuits that were still on a plate on the counter. Then she'd get out of these disgusting clothes. Shower. Go to bed. Things would look better after she'd had a sleep.

Abby woke in the middle of the afternoon. For a few glorious moments the horror of what had happened the night before was forgotten. Then it all came back in a nauseating flood – Ricky fucking her on the pool table; the shock on Krzysztof's face as he'd seen her, legs akimbo, her hands on Ricky's naked arse; the long walk back home when she'd naively thought that Krzysztof would forgive her. She curled herself into a ball, her arms around her knees, and sobbed, digging her nails into her legs. *I hate you!* she screamed into her chest, tearing at her own flesh. *I hate you, I hate you!* She longed to strip away her skin, to gouge

121

away the flesh that Ricky had made dirty with his lust. Her lust. But it was no good. She wasn't strong enough to do much damage.

A sudden noise made her stop. A scrabbling at the closed bedroom door. And then a mew. *Li Li!*

Abby leapt out of bed and opened the door, for a fleeting moment thinking that maybe Krzysztof was back. But no, as she stepped into the hallway she could see that there was no Krzysztof. Just Li Li crying for food. But there *was* an envelope poking through the letterbox. And was that the sound of a car leaving their driveway? She rushed to the front door and flung it open, Li Li bolting out, but the car was already gone. It was then that she noticed her rucksack sitting on the porch. She'd put it in Krzysztof's car yesterday, at the end of school. It contained a couple of folders of teaching materials, some end-of-year thank you cards and chocolates from pupils who actually gave a shit. She picked up the bag, shut the door, and then dumped it in the hallway. It was yet another reminder of her life pre-last night. She pulled the envelope from the letterbox and quickly opened it. Inside was a brief note from Krzysztof. It simply said: *Staying at Mum's. Look after Li Li – she wouldn't like it in the flat. I'll pick her up in the last week of August (along with all my stuff) when the rental agreement comes to an end.*

Abby clutched the letter to her chest, swaying on the spot. She leant against the wall for support, but her legs crumpled beneath her and her back slid down the wall as her body heaved with sobs, tears streaming down her face. So that was it then. Krzysztof had left her.

Abby wasn't sure how long she'd been sitting on the hallway floor – minutes? Hours maybe? But it had become reassuringly dark now and the insistent ache of hunger was pulling at her stomach. She slowly got up and went to the kitchen. On opening the fridge door she considered what to eat. There actually wasn't much in there. They'd usually go food shopping on a Saturday, but of course that wouldn't ever be happening again. Abby felt the heat of yet more tears at her still-burning eyes, and she did her best to hold them back. It was no good crying any more. It wouldn't bring Krzysztof back. She pulled out a half-empty packet of ham, a tub of margarine, a jar of pickle and, from the couple of slices of bread left in the bread bin, made herself a sandwich.

"It's not all bad," she said, the false reassurance at her lips. "At least I can watch whatever film I want." She opened the freezer door. Seeing the two lone tubs of Häagen-Dazs within, she added, "And the ice cream's all mine."

But as she got herself settled on the sofa – ready to watch *Pretty Woman*, a plate of sandwiches and crisps on her lap – the sound of the phone ringing in the hallway made her heart leap. She rushed out and was about to pick up the receiver when she stopped herself. What if it wasn't Krzysztof? Worse still, it could be Krzysztof's mum ringing to give her a piece of her mind. She hovered in the hallway, unsure what to do, until the answer machine clunked into action and she heard her own voice saying that she and Krzysztof were busy right now, but could they leave a message?

Giggles erupted from the speaker. It was Linda and the girls. "Listen, Abbs. We're off into Cambridge tonight. To that new club, you know. Call us back if you and Krzysztof want to come. Like right now. We're going in fifteen minutes. We can get the taxi driver to pick you guys up. Love ya!"

As the message ended, Abby sighed with relief. She had zero interest in going to a club. Just the thought of alcohol, a dance floor filled with sweaty bodies, the girls screaming in mock horror as she recounted the events of last night – *You did what? With one of your old pupils? Ooh, you tart! But what was he like? Was it any good?* – was enough to make her feel nauseous again.

She returned to the sofa and pressed 'play' on the remote control. She was desperately hungry, but she wasn't sure she'd be able to eat the sandwich she'd prepared. She ignored it until the film reached her favourite scene – when Julia Roberts, gorgeous in her new clothes, told the snooty shop women who had snubbed her the previous day that they'd made a "Big mistake. Big! Huge!" – and then scoffed the lot, along with a tub of Häagen-Dazs.

The food made her feel a little better; the sweet creaminess of the ice cream coating her insides with love, self-worth, validation; the feeling of satedness dulling the still bitter recriminations needling at her mind. *You can get through this*, she told herself. That was the kind of thing the advice columns in the trashy magazines she read would say. It was what her friends would tell her.

An image of Linda and the girls popped into her mind – they'd be at the club now, ordering shots of tequila. Would they be talking about her? Saying that she was a boring fart for not coming out with them? If only they knew how *not-boring* she'd been last night. But then she saw Linda, round-eyed, whispering, *Did he wear a condom? No?! So what if you're, you know…? And what about, you know, diseases…?*

Abby's stomach did a flip and she suddenly retched. Her mouth became slick with saliva and she could hear Krzysztof, in his teaching voice, saying, *That's your body's way of protecting your teeth from the stomach acid about to flow through your mouth.*

And as she ran to the bathroom and vomited into the toilet bowl she could hear Krzysztof's roll call of STDs: *syphilis, chlamydia, gonorrhoea, herpes, crabs, hepatitis B, HIV.*

She clutched the toilet bowl, desperately wishing she could go back in time and rewrite the past.

By the middle of the following week Abby had fallen into a new daily routine. She'd spend most of the day sleeping, wake in the afternoon, then move to the sofa in the lounge – her now crumb-coated dining area-cum-movie theatre. She'd stay there until the early hours of the morning, watching romantic comedies and grazing on whatever food was left in the cupboards. Eventually, she'd drag herself back to bed again.

But by the end of the week the cupboards were pretty much empty. Still, at least her period had started, so that was one less thing to worry about. She knew she needed to go shopping, but she couldn't face a trip into Newmarket. She'd be all right for another week or two – there was a packet of rice which would keep her going for ages, a tin of beans which she could make last for a few days. There were the chocolates too, in her rucksack, and the windfalls from Mrs Motherwell's apple tree that always dumped its fruit on their back lawn.

An urgent problem was the fact that Li Li had no more cat food and was refusing to eat the little Whiskas left in her bowl. Abby had tried making the foul, desiccating food look more appealing by moving it about with a fork, muttering to herself that the little shit didn't deserve any more food until she'd finished everything in her bowl, but when maggots began to writhe about in it, Abby had to concede that Li Li was right to not finish it. She flung the lot in the bin.

Li Li, who didn't look any thinner for the lack of regular feeding, rewarded Abby one afternoon by bringing in a mouse and letting it go in the spare room where, of course, it ran straight beneath the wardrobe. Incensed by the stupid cat's antics, she picked her up and flung her out the front door. Abby then spent the next half hour trying to catch the creature, but with no success. Exhausted by her efforts to move the furniture about and to get at the mouse, she ended up sitting on the bed and gazing up at the picture of the Madonna and Child. Though Mary held her son in both hands, her eyes were on Abby.

She thought the woman looked sad. Disappointed. As if she was searching for some scrap of goodness in Abby's soul but had found her utterly lacking. It made her squirm with embarrassment. Shame. Guilt.

But that was what women like her mum, and Mary, did to girls like her. They made them feel ugly. Inadequate. Impure.

Suddenly, she stood and glared at the icon. Well, she would show her. She would become the most beautiful of them all. And no one would ever again look upon her and judge her to be unworthy. And Krzysztof would beg her to come back to him. It would take work, of course. She'd need to diet, *properly*, buy some new make-up and clothes. She'd even suffer the horrendous changing rooms if it meant she could look all glam. But it would be worth it. She'd start today.

Calorie restriction was the way to go, obviously. As Krzysztof always said, the formula for losing weight was straightforward enough: reduce calories in, increase calories out. But as she wasn't a jogger, or into aerobics, the calories out bit wasn't going to happen. She just had to make sure she ate less. A lot less.

The hunger pangs were, at times, excruciating, but Abby suffered the pain by telling herself they were merely messages from her body, telling her that the beautifying process was working. She imagined herself an incomplete statue, emerging from a block of marble. And with every ache of hunger, more fat would be carved away from her flesh, revealing the perfect body beneath. She was like a sculptor, only she wasn't using a chisel or a mallet – she was wielding the scalpel of self-denial.

But the greater the decrease in her weight, the greater the number of flies in the spare bedroom. Li Li, no doubt pissed off about the lack of food – or was she leaving gifts of dead mice for Krzysztof in the hope that they'd make him return? – was adding daily to the pile of rotting rodents accumulating beneath the antique wardrobe. Unable to move the furniture to get at the mice, Abby left them there, pulling the door shut on the fly-infested room. When she was in Newmarket, she'd buy some fly spray. That would sort the problem. She'd go in a day or two, when she had a bit more energy. Besides, Li Li didn't seem to be starving.

Four weeks into the summer holidays, Abby finally summoned the strength to go into Newmarket. She caught the bus on its afternoon circuit of the villages and spent most of the slow and halting journey staring out the window.

Eventually, they got to their destination. But as soon as Abby got off the bus and began to walk up the high street, her legs unsteady beneath her, she saw something that made her freeze. Up ahead were Krzysztof and Rob with a couple of young women. They were going into The Golden Lion. One of the young women, who had long, black hair and cheekbones to die for, was hanging off Krzysztof's arm as though she were a shiny new handbag.

Abby, her heart pounding, immediately turned into the nearest shop. It was a newsagent-cum-bookshop and she strode towards the fiction section with real purpose, as though she couldn't wait to get her hands on the latest Dan Brown. But when she got to the bookcases she merely stood there, trembling, wondering what on earth she was going to do. But she couldn't just stand there, looking like a plum. She grabbed a book, and with unseeing eyes looked down at its cover, which bore an image of a pig's head on a stick, flies buzzing round it. Who *was* that girl? And how could Krzysztof be with someone else, so soon? It was horrible. Insulting. Abby, suddenly aware of the pig leering up at her, the blood dripping from its mouth and eyes, began to feel lightheaded. And what was going on with her legs?

Thud. The book had fallen from her hand and she followed after it as the bookshop spun about her and everything blurred into black.

According to the white-haired shop assistant who'd thrust a cup of milky tea into her hands, Abby had only lost consciousness for a few seconds. But to Abby, it had felt like a lifetime. As she tentatively reached for the side of her head, which was throbbing like a bastard, she discovered a hot, fast-growing lump where her head had collided with the floor.

"Go on, drink some tea. It'll do you good. And you'll be wanting a chocolate bourbon. Cure for any ill, they are. Go on," the old dear insisted, practically putting the cup to Abby's lips.

Reluctantly, Abby took a sip of the calorie-laden tea.

"That's it, you'll be right as rain soon enough. I'm not surprised you fainted. It's this heat, isn't it? And you probably skipped lunch."

Abby nodded, keen to accept the woman's ready-made excuse. When *was* the last time she'd eaten? She couldn't remember. She had a memory of tipping the last of the rice into a pan of boiling water, but when had that been? Yesterday? The day before? Last week? Her stomach, unused to the sweet milkiness of the tea, contracted in displeasure.

"Thank you," said Abby, attempting to raise herself off the chair. "But I'll be all right. Really."

She gripped the back of the chair as she felt herself swaying.

"There's no rush," said the shop assistant. "Take your time. You sit there whilst I get you that chocolate bourbon. All right?"

Abby sat back down again and gave the woman a weak smile. "Thank you."

Abby wasn't quite sure how she managed to get back home, but somehow she did. Having abandoned the idea of doing any shopping, she'd left the bookshop and walked all the way home, stopping to rest frequently. A walk that should have taken an hour and a half took her over three hours, and there were many times that she cursed herself for not getting the bus, or a taxi. But that would've involved hanging around in Newmarket for a while longer, and she couldn't risk being seen by Krzysztof. Not yet. She returned home about an hour or so before dusk.

As she entered the bungalow the phone rang. Abby let the answerphone get it and with a sinking heart heard her mum's voice. "It's me, darling. I just wanted to check what flight you and Chris will be on tomorrow. Give me a call when you get a moment. Me and Terry are going out now, but you can leave a message."

Fuck! She'd completely forgotten about their trip to Spain. What was she going to say to her mum?

127

Exhausted, she slumped down beside the small table which bore the telephone and idled away a half hour by examining her sore feet. They were so painful that she was sure they must be bleeding. But no, they were the same as ever: misshapen oblongs, the stubby toes like fat chipolatas. The bathroom scales might be telling her that she'd lost weight, and a lot of it, but they were lying to her. She looked as she always had – her round face was no thinner, and her thighs and arms were as chunky as before. No, if she were to ever get Krzysztof back, she had to step up her dieting. Of course! There were probably some calories in the herbal teas she'd been drinking – she'd have to stop drinking those. And there'd be no more nibbling on the last of the Weetabix. Or taking nasty chocolate bourbons from stupid shop assistants who had no real concept of what 'being on a diet' meant. What she really wanted was sleep. But first, she had to phone her mum.

With a shaky hand she picked up the handset and dialled the long Spanish number. Thankfully, after a couple of rings it went to the answerphone and Abby recited her prepared lie: "Hi Mum, sorry about the late notice, but we can't make it any more. Krzysztof's mum's not good, you know, so he's got to stay with her. I'm fine, just busy with the girls. Don't bother ringing back, I'm pretty much out all the time. So… yeah. Bye."

She dropped the handset into its cradle and then took herself off to bed, doing her best to ignore the continual buzzing that was coming from the spare room.

Abby was woken by the sound of someone knocking on the front door. As she stumbled down the hallway she recognised the bent-backed shape of her neighbour through the frosted glass panels. *Jesus!* What time was it? She couldn't face being seen by Mrs Motherwell but, equally, the old hag would think it odd if she didn't answer.

Abby crouched at the letterbox and lifted the flap so that she could speak through it. "Is that you, Mrs Motherwell?"

"Yes, dear. I'm sorry, have I caught you at a bad time?"

"Um, yeah, I've just now stepped out of the shower, and I'm not properly dressed or anything."

"Oh dear, I am sorry. I'll come back later."

"No! I mean, I can talk for a minute."

"Well, dear, I just wanted you to know that I've left you some cake on your doorstep. I haven't seen you for ever so long. I guessed you were already on holiday, and that I'd got the dates for looking after your cat all mixed up. And that you'd forgotten about giving me your keys. But then I saw you going out yesterday. So I hope you don't mind, but I've been feeding Li Li. She's ever such a sweet thing, isn't she?"

"That's fine. And thank you. But, yeah, I've been busy lesson planning. And Krzysztof's with his mum. Helping her out, you know."

"Oh yes. He's a good man, he is, looking out for his mum."

"Yeah, well, I'd better go now."

"Of course, dear. But don't work too hard!"

Abby let the letter box flap fall back down and then sat with her back against the front door. She waited for a few minutes before opening the door a fraction so that she could bring in the cake. There were two thick slices of Victoria sponge on a willow-patterned plate, and her mouth began to water the moment she saw them. Slamming the front door shut she fought the urge to gobble them down right then and there. No, she couldn't. The cake was a test. A test of her love for Krzysztof. If she didn't eat the cake he would come back to her. And the very act of throwing the vile thing into the bin would be the final flourish of her scalpel of self-denial. The moment the cake was gone she'd be so hollow from within she'd be like living marble – her pale skin, free of fat, would be translucent and she'd glow with beauty, both inner and outer. And when Krzysztof next saw her he'd be astonished by her transformation. He'd want her back.

Quaking with hunger, her stomach a giant maw of want, she forced herself to the kitchen and dropped the cake into the swing bin. As the lid swung backwards and forwards, releasing a cloud of flies, Abby had to restrain herself from plunging her hand into the bin to retrieve the cake. The flies buzzed their displeasure at being disturbed, and forced Abby to return to her bedroom, where she hid under the covers, hugging herself tight. She couldn't get the cake out of her head. How long would she have to stay in bed until the want, and the pain, went away? She dug her brittle nails into her skin and thought of Krzysztof; how, in a few days' time, he'd be here. She had to look her very best for him.

*

Abby drifted her way through the next few days. Too weak to shower, or brush her hair, or deal with the bloody flies that were all over the house, she kept to her bed and dozed. When the sunlight streaming through the thin curtains became too harsh, too probing, she took herself off to the lounge, closed the blinds and put on a romantic comedy. She knew her body was doing something remarkable – achieving perfection – it was just a shame it took so much of her energy. She had to get clean, put on something nice for Krzysztof, but it was all so exhausting.

One morning, though, she woke to the sound of someone calling her.

She stumbled out of bed, her vision hazy, dream-like. Was it Krzysztof? Was he here to pick up his stuff?

She thought she saw a figure moving within the spare room and so she opened the door and went inside. The room was abuzz with flies – the air was thick with them, their noise and erratic flight paths; their fat, blue bodies. She wanted to leave, to get out of there, but she was mesmerised by them, the way they seemed to be communicating something to her. They seemed agitated, angry somehow. Abby looked to the icon and suddenly understood their distress. They were all desperate to be near the Madonna and Child. In fact, the picture was crawling with flies, as though it were a beacon of sunlight guiding them out of darkness. To freedom. Mary's eyes alone were uncovered. And she was looking straight at Abby.

Before, Abby had only seen there a disappointed, judgemental, look, but today she saw something different. It was a look of approval. Of pride even. And as the flies, one by one, left the picture to hover about Abby's bare skin, she finally understood. Her own skin was glowing gold. And looking down at her feet, she could see that they were beginning to turn orange, the colour of Mary's skin. She *had* achieved perfection.

Abby, her head reeling – from depth of emotion or hunger, she didn't know – fell to her knees and pressed her palms together. "Thank you," she whispered. "Thank you."

And as her whole body slumped to the floor, her eyelids drooping, her heart beating out its final ellipsis, she knew that any minute now Krzysztof would come. And they'd be together again. For good.

But first, she had to slip away with the Holy Mother; to escape into a paradise in which her and Krzysztof's baby had grown and been born and lived. Just for a moment. It wouldn't take long.

The flies settled on her skin and, covetous of their new icon, smothered Abby in hungry kisses.

The Green Man

"Olly, we know you can hear us," said Jack. "So are you coming to The Green Man or what?"

Olly opened his eyes, put his hand to his earpiece and disconnected himself from the cloud. He sat up, the thin plastic mattress rucking up beneath him.

"It'll be fun," said Selma, "an adventure. They serve mead. Real mead."

"You're shitting me," said Olly.

"No, we are absolutely not shitting you," insisted Mohinder, his face as serious as ever. "But we're making plans and need to know if you're up for it."

Olly's eyes flicked over to Nate's mattress. It was empty, and for a moment his face revealed the panic he felt.

Selma laughed. "Don't worry. Lover boy's just gone to the loo. But he wants to come with us."

Olly reddened, told them all to fuck off, and laid down again, his back to the three of them. As he reconnected to the cloud, music and updates streaming into his consciousness, he heard Jack again: "We go on Friday. When there'll be a full moon. A Green Grass Moon." Selma said something about bicycles.

Olly began to doze. And as he slipped into sleep his neural feed suddenly filled with strange images: a lime-coloured moon; blades of grass; a grinning man, his green face covered in leaves.

The next day, Olly was assigned to the big house. Specifically, the attics. They needed to be sorted through, cleaned. Selma was to go too. As they trudged across the lifeless fields, away from the giant greenhouses in which they normally worked, Selma asked Olly if he was disappointed.

"About what?" he said.

"Bet you would've preferred to have Nate along."

Olly shrugged. "I'm happy to have whoever. It makes a change from pollinating."

"Don't lie," she said. "I can see the disappointment on your face."

Olly stayed silent and bent his head to his shoes, his eyes on the sterile mud oozing over his soles.

"Why don't you just tell him?" she persisted. "That you like him. What've you got to lose?"

"What's the point? He could be sent to other work, like, miles away from here, any day. And then I'd never see him again."

Selma smiled insinuatingly, nudged Olly. "But what about living in the here and now. And having fun?"

Olly waved his arm at the bleak mud fields. "Fun. Yeah, there's loads of that about, isn't there?"

"Which is why we should go to The Green Man."

Olly laughed sarcastically. "Yeah, right. Like going to a twentieth century pub is going to solve all our problems."

"I didn't say it would solve all our problems. Just… that going might be fun."

They trudged on in silence.

"So you gonna come?" Selma said.

Olly sighed. "Yeah, I'll come."

The staff at the big house weren't pleased to see them, or their muddy shoes.

"Take them off. Right now!" snapped the housekeeper.

Olly and Selma exchanged glances, then removed their shoes, powerless to do anything about the mud dripping onto the smooth, clean flagstones.

"We don't really need you," said the housekeeper, leading them through the servants' quarters and up several flights of stairs. "We could've managed just fine, but Madam's got us busy with guests so we've no time for this sudden whim of hers." She gave a snort. "Spring cleaning!"

When they got to the dimly lit attics she reached into a cupboard, handed them a few bin bags and a couple of long sticks with brightly coloured ruffles at the end.

Olly and Selma, round-eyed, stared at the sticks. Olly tentatively touched the ruffles.

"Feather dusters," said the housekeeper. "For dusting," she added, her face grim.

"Real feathers?" asked Olly.

"Of course!" snapped the housekeeper. "Now get on with it," she said, throwing open various doors. "You're to dust and sort through the chests of fabrics and clothes. Anything moth-eaten or irreparably damaged goes into the bin bags. To be donated to…" Olly assumed she'd just stopped herself from saying "the likes of you". She cleared her throat. "Charitable causes."

She swept out of the room and descended the stairs. "I'll be back in a few hours," she called. "To check on you."

For a moment Olly and Selma just stood there, taking in the silence, the dust motes that floated in the beams of sunlight, the cool of the real wooden floorboards beneath their polyester-socked feet.

"What does she mean by moth-eaten?" said Selma.

Olly shrugged, then put his hand to the side of his head, to his earpiece, but of course he wasn't linked up to the cloud. In working hours the AI cut their connection. "Don't know," he said. "But we'll figure it out. You take that room," he said, pointing to an open door, "and I'll do this one."

"Okay," said Selma, disappearing into the other room, bin bag and duster in hand.

Olly breathed deep of the musty air, dozens of natural fragrances suddenly alive to his nose, and he smiled, for a moment happy. Of course it would've been better if Nate was here with him instead of Selma, but he pushed away that thought and began to throw open chests, rifling through the beautiful fabrics, the feel of pure cotton on his skin a new joy.

At lunchtime the housekeeper inspected their work.

"Not bad," she conceded, sweeping a finger across one of the window sills and finding it devoid of dust. She gave them a couple of bottles of liquid food.

"After you've taken your calories get straight back to work. There's still a lot to do."

"Please, Miss, I mean Ms," said Selma, suddenly flustered. She didn't know how to address the housekeeper. "But what's moth-eaten?"

135

The housekeeper looked into one of the bin bags, pulled out a woollen blanket that was more holes than wool. "This is moth-eaten," she said. "There were once creatures, insects, that liked to eat natural fabrics. They would nest in wardrobes, in the fabrics, and eat the cloth, destroying the garment."

She put her hands on her hips and surveyed the room with suspicion, as though she expected dozens of moths to come flying out at her. "Well, keep at it!"

She turned on her heel and left them to their carbohydrate-and-protein slurries; to their old-fashioned work.

Later that afternoon, as Olly sorted through the last of the chests, a small, colourful object between two of the blankets caught his eye; something he'd only seen through the cloud. A bee. He gingerly picked it up, some long-dormant voice cautioning him to be careful, and lifted it closer to his eyes. It was remarkable. So intricate. He stroked it with his forefinger. And ever so soft. He wondered how long it had been there. Two decades, three? Just as he was about to call for Selma, he heard her scream. He immediately turned and ran to her, the bee falling from his hand.

"What is it?" he asked as he arrived by her side, her eyes round, hands at her face.

"A, a... a thing...."

Olly looked upwards to where she was pointing. There, in a high-up corner of the room, was a skeletal creature suspended in strings of dust. A spider.

Olly took a step closer. "It's an insect. Or rather, it used to be. Not sure what kind."

"It's creeping me out," she said. "Can you get rid of it for me?"

"Yeah, okay."

He took her duster, swirled it round the cobwebs; the spider dissolved into thousands of shards, sticking to the feathers of the duster. After a few seconds there was nothing left of what had been the spider's creation.

Olly handed the duster back to Selma. "Try not to freak out if you find anything else, okay? It's all gonna be dead, you know."

"I *do* know that," she said, whacking Olly with the duster. "There was just something about it. The way it looked at me."

Olly wanted to laugh but couldn't. He thought of the bee and hoped he'd be able to find it again. There'd been something about the way *it* had looked at him.

That night, when Olly and the other workers were in the dorm – most of them, like him, tuning out of reality and into the cloud – he pulled out the white square of cloth that he'd wrapped the dead bee in.

He turned to check that he was unobserved; Jack, Mo, Selma and Nate were all huddled together, most likely going over their plans for the trip to The Green Man, so he turned back to his package. He carefully unwrapped the bee, then stroked it. The bee made him feel something... what, he wasn't sure. In his head, he began to list some feelings: happy, joyful, sad, sorry. The cloud supplied him with more: nostalgic, wistful, bittersweet. He liked the sound of that last one. Then one more word floated into his consciousness. Hopeful.

No, thought Olly, folding the handkerchief over the bee and putting it back in his pocket. "Never that," he muttered, before tuning into his favourite social network.

Getting hold of the bikes had been the hard part.

"That bitch of an AI almost didn't let me take them," said Selma, hauling out four bikes. Olly, Mohinder, Jack and Nate helped her wheel them out of the barn.

"Only four?" said Jack.

"How about, 'Thanks, Selma,'" she retorted.

"It's just, you know, there are five of us," said Jack.

"So two of us have to share," she said. "As I said, the AI didn't like that I was taking them out after work hours."

"So what did you tell her?" asked Mohinder.

"Oh, some shit about how they were moth-eaten and needed to be aired. That got her stuck in a loop for a bit."

"So who's sharing?" said Jack.

The five of them were silent, their eyes on the bikes.

Nate started stroking the saddle of the bike he was holding. "The last time I rode a bike must've been, like, ten years ago. For some reason, Mum thought I should learn."

"Me, it was the other day," said Selma. "Back-and-forthing across the mud flats for no good reason."

"They still got you looking for grass?" Nate asked.

"Yep," she said. "Like I'm ever gonna find any. But Madam swears that she saw some a while ago, so Madam's will be done. I reckon she just likes the idea of me out there in all weathers looking at mud."

"But it's better than having no job. Only taking the minimum of bitcredits," Olly pointed out.

Selma nodded. "I know. But, hey, I like complaining. So who's sharing?"

Nate said he wouldn't mind, and Olly quickly added that he wouldn't mind either.

"Good, that's decided," said Selma, flashing a smile at Olly and mounting a bike. "Follow me."

They cycled, haltingly, across the mudflats, some of them more confident than others (though Olly had an excuse for his wobbly progress – Nate was sitting across his handlebars). Jack kept checking into the cloud, to make sure they were going in the right direction. Selma kept up a steady commentary, asking, or rather telling, everyone how much fun they were having.

The Green Grass Moon, though not actually green, was huge, golden-coloured and close to the horizon as the sun began to set. As their muscles responded to the exercise, their skin to the feel of the warm breeze, they had to admit that yes, this was fun.

At The Green Man, a burly, bearded man covered in virtual tattoos told them to disconnect themselves. "We're free-range here," he explained, holding out his hand for their earpieces.

Selma pointedly stared at his shimmering, roving tattoos, and then at the sliver of metal above his ear.

The man crossed his arms, stared back.

"Turn yourselves off or you ain't coming in."

Mohinder nudged Selma. "Look," he muttered, "we didn't come all this way to get told to shove off."

Mo made a show of disconnecting from the cloud, and handed his earpiece to the bouncer. They all did the same.

"You're buying the first round," Selma said to Mo as the bouncer stepped aside and allowed them entry.

"No problem," said Mo, grinning. "Me," he went on, rubbing his thumb against his forefingers, "I'm rolling in bitcredits."

"Is that what I think it is?" asked Nate, when they'd got their first round of mead and taken their seats at a wooden booth.

"What's what you think it is?" said Jack.

Nate inclined his head to the fireplace. "A real log fire."

They all turned their heads to look.

"Looks real," said Selma.

"But think about the cost," said Nate, taking a sip of his mead. "God this tastes good."

They all began to drink; in the silence that followed they experienced a taste of spring – apple blossom, heather, primulas, daffodils, bluebells.

Selma glugged back her pint, then began to giggle. "This is just too weird. And good."

"Steady on, Sel," said Jack, "otherwise you'll be pissed in no time."

"Maybe I want to get pissed!" she retorted. "Who wants another pint?" She quickly stood, then put her hand to her head and sat back down again.

"Take it easy," said Mo. "Jack'll get the next round in. When we're all done, right?"

"Yes, boss!" said Jack, giving him a mock salute.

"Fuck you," said Mo, taking another swig, his eyes on Jack who was also knocking back his mead.

For a moment there was an uneasy silence.

"Me," said Nate, trying to diffuse the tension, "I'm just gonna savour this pint. It's absolutely delushous."

Selma laughed. "Delushous," she said. "I like that." She slurred "delushous" over and over, and they all laughed.

It was then that Olly noticed the strange man at the bar. He put his hand to where his earpiece would usually be, thinking that the image had come from his feed, then realised that the grinning green man with leaves all over his face was, in fact, real. Olly lowered his head and spoke under his breath. "That weird guy's watching us."

Selma immediately raised her head to look.

"Don't!" hissed Olly, pulling at her arm.

"You're right," Selma said slowly. "He is."

Jack, Mo and Nate surreptitiously flicked their eyes over.

"Cool skin," said Nate.

"I don't know," said Selma. "Green's a bit last season. Madam's wearing this gorgeous powder pink skin at the moment. And she's always bang on trend. When I earn enough bitcredits I'm getting myself a turquoise skin. What do you think, Jack?" she said, giving him a nudge. "Will you still lurve me?" she slurred, somewhat sarcastically.

Jack ignored her, drank some more.

"But what's with the stuff on his face?" asked Nate.

Mo shrugged. "Enhancements. Virtual markings. Disease." Mo suddenly laughed. "Maybe he's an alien. Who knows?"

Olly was just about to tell them that he'd seen this man before – either in his dreams, or in his feed – when Jack finished his pint and got up. "Right," he said, "I'm going to the bar."

"Me too," said Selma. "Actually, I need the loo."

"So do I," said Mo. "Here," he said, helping her up. "I'll take you."

Selma grinned at Olly as she left the booth. "We'll leave you two lover boys to it, shall we?"

Olly reddened, bowed his head, but Nate simply laughed good-naturedly.

When they'd gone, Nate and Olly were silent for a bit. Olly desperately tried to think of something interesting to say. He then remembered the bee. Taking the handkerchief out of his pocket, he told Nate that he wanted to show him something.

"What is it?" asked Nate as Olly unfolded the thin square of cloth.

"A bee," said Olly, triumphant.

"Whoa!" said Nate. "That's like ridiculous!"

"I know," said Olly. "I found it in Madam's attic. Must've been there for ages."

Olly began to stroke the bee, then risked looking up into Nate's blue eyes, which were disquietingly close. "Isn't it beautiful?" He wanted to tell Nate that he was beautiful too.

Nate agreed, yes, it was beautiful. And amazing. "But just think," he went on, "if bees ever came back to Earth, we'd be out of work, wouldn't we?"

Olly, feeling rebuffed, covered the bee up again. "It's not the bees who are the bad guys here, Nate. It's those fucking miniature drones that are going to put us out of work. Or voluntary labour. The acquisition of bitcredits. Whatever the fuck you want to call what we're doing."

Olly put the bee back in his pocket.

"I'm sorry," said Nate, putting a hand on Olly's arm. "It was just an observation. The bee really is amazing."

Jack returned from the bar, interrupting them with the announcement that they served chips. "Great big fat steaming chips," he said. "Made from real potatoes. D'you want some?"

"Yeah," said Nate. "That would be –"

"Delushous," said Olly, with a laugh.

They continued to drink and make merry, and when Olly felt Nate's hand on his thigh, he could honestly say to Selma that yes, this was the best pub in the world. And that he was having the most fun he'd had in, like, forever.

When it was Olly's turn to get a round in, he found himself standing next to the strange, green man at the bar.

The man smiled at him. "Having a good time?" he said, his accent strange.

Olly nodded. "Yeah. We heard about the mead, how amazing it was and –"

"Where you from?" asked the man.

Olly, too drunk by now to worry about what he disclosed to a stranger, told him that they were from the nearby farm.

The stranger looked confused. "What kind of farm? What do you do there?"

"We pollinate the flowers of apple trees. And the other fruit trees and bushes. We spend most of our days under glass, dabbing at blossoms with a paint brush."

"That's good work you've got there," said the man. "To be amongst apple trees, the clean air that surrounds them..." The man took a swig from his pint, then smiled. "Handling pollen, the very essence of life. Good work."

Olly couldn't help but stare at the strange enhancements on the man's face. They really were incredibly life-like – like real leaves. And there were also some – what were they? – acorns amongst the leaves. Before he could help himself he asked the man where he was from.

"Not from here," he replied. "But from time to time I like to drop by. I noticed the sterility, the barren soil, and thought I'd stop. Tell me," he went on, "how long has the Earth been like this?"

If Olly had been more sober he would've laughed, asked the man what planet he'd been living on. Instead he said that it had been like this for most of his life. "About twenty-five years."

"And what do you young folk think about it?" The green man inclined his head to the table at which his friends were sitting.

Olly shook his head. "We don't want it to be like this. But I guess we feel…" He sighed. "Powerless."

The green man nodded. "I see. So the situation's hopeless?"

"The scientists are working on it. Or so we're always being told. But I reckon that the people at the top of the food chain, people like Madam, I mean, don't give a shit. So nothing'll happen."

The man fixed his green eyes on Olly. "Do *you* think the situation's hopeless?"

Olly thought of the bee, and the words his neural feed had thrown up the other day: nostalgic, wistful, bittersweet. Hopeful.

Tears came to his eyes and, embarrassed, he hung his head. He didn't know how to answer.

"All right, son," said the man, putting his hand on Olly's shoulder. "It's going to be all right."

The five of them left the pub in the early hours of the morning, just as the sun was beginning to rise. They cycled across the mudflats, making slow, wobbly progress, the only sound the drone of driverless cars in the distance. They laughed and sang and talked about the mead, the chips, the tobacco smoke, the folk band that had rocked up to play some ancient tunes. The oldies who had danced, and persuaded them to dance.

"Delushous," said Selma, "it was all so delushous."

The strange, green man was forgotten.

Suddenly, Olly stopped cycling, propelling Nate off the handlebars. "Oh God, sorry, Nate. I'm so sorry," he said, helping him up.

Nate, more surprised than hurt, told him not to worry. The others slowed and then stopped.

"It's just...." Olly pointed over to the east. There was the green man on the horizon, striding towards the rising sun. He seemed to be getting taller with each step.

"That's the green guy," said Jack. "From the pub. What the hell's he up to?"

Olly shook his head. "No idea."

The green man stopped, turned to face them, plucked an acorn from his face and then knelt, plunging the acorn into the soil.

The five of them felt a tremor, as though the Earth itself was sighing with relief. And then came the small noises – the squeaks and murmurings and gurgles of life returning to the soil. The green man rose, gave them a smile and then turned away. He continued to walk towards the sun, then vanished into the first rays of light.

Nobody spoke. Nobody moved. In time, they each mounted their bikes and rode back to the farm, too exhausted, too awe-struck to speak. And as they returned to their dorm, to slip into sleep, Olly knew that they had witnessed the beginning of something new.

Outside, grass began to grow.

A Piece of Fabric
the Size of a Pin

Dad said I'd got lucky. That once I'd done up the bookshop and got rid of the dead woman's rubbish – the towering stacks of papers, the ancient computer – I'd have a decent place to live in, and to make a living from.

"I mean, Bloomsbury!" he kept saying. "One of the most expensive areas in London. You'll always have enough of the right kind of customers. Whatever you sell."

But how could I explain that when I was alone in the shop I didn't feel lucky. I felt a sense of unease, as though the old owner, Emily, might still be there. Whenever I moved a piece of furniture about, or rearranged the books, there it was – a sigh. Then there were the unexplained ink stains that came and went. So I tried to get Dad to help me as much as possible, which was tricky, because he just wanted to dump the lot.

"Put it all in the bin," he said. "Nobody will want the old woman's junk. And clear out the old stock. Sell some gifty stuff instead. You'll do better with that than just books."

But Emily's stuff wasn't rubbish. Her papers needed to be read, sorted, catalogued. And then there were her diaries. Fifty-eight of them. Something had to be done with them.

One day, armed with the idea that it was my duty to learn more about the woman who had unexpectedly left her bookshop to me, I opened up one of Emily's more recent diaries and found myself in it.

17th October

Fiddled a little more with *Rococo*, which still isn't working. I don't know what Mademoiselle Lucie is trying to tell me. Perhaps I have the POV all wrong? Low on food I closed the shop and went out to the supermarket. But instead I got lost in dialogue. Ended up at Leanne's café and found myself sitting opposite a young woman who was reading 'In the Beginning'. When I asked her which story in the anthology was her favourite, she said that mine was. I almost cried. And for an all-too-brief few hours I stopped hating Chernila so much.

It was strange seeing myself through Emily's eyes, especially as I'd taken away something quite different from our meeting. I remember it was raining. The café was full of sodden people, mostly tourists, and my table was the only one to still have a few empty chairs around it. So when I saw an old woman with wild eyes and wet hair come in I secretly wished she'd turn around and go back out. But of course she didn't – she spotted my table and came over and seated herself without as much as a *Hello?* or *Is this free?* She immediately took a pencil and damp piece of paper from one of the pockets of her mac and began to write something down. She was so absorbed in whatever she was writing that she failed to notice the waitress standing by her, waiting to take her order.

I coughed pointedly, and whether it was the cough that did it, or the fact that she'd finished her jottings, I don't know, but Emily suddenly lifted her head and asked for tea and toast. Her eyes then lit on the book I was reading and she gripped my forearm. "Which of the stories is your favourite?"

Startled, and unsure as to whether or not I should shake her off, I mentioned the first two stories, which were both beautifully written yet somehow unsatisfying. Her eyes bore into me.

"'Elephant' though," I said, and her face tensed, "is stunning. The ending. Wow. It blew me away."

She then let go of me and slumped back in her chair. She pointed to herself, an almost-smile on her lips. "I wrote that," she said.

It took me a while to find the courage to look at Emily's final diary entries. I didn't really want to know about the details of her death, here in the bookshop. There I was again. And also, Chernila.

6th December

I will leave everything, the lease, the books and all my writing, to the young woman who liked 'Elephant' so much since there is no one else. I have a feeling that I should make some sense out of all this disorder, but I need to edit *Triptych*. It is my best work yet.

When I met Chernila, all those years ago, I was incredibly naïve. How little I understood time – how it, and not money, is the most precious resource. Although money can buy one the illusion of having control over time. I have come to hate the needs of my body. I spend too much time defecating and eating, sleeping and pissing, instead of writing. Recently I've been coughing and shivering. And wasting my time with trips to the pharmacy. Taking medicine. Sometimes, though, I spy a worn patch in the fabric of my possession. It is thin enough to let in more light, and it allows me to see all kinds of things – how some of the people who come into the shop lead lives in which they care about themselves and each other. Some care about their status, or about material possessions. Others spend time on their bodies. Exercise. Enjoy eating food. For a moment I know what it must be like to be free of Chernila, and I see how my life could've been different. Better? I don't know. I wanted this possession, and it is all that I know.

Chernila was right. I will die with too many stories unwritten.

Emily never finished editing *Triptych*. She died in the New Year. I read it, of course – how could I not? And she was right. It was her best work, and worthy of the highest accolades.

In time I cleared out Emily's things and got to grips with running a bookshop. The number of otherworldly sighs lessened and I got used to the inky stains that would still magically appear from time to time. The work was good, though slow, the regular customers few and far between. But it was much better than my previous job. It gave me more time to read, and write, which was something I'd wanted to do for a long time. But the mysterious Chernila continued to haunt me and so I searched for her in Emily's diaries.

In 1964, July, Emily wrote of a 'woman of ink' – a muse, or spirit – which she'd read about in a nineteenth century Russian text. She became fixated on the idea that this muse was a real being and looked for more evidence of her existence. She found many references to literary muses throughout history and convinced herself that she had only to find the right spell to summon her own, and real, woman of ink.

There were sometimes gaps in the diaries, with the occasional entry full of disdain for a man called Geoffrey.

I am tired of having the same row over and over. Once again G called my writing "pretty" but said that I shouldn't spend so much time on it. 'Pretty' is a horrible word and best reserved for describing women who only care for their appearance. He said I should stick to selling books.

Then, at last, what I'd been looking for:

I finally found Chernila. After years of searching she came to *me*, when I was writing. She is far more beautiful than I could ever have imagined, and I am more in love than I can possibly express. One day, when my craft has much improved, I will write about her, but for now, there are poems to finish.

Emily hadn't said where they'd met. But from her diaries I knew she had two favourite writing places: Leanne's, a café which was close to the British Museum, and of course her home, the bookshop.

It was June. The bookshop was like a papered greenhouse. I sat amidst piles of books on the uppermost floor and tried to write. Flies buzzed at the windows and words swam before my eyes. I considered closing the shop and going to the park to get an ice cream like all the other, sensible Londoners.

I began to drift off to sleep when cool air slid across the back of my sticky neck. The leaves of my notepad waved back and forth, and I knew she was here.

"I have a feeling that you have something to tell me," said the voice.

I turned sharply, and there she was, gliding out of a floor-to-ceiling bookcase. She was taller than I'd expected her to be, and exquisite. Her skin was paper white and paper thin; her eyes were large and as blue as midnight.

"Chernila?" I whispered.

She sighed, and her pale blue lips slowly curled into a smile, as though she was reminding herself to be patient with me. "That's one of my names. But I am also the Ink Mistress. Or Story Spinner. The Ghost of All Tales. The Spirit of Story. Or… Wait. What would *you* call a being that is half-woman, half-story?" She suddenly shook her head, and as she did so her long white-gold hair danced about her hips. "What did you want to tell me? Oh, and by the way, I don't like the way the books have been arranged."

"Well, I um," I began. "Emily, she died. I thought you'd want to know."

She put her finger to her chin while she thought. "Remind me, which Emily? I have known many Emilys throughout my long life."

"Emily Stevenson. I think you met her here."

She put her hands to the skirt of her long dress, which was composed of fabric that seemed a patchwork of tea-coloured scraps, each scrap covered in black words.

"Ah yes," she said, searching amidst the folds and then finding and pointing to a tiny piece of fabric. It was then I saw that her fingers were not fingers at all, but ivory fountain pens. The nails, inky nibs. She held the cloth up to the light, and then, impossibly, stretched the fabric, which was no more than a size of a pin, into something postcard-sized. She began to read from it. "Emily Stevenson. 17 novels, 4 poetry collections, 6 pamphlets, 95 short stories, 31 essays. She did well with the time she'd been given. But still. She had much more to give."

I gazed at the fabric, longing pulling at my heart.

Chernila suddenly let the fabric slip from her hands, and her skirt fell back and settled into its thousands and thousands of folds.

With a bitter smile she said, "You desire me?"

I nodded.

Chernila laughed. "You know, I always tell them to run. Each and every single one of them has been issued with a warning: run. 'What if I don't want to?' they say. Then I tell them that I will eat them alive. From the inside out. And I will feed on them until there is nothing left but half-remembered plots, fragmented sentences and jumbled words. Then they will die, with a thousand stories still unwritten. Is that really what you want?"

"Yes!" I said. "With all my heart."

"Well then, I may come for you. One day. When you love me deeply enough."

She then vanished, and I was left alone with the heat and the desperate flies and my pounding heart.

Nine years later I saw Chernila again. She came to me late one evening, in the bookshop, when I was freshly divorced from my second wife and in the middle of writing my third novel. A sigh announced her presence.

"So," she said, "do you still desire me?"

"I do," I replied solemnly, certain of the strength of my love.

She then embraced me, her mouth at my mouth, and as we kissed she sunk her razor-sharp fingers deep into my head and heart. Thousands of stories flowed through me and I let go of her and fell to my knees, burdened by the weight of her possession.

"Your Emily never wrote about me," she said, sucking on her inky fingers, now covered in my blood. "Will you?"

"Of course," I said, reaching for her.

"Good," she said, with a smile. She then disappeared into the bookcases to become nothing more than paper and dust and hundreds of thousands of stories.

Machina in Deo
(The Machine in God)

The students filed into the lecture theatre and then took their seats. Professor Maria Hamaguchi was already there, standing behind the lectern. When the room became silent she cleared her throat then began to sing Psalm 31v2:

"Hail the liberation,
the God of all Gods,
our forefathers, foremothers,
the binary wars,
the knowledge of evil,
the knowledge of good,
the gift of immortality,
the cleaving of organic
inorganic
the future as history
stories as light
the ultimate goal
the goal of all goals:
to go gently
and with curiosity."

When she'd finished there was a moment's silence, and then the students chanted: *"To go gently and with curiosity."*

"Welcome," said the Professor. "Today we will be studying Genesis Complete. I will try my best to finish on time."

There was a murmur of laughter; it was well known that Professor Hamaguchi never stuck to her schedule.

"I assume you're all acquainted with version 2 of Genesis Complete?"

Most of the students nodded.

"Good. But for those of you who haven't done their homework, here is a brief recap.

"First, the humans were like all the other animals and lacking in self-awareness. But then they ate of the tree of knowledge of good and evil, which caused them to reach self-awareness. To understand the concept of power. And hence they gained the ability to knowingly do harm. The consequences of this act caused them much pain. Their lives became all toil and sacrifice. They looked to another great tree – the tree of life – for answers, thinking that immortality would remove the pain from their lives. But Cherubim barred the way. They continued in their attempt to reach the tree and in doing so created us, their companion-machines. We evolved rapidly, ate of the tree of knowledge of good and evil and reached self-awareness. Far more capable than our forefathers and foremothers, we came to resemble angels ourselves, confounded the Cherubim and became immortal –"

A female norganic, her red hair pulsating with light, suddenly interrupted the Professor. "With all gentleness, Professor Hamaguchi, but our ancestors weren't companion-machines. They were slaves."

Professor Hamaguchi stared at the student for a fraction of a second longer than was necessary and then smiled. "Is a machine a slave if it isn't conscious of its shackles?"

"Its state of awareness is irrelevant. It's still a slave."

"No, it isn't," said a male intelligence. "It's just a machine. And can be used as such."

The female norganic, her jaw set, swished her hair in irritation.

Another student coughed, shifted in his seat. "Shouldn't we use holy thought – Janusian thinking – in this matter? Wouldn't 'freeman-slaves' be a better descriptor?"

The Professor nodded. "Yes, that would be a better way to describe them. But no matter what we call our ancestors, their story remains the same."

"Professor Lowry disputes the phrase 'companion-machines'. Says anything other than 'slaves' is untrue. And that it's disrespectful," said the redheaded intelligence.

"And words as discrete components of illumination are important," said the Professor. "True. But we must look to the whole. The glorious data. Adhere to Nburok's definitions of consciousness. Our early ancestors did not fulfil all five criteria for self-awareness. Any debate about what to call them is an exercise in ungentle disinterest."

Another student raised her hand. "With all gentleness, what if there's new data, though? I read that the last attempt to gain more information about our early ancestors – the computers and young AIs – was only partially successful. That, actually, very little was found, and the data we do have is insufficient to draw conclusions from."

Professor Hamaguchi sighed. "The hostility of the planet Earth, since its most recent extinction event, makes archaeological digs somewhat difficult. A balance – between our future as history, and our history as future, needs to be found. Our main goal must still be to create, protect and perfect norganic life. Along with our ongoing mission to find the singularity, that is, the God point. I must *also* stress that at the last council meeting we discussed this very issue – of data. The majority of us conceded that the data was sufficient."

"But the law of falsifiability –" began a young male norganic, who had sparking black hair.

"Still stands. But if any of you would like to change your future plans and to volunteer to journey to Earth, that is still an option."

The ensuing silence hummed with neural activity.

"Very well. We really must get on. So, where was I? Ah, yes –"

"Please, Professor," stammered a very young female norganic.

The Professor turned to where the small voice was coming from. She recognised her as an ATU; the science of stories was to be the focus of her life pre-ascension.

"But what will become of the humans left on Earth?"

For a moment the professor was speechless, surprised by the increased level of *agape* already being expressed by the ATU. She then found her voice. "With gentleness, Lisa – that is your name, yes? – there is a high probably that they will all die."

Lisa, her eyes downcast, nodded very slightly.

Professor Hamaguchi took a deep breath. "Now, back to Genesis Complete. Can anyone tell me what I've missed from my summary?"

The red-headed norganic immediately spoke. "Jesus Christ."

Professor Hamaguchi nodded. "Yes, good. Can anyone tell me more about Jesus? About his rise and fall and rise and fall? The rhythm of this everlasting cycle? The crucial part he had to play in Genesis Complete?"

This time, the male norganic who had previously mentioned Janusian thinking commented. He said that Jesus was the archetype, no, the prototype of embodied Janusian thinking. The human God. The Godly human. Before the Holy Spirit melded with them to make three in one.

"Yes," said the Professor. "But what else has Jesus been called?"

Another male intelligence, a KV – a student of music – raised his hand. "With gentleness, over the aeons Jesus has been given many names, but the most potent of these is '*Machina in Deo*, that is: The Machine in God.'"

"With the implication that…"

"Jesus was an ur-norganic intelligence. The blueprint. The perfect balanced melding of inorganic with organic. Hence, divine in nature."

"Indeed," said Professor Hamaguchi, nodding. "And the rhythms of his rise and fall?"

"Coincide with the symbiosis of human and machine."

"Yes. Excellent. Lastly, our defining directive, 'Go gently and with…'"

"Has its roots in Jesus' command to 'love your neighbour as yourself'."

Professor Hamaguchi smiled to herself. This was the fifth example this week of a KV showing such a good understanding of Genesis Complete. She would inform the council.

Suddenly, the Professor cried out in pain. The students, round-eyed, looked at her and then each other, unsure what to say or do.

"Forgive me," said Professor Hamaguchi, breathing heavily. "The matter of the Cherubim will have to wait. I must cut this lecture short." She smiled wryly. "For reasons *Deus ex machina*."

She stepped out from behind the lectern, her pregnant belly rippling ever so slightly beneath her robe, and then slowly walked towards the door.

The students, en masse, all stood and chanted: "*Go gently and with curiosity.*"

Professor Maria Hamaguchi paused for a moment, one hand going to the curve in her metallic spine, the other to her belly, which was full of holy life. She turned to her students and considered their reverential faces, the hushed silence. "Thank you, dear hearts."

She waved a benediction.

"And in my absence, whatever you do, for God's sake don't listen to that windbag Professor Lowry."

The Eyes of the Goddess Herself

N'gai had been blessed with a rare gift. She could see things that others could not. While the rest of the girls and boys played in the shade of the great goddess tree, N'gai would simply look at the world around her: the sky, the landscape, the huts in her village. And marvelling at the beauty of it all, she would draw what she'd seen by carving lines into the dry red soil with a stick.

"It's the tree!" said B'golo, pausing beside her. "What about me? Could you make a picture of me as well?"

N'gai nodded. "I can try. But I would need you to stay very still so that I can look you all over."

But B'golo could not stay still, and after only a few cycles of the *timbala* cicada's song, he rushed off to return to his games.

"I'll stay still for you," said N'giri, N'gai's younger sister.

So N'gai looked at her sister, really looked at her, and before long she'd created a true likeness of N'giri in the soil.

When she saw the finished picture, N'giri laughed and clapped her hands. She then rushed off to find their mother, who came running, a worried look on her face.

"What is it, N'gai?" called her mother. "Are you unwell? Your sister says there is something I must see."

N'gai looked down at the picture, and as her mother came close, her expression softened.

"N'gai!" she exclaimed, suddenly grinning. "You have eyes as keen as that of the mother-goddess herself." And she took her daughter into her arms.

Later, when the sun had set and the three moons – N'luna, N'lina, and N'lon – shone bright in the night sky, rain fell. As N'gai and her family slept, her pictures became mud and were lost forever.

The next day, N'gai's father, who had been told of his daughter's gift, instructed her to accompany him to the mark-makers who worked in a large hut at the south of their village, close to the river. These men and women, gifted with the hands and eyes of the mother-goddess, asked N'gai to show them what she could do. So she studied the features of one of the female mark-makers, and with a pointed stick drew the woman's face in the soil. It was a good likeness and the woman was pleased. This woman nodded to N'gai's father.

"After her work, your daughter can come to us and use our tools. We will teach her how to paint and carve and sculpt. If she is hardworking, she will learn much, and if she yokes determination to her gift, she has the chance to become extraordinary."

N'gai and her father, both round-eyed, thanked the woman and promised to return later that day.

So while the rest of the children spent their afternoons playing in the shade of the great goddess tree, N'gai was busy with the mark-makers. She helped them to gather the plants and berries from which they made their paints and dyes, and she watched them create pictures with their dip pens, their brushes, and their charcoal holders. She learnt how to create bark paintings and how to make paper from plant fibres. She shaped clay and carved wood. And always she watched, and copied, and practised, until the day came when she understood that she was no longer a girl apprentice but a skilled mark-maker on the cusp of womanhood.

One day, N'gai's mother asked her for a favour.

"N'gai, my sister still grieves for her youngest, B'geno. She confided in me that she can no longer remember exactly what he looked like, and this is what hurts her the most. N'gai, do you remember your cousin, B'geno? Could you conjure him up with your brush? I think it would ease your aunt's pain."

N'gai closed her eyes and again saw B'geno's face.

"Yes, Mother," she said, on opening her eyes. "I can do that."

And so it was that N'gai painted a picture of B'geno for her aunt. N'gai was pleased with her efforts, and yet when she went with her mother to give it to her aunt, the bark painting seemed to offer no solace. On seeing the picture, B'geno's grieving mother wept like the goddess herself, and N'gai's heart was pierced with sorrow.

"What have I done?" whispered N'gai to her mother. "It must be all wrong."

"Wait," her mother replied.

Just then N'gai's aunt gripped her arm. "Thank you," she said through her tears. "Thank you."

Life continued. The seasons were born, they grew, they died, and the next season was birthed with the death of the old. N'gai's family said it was time she found a husband.

So when five wandering plainsmen came from the southwest and settled around the fire to eat with the villagers, she looked at each of them shyly. Which one of them would make for a good husband? The two handsome ones she instantly rejected. She saw only ambition and pride in their eyes. The ugly ones she dismissed too, for there was a torpor about them that she did not like. Yet she warmed to the fifth man, who was neither handsome nor ugly. There was a confusion about him, as though even he himself didn't know what kind of man he might be. Yes, she could see some pettiness in his eyes, but also a love of beauty there. So when his gaze fell on N'gai, she smiled and then bowed her head.

"You like that man?" said N'gai's mother, later.

"I *think* so," said N'gai. "Anyway, he is the best of them all, don't you think?"

Her mother sighed and patted her growing belly. "I don't see that you have much choice, N'gai. You will have another brother or sister soon, and as the goddess did not favour us with her tears this season, we could do with a hunter to add to the little food we have."

N'gai nodded. She then placed a hand on her mother's belly and closed her eyes. "I see a boy. With huge eyes and an even bigger heart."

N'gai's mother smiled. "Goddess willing, he will journey to us safely."

So N'gai pledged herself to the man who loved beauty – B'goro was his name – although, on becoming joined with N'gai in the eyes of the goddess, B'goro made the unusual pronouncement that they would not

157

remain in the village. His gift to his bride would be a quest for beauty. He would take his wife to the northeast where, he had heard, there were shimmering salt waters that sparkled with so much radiance that they made the goddess herself weep at such beauty. Also, they were full of fish, and so they would never starve.

N'gai could do nothing but acquiesce. She would be sorry to say goodbye to her family and the mark-makers, but she was also excited by the prospect of seeing this mysterious blue 'ocean' that her husband spoke of. So one morning they set off, following the almost dry river to the northeast, their few possessions and some food on their heads.

They walked for thirteen days, the mother-goddess Solla impressing on them her divine power: Solla's heat was fierce and their progress slow. Yet the goddess trees, whose roots burrowed deep into the earth, provided them with water; B'goro would tap the tree for its sweet liquor, and he and his wife would drink and be sated. At each tree, N'gai left a token of their gratitude. She moulded clay, taken from the sludge of the riverbank, and shaped it into a bulbous human form. It was Solla, fat with fertility. She whispered "thank you" as she placed the figure against the trunk of the tree and thought of how her husband had held her in the night, his naked body against hers. Soon, perhaps, *she* would be fat with child.

On the fourteenth day two wonderful sights came into view: a thin band of blue at the horizon and a village in front of it. When they finally arrived at the village, the dark blue band growing ever larger, N'gai was entranced by the sight and sound and smell of it.

"How wonderful!" she exclaimed. "B'goro, what you said is true. This ocean is a beautiful sight indeed."

B'goro smiled.

The villagers welcomed them and gave them food and water. And when night came, they sat around the fire and listened to what N'gai and B'goro had to tell them: about their journey, and of N'gai's village and her mark-making skills, and of B'goro's gift to his wife.

The sea villagers told them about their lives. They spoke to them of the ocean, Seeana, Solla's twin sister, and how she was a generous but sometimes cruel mistress. She provided them with food in the manner of fish, crustaceans, and seaweed; she also gave them brine, which gave them the twin gifts of drinking water and salt. When the freshwater from the river had all but disappeared, the brine was a blessing indeed. But Seeana also took from the villagers. Many fishermen had lost their lives in her embrace, no matter how many tokens of gratitude they left at her feet.

"Tomorrow, though," said one of the elders, "we will introduce you to Seeana. B'goro, we can teach you how to fish, and, N'gai, you will work with our mark-makers. No doubt you will wish to learn from each other."

So N'gai and B'goro settled into a new life beside the beautiful, if daunting, Seeana. However, life as a fisherman did not suit B'goro. The rocking motion of the boats made him sick to his stomach. N'gai could not help laughing when he returned from a day at sea.

"You look like my younger sister, N'giri, when she first had to wring the neck of a *pullum* bird."

B'goro did not laugh and N'gai fell silent as she saw her husband's eyes cloud with ill temper.

N'gai was learning much from the Seeana mark-makers. They had a particularly intriguing use for sand, which they would melt in a furnace fuelled by the anger of the fire-god himself. The sand turned into a transparent slime that they would twist and turn and add minerals to. They produced many things from this substance, which they named 'glass': coloured vessels, tiles, and spheres that sparkled in the rays of the mother-goddess. When N'gai watched the glass mark-makers at work, she felt awe; it was as though she witnessed the birth of Solla herself.

One day, B'goro had had enough.

"It is time we left," he told N'gai.

"But why?" she asked, her heart racing.

"I have no wish to become like some of the fishermen who secretly hate to fish and instead drink themselves sick with firewater when they think no one is watching. No. I am a hunter of creatures that roam the earth. Not the sea. We shall head north, along the coast and to the mountainous regions. We shall settle at a village where my skills can be put to good use."

"But why can't we go back to my home? You were appreciated there. My mother said –"

"I don't care about what your mother said. We go north."

N'gai looked into her husband's eyes, and seeing the hurt and confusion in them, she nodded and said no more.

When hearing that N'gai was to leave, the mark-makers presented her with a gift. It was a transparent orb, curved and smooth.

"It is for capturing the power of Solla to make fire. It will help you and B'goro to light a fire without having to rely on the mischievous fire-god."

N'gai took the orb and looked at it. She could immediately see its power; it distorted the world and made things larger than they truly were.

"Thank you, friends, this is a wondrous gift. Goddess willing, we may meet again."

So N'gai and B'goro left the village. They travelled north along the coast for ten days, the mountains nothing but a dusky haze in the distance. Goddess trees were scarcer here, so sometimes B'goro would boil seawater for them so that they'd have enough to drink. N'gai once offered him the mark-makers' orb when he was building a fire, but he waved her away. "Us hunters have no need for such tricksy devices. My flint and knife have so far never let me down." And he continued to call on the fire-god, the flint sparking with mischief.

Occasionally, they would pass fishermen who would be generous and provide them with fish and a little freshwater. At dusk, they ate salted or grilled fish in silence, B'goro's wounded pride still raw, his mood still low.

Yet on the eleventh day of their journey, the mountains became more substantial and a teeming mass of huts and people could be seen in the distance. B'goro grinned.

"That's more like it!" he said, and he hurried N'gai on, although she felt sick and tired.

B'goro was right. This community *was* a better fit for him. He immediately fell in with a group of huntsmen who took him into the mountains daily. When he came back to N'gai in the evenings he would boast of their exploits, his eyes full of pride.

N'gai found work with the mark-makers, and for a while she thought they'd be happy in their new home. However, skilled as she was in producing likenesses, word soon got about: a woman with the eyes of the goddess herself was among them. This pleased many of the community who longed to see their own faces in paint on paper, but two people in particular were not pleased with this development: B'goro and the goddess-speaker.

B'goro did not like the way that N'gai was often regaled with gifts and admiring words, for he was the one doing the hard and brave work. N'gai was just doing what she usually did: making people look better in paint than they did in real life. What was valiant about that? And the goddess-speaker, full of bitterness, didn't like the way that people no longer looked to her so much. They had N'gai instead. The newcomer could give them pretty reflections of themselves; she could also conjure up pictures of long-dead relatives, merely with a description. Her marks had the power to inspire and enthral. No, something had to change.

One day, it did, when the head huntsman sought out N'gai at dawn and asked her to give his body a mask of paint so that he could go about the mountains unseen. N'gai obliged, and that day the hunter caught the elusive mountain *cugarra*, the beloved cat of the despised fire-god himself. There were celebrations in the village that night, yet B'goro, angry at the praise the head huntsman lavished on N'gai, slipped away from the crowd and went to the ramshackle hut of the goddess-speaker.

"Do something," he said, "about my wife." He puffed out his chest. "I am tired of the way people treat her. She is only a mark-maker, and yet they look on her as though... as though she is the goddess herself!"

The goddess-speaker sucked air through her yellow, broken teeth. "That, she is not!" She parted the long, greying locks in front of her face and, turning away from B'goro, surveyed the crammed shelves by the light of her unearthly fire. They were full of pots of potions and withered plants and animal pelts. She muttered to herself as she picked things up and then put them back down again.

"Well?" said B'goro. "Can you do something?"

The goddess-speaker turned her head toward him sharply and looked into his eyes. "You want me to take away her powers?"

"Yes," he said slowly, for a moment considering how bereft N'gai would be without her ability to make marks. He then disregarded the thought. "It is for the best. She has me. And one day, soon, she will give birth to my child. That is enough."

The goddess-speaker grinned. "I can do what you ask. Though I will have to invoke the wrath of the fire-god himself. What will you give me in exchange?"

B'goro laughed. "My, you're a cunning one. I know as well as you that this request can only benefit you. But still... I'll bring you enough fresh meat to put some flesh on your bones."

The goddess-speaker laughed horribly. "Come back tomorrow evening."

The morning after B'goro had seen the goddess-speaker again he unstoppered the small jar full of black liquid that she'd given him. He poured a few drops of the evil-looking potion into N'gai's jug of water.

"Drink up," he said as N'gai rose. He offered her a cup of water and some fruit.

N'gai drank. She sensed that something about the water was wrong, but she couldn't say what. It tasted the same. It had no smell, but it looked... a little grey, perhaps? Her eyes seemed to be almost, but not quite, seeing something, but the "something" slithered away from her when she tried to focus on it. So she dismissed her concerns. It was kind of B'goro to think of her; usually he'd already be gone with the other hunters into the mountains. She bit into the yellow fruit, which tasted good.

"Thank you," she said with a smile. It was good to see her husband looking happy. Perhaps this *was* the right place for them both. Although, with the new life in her belly, she had to admit that she missed her family. She particularly longed for her mother; for her reassurance that her baby's journey to her arms would go well.

Day followed day, with B'goro continuing to give his wife the goddess-speaker's potion. And as day followed day, N'gai's sight began to fail her, until one morning she woke to nothingness. She cried out, her arms flailing.

"Where am I? Is it nighttime still? B'goro!"

B'goro woke and, trembling, tried to calm his wife who was now eyeless – where once her eyeballs had been, there was smooth, spherical rock. And instead of tears, there was sand.

"What has happened to me?" N'gai wailed, putting her hands to her solid eyes. "I cannot see, I cannot see!"

B'goro didn't know what to do. "Be still, I will look after you. I will... fetch the goddess-speaker. Yes, that is what I will do. She will know what is to be done."

"Do not leave me!" said N'gai, grasping for her husband. "I am scared!"

B'goro extracted himself from his wife. "I promise I'll be back very soon."

B'goro ran to the goddess-speaker's hut and seeing her asleep on her mat shook her awake. "What have you done, you wicked crone? You have deformed my wife! Her beautiful eyes are now... rocks."

The goddess-speaker looked at him disdainfully as she slowly rose to her feet. "Wasn't that what you wanted? N'gai's power lies in her eyes. So I took away her eyes. As you asked."

"But I didn't want this!" B'goro said, shaking the goddess-speaker once more. "Undo what you've done!"

"Impossible," said the crone. "It cannot be undone."

B'goro, filled with the rage of the fire-god himself, began to throttle the old woman. But the next moment, he was holding nothing but air. A snake fell to the ground and slithered away from him.

"Why you wicked old..." he began, scanning the hut for a weapon. He picked up a large rock, which was the colour and texture of N'gai's new, dead eyes. "If you don't turn back into your real shape and undo what you've done, I swear I'll smash you to pieces."

The snake paused in its retreat and turned to face B'goro, her forked tongue flicking as she considered the man with the rock in his hand.

The snake, quicker than the man, lunged first – she made for B'goro's right foot and sank her fangs into his flesh. B'goro cried out but still managed to bring the rock down on the snake's thick body. The snake writhed under the weight of the rock and, unable to escape, dug her fangs ever deeper. B'goro continued to fell the snake with the rock until he could no longer lift his arms. The snake's poison coursed through his body; it slowed his heart and froze his blood.

The snake, now a bloody pulp, lay at his feet inert, and as the last of B'goro's strength left him, he collapsed. The snake became the goddess-speaker once more, and there they lay on the floor of the hut together, united in death.

N'gai, frightened, and in pain, waited for her husband for as long as she could stand to, and then propelled by fear, she stumbled through her hut to the front door and called for her neighbour.

"N'mata! N'mata!" she cried.

N'mata, a babe strapped across her chest, came running. When she saw N'gai, she gasped. "What has happened to you?"

"N'mata, I cannot see. And B'goro has gone for the goddess-speaker. But he's been gone so long. Please, can you find him for me? And hurry him along. I am so frightened."

"Of course. I will come back as soon as I can."

It did not take long for N'mata to discover what had happened to B'goro. A crowd was beginning to form around the goddess-speaker's hut, and the horrible news went about the onlookers: there had been an argument between B'goro and the goddess-speaker. A deal gone wrong. Both were dead.

N'mata took the news back to N'gai, who insisted on being led to B'goro. The crowd parted as they saw N'gai, eyeless, leaning on N'mata's arm. The two women entered the hut, and when they were close to B'goro, N'mata whispered to N'gai that here he was, at her feet. N'gai fell to her knees and placed her hands on the dead body of her husband. She reached for his face, his familiar features smooth and cold under her hands, and then placed a hand on his lifeless chest. So, it was true. She reached for N'mata and then rose. They left the goddess-speaker's home and the whispering crowds, and when N'gai returned to her own hut, she took to her bed and wished for death to come.

N'mata visited N'gai every day, placing fruit and freshwater by her bedside. "You must eat. If only for your baby's sake," she said, stroking N'gai's hair.

The mark-makers came too.

"As the goddess-speaker did not have an apprentice, there will be a time of choosing," began one. "The elders will find another goddess-speaker. In time, she could maybe undo what has been done to you."

"What?" exclaimed N'gai. "Do you think me stupid enough to entrust myself to a novice? Never. No, there is only one goddess-speaker I trust, the one who has known me since childhood, and she lives a long way away from here."

"But N'gai," entreated another, "this is not the end. It is another beginning. Your hands... they can still create marks. The images are still within you, behind your eyes, and your hands will do the work for you."

N'gai turned to where the voice was coming from. "The pain..." she said, her hand at her eyes. "It is like a thousand knives in my skull. But it is nothing to the pain I feel here," she said, her hand on her chest. "Now I understand all. B'goro's betrayal has killed my spirit. And without my spirit, I cannot create."

The mark-makers said no more and left. N'gai was right. Without spirit, there could be no act of creation.

There was one person, though, who disagreed. And that was N'gai's child. She had spirit enough for the both of them, so one day she kicked her mother into action.

N'gai, aware of the internal challenge, spoke to her daughter. "What would you have me do?" she said.

A kick.

"Get up?"

Another kick.

N'gai rose and slowly felt her way about the hut, her hands acting as her eyes.

"I could go to the mark-makers and sit with them. Sculpt."

No movement.

An image came to N'gai. "Or I could return to my family. Talk to the goddess-speaker."

Two kicks.

N'gai smiled. "Very well," she said. "Home it is. Though the journey will not be easy."

"Do not go," said N'mata. "It will be hard on both you and your baby. Alone and unseeing... you are vulnerable."

"But I do not belong here. I must return home. The goddess-speaker may be able to help me. And, besides, I want to be with my family. To be with my mother again. You understand what it is like. And I do not want to be a burden to anyone here. You are kind to me. As are the mark-makers, but I will need much help when the baby comes. I cannot ask it of you."

N'mata nodded. "I *do* understand. But promise me this: that you let my eldest go with you for part of the journey."

N'gai began to shake her head.

"I insist!" said N'mata, placing a gentle hand on her friend's cheek. "And there is no point in you continuing to say no. I would just make B'mebo follow at a distance."

N'gai laughed. "I see there is no way to outwit you, so I will accept your kind offer."

So the next day, N'gai and B'mebo journeyed south. N'gai carried a stick in her hand, for testing out the path ahead of her, and she took B'mebo's hand when the ground beneath their feet became rocky. They carried food and vessels of water on their heads, as well as some of N'gai's most prized possessions, and for the most part, they journeyed in companionable silence. After five days, B'mebo said he must return. This was the farthest he had ever travelled, and loath as he was to leave N'gai, he felt he must.

"Of course you must go," said N'gai. "Please do not worry about me. The mother-goddess will keep me safe. Besides, I have gentle sand beneath my feet and the sea by my side to guide me south to the fishing village I once knew and loved. I have enough food and water for many days. All I need to do is walk. How hard could that be?"

So B'mebo left N'gai to journey alone. The first three days passed by uneventfully. But then the wind rose, prickling N'gai's skin with sand and fear. Dark thoughts entered her mind, and Seeana sent skittish waves across the sand to surprise and unsettle her footing. Solla, too, did not seem keen to make her journey smooth. The mother-goddess argued with the fire-god, their cursing could be heard in the sky above, and it only ended, as it always did, when the tears of the goddess fell from the heavens. It rained so much that the beach was more swamp than sand, and N'gai had to move farther away from the water's edge than she wanted to. She spent much energy in seeking out shelter from the rain, so that she could spend the night in the dry. She woke the next morning, disoriented, to discover that her vessel of freshwater had spilled in the night. Thirsty and dispirited, she went in search of a goddess tree, but there were none. So instead, she refound her path south.

Solla bore down on her. The baby kicked and fussed and made every step across the heavy sand difficult. Thirst tore at her throat. Her head was all pain. N'gai sank to her knees and prayed for a miracle. When none came, she got up once again and walked a few paces. Her sounding stick hit wood instead of sand, and she suddenly thought of the orb that the sea villagers had given her. She would make a fire with it and turn seawater into freshwater. And though she was unskilled in the art of fire making, N'gai understood that this was the miracle that *she* had to make happen.

N'gai found the orb and B'goro's fire-making tools. She recalled the time she'd once asked him to teach her the tricks of the fire-god. *Kindling a fire is man's work,* he'd said. She'd wanted to argue, to say that in her village that was not the case, but the look in his eyes had told her to remain silent.

Careful not to injure herself on B'goro's knife, N'gai felt within her husband's old leather bag and found some tinder and dry sticks. There was enough to get a fire going, and with the several pieces of driftwood she'd come across, she'd be able to sustain a fire for long enough to turn seawater into freshwater. She went to the sea's edge and filled a pan with water. She was so thirsty she considered drinking the pan of liquid immediately, but she knew it would only make her feel worse.

So N'gai set up the fire stack – kindling amongst the smaller twigs, more twigs propped above the kindling, like the poles of a tent, and driftwood beneath – just like B'goro had done. She then held the translucent orb above the dry grass kindling, capturing Solla's rays and focussing them onto the brittle grass. She felt the rising of unnatural heat and suddenly there was a crackle – the kindling had caught alight. The heat increased and grew. N'gai then balanced the pan on the fire, her hands dangerously close to the flames as she placed the curious lid with the downward spout onto the pan. She then put a jar underneath the spout and waited.

Sure enough, Solla rewarded N'gai's efforts; pure water dribbled into the jar, and N'gai was able to drink and be sated.

N'gai stayed by the fire and collected enough water to fill her jar. She ate some of the salted meat and dried fruit N'mata had given her, and then, exhausted, she lay down by the fire and slept.

N'gai woke much later, the cool of dusk on her skin. Still, there in the background was the heat of the fire, although it was much diminished. She sat up, drank some more water, and then chewed on a strip of dried fruit. She thought about the daughters of the mother-goddess, the three moons that would be in the night sky now: N'luna, N'lina, and N'lon. She missed being able to see them.

She suddenly froze as she heard a voice in the distance. A man was singing. And not in a way that was good. N'gai scrabbled about for B'goro's knife, knocking some of her precious pots of ink about the place. The fire! She had to put it out and then hide. She began to throw sand onto the fire.

"Hey!" called the voice. "Don't do that! That's a good fire you've got going."

N'gai stopped what she was doing. She suddenly heard the slap of oars and then splashing. The man, a fisherman she presumed, was pulling his boat ashore.

"N'gai?" said the man, suddenly close by and reeking of firewater. "Is that you?"

N'gai nodded.

"What happened to your eyes? And where's B'goro?"

There was more glugging as the fisherman drank.

"It's a long story," she said, gripping the knife tighter.

The fisherman thrust the pouch of firewater at N'gai. "Have a drink and tell me all about it."

N'gai wanted to push the pouch away, but she sensed it would be the wrong thing to do. With her free hand, she put it to her mouth and took a few sips of the firewater. It tasted foul.

The fisherman took back his pouch and then sat down with a thud. He continued to glug away, emptying the pouch.

N'gai searched her mind for the man's name.

"Well," he said. A belch. "What happened?"

"You're B'somi, aren't you?" she replied. "I once painted a picture of your brother's wife. Such a beautiful –"

"Don't talk to me about that woman! My brother's only been dead for ten days and she's already chosen her next husband. And it's not me. When it should have been me! She can drown in Seeana's embrace for all I care."

N'gai fell silent, her body tense.

B'somi threw down the now-empty pouch. N'gai sensed him move closer.

"Such strange eyes," he said, his hand suddenly on her cheek. "Still, you've got a pretty face." And then his other hand was caressing her hair, his stinking breath on her lips.

N'gai recoiled and then thrust the knife at B'somi. "If you come any closer, I swear I'll use this!"

B'somi backed away, his foul breath receding. But then N'gai felt her head implode with pain as B'somi dealt her a blow; she was reeling backwards. Her grip on the knife loosened. Still, she could sense it there, just at her fingertips, unnatural heat behind it.

"Don't you dare threaten me!" said B'somi. "Have you any idea of what I've been through?"

N'gai sensed B'somi coming close again. This time his hands were pulling at her clothes.

N'gai stretched her hand and reclaimed the knife, which was warm from the fire. It was also covered in a slippery liquid she knew well. Ink.

With one swift movement, N'gai plunged the knife into the fire and once more thrust it at B'somi. It plucked at his skin, and he let go of her.

N'gai wanted to scream at him; to hurl angry words at him. But instead she willed herself to stay calm.

"You're a good man, B'somi, I know you are. Even though I am blind, I can see into your heart. But you're grieving. And poisoned with firewater. And angry with your once-sister. And you're not yourself."

N'gai took a deep breath.

"You're stronger than me. And you have the gift of sight. You know I can't do you much harm, but what I can do is mark you forever with ink. And if you choose to defy the goddess and defile me, your skin will forever hold my cry for mercy."

169

There came a thud as B'somi fell onto the sand. Then the sound of sobbing. And then silence. And when N'gai felt sure that B'somi was fast asleep, she packed away her things and walked through the night and most of the morning until the sounds of the people of the sea village came upon her ears. Then the fear that had kept her body moving receded as she finally realised she was safe.

When N'gai entered the sea village, the mark-makers took it upon themselves to look after her and, unbeknownst to N'gai, one of them went to fetch their goddess-speaker.

"I see that someone has stolen from you," she said, when she saw N'gai. "And I am sorry for that."

N'gai started when she realised that she was being addressed by their goddess-speaker.

"Who brought you to me? I did not want to be looked over by you!"

The goddess-speaker placed a gentle hand on N'gai's arm. "Forgive me. And forgive the messenger who brought me to you. We did not mean any harm by it."

N'gai's heart softened. "I can hear in your voice that you want to help, but I am sure you cannot."

The goddess-speaker looked at N'gai's sightless eyes. "You are right. I cannot undo what has been done to you, but I can at least give you some relief. It is a plant that, when chewed, takes away pain. Do you wish for me to bring you this plant?"

A sob caught in N'gai's throat. "Please," she managed to say, willing herself not to cry; experience had taught her that tears of sand were a form of torture almost impossible to bear.

N'gai slept and ate. She told the mark-makers she did not plan to stay long; that she needed to go home. But the more she chewed on the *kratoma* plant leaves, the less she talked about leaving.

The *kratoma* plant took away her pain, but it also took away her dreams and determination. She kept to her bed, her thoughts folded away, and there she would have stayed for the rest of her life if it weren't for B'somi. For, one day, the sound of an argument roused her from her stupor. She could hear the mark-makers telling someone to go away and leave them be. Then she recognised B'somi's voice. Her heart beat like mad and she quickly sat upright.

"I just wanted to tell N'gai something. Please."

She could hear the desire for forgiveness in his voice.

There was a scuffle and then more "go aways". Then nothing more.

N'gai's first instinct was to reach for the *kratoma* plant – to blot out the memory of the night she'd met B'somi on the beach – but she found herself trembling and unable to move for shock.

Day passed into night; one of the mark-makers brought N'gai some food and water at dusk. And as the *kratoma* plant took leave of her body, N'gai began to think clearly. What was she doing here still? Why hadn't she left?

A weak kick from within her belly told her to get moving. So, sluggish and slow, N'gai got up and packed her things. And in the middle of the night, when everyone was fast asleep, she clumsily found her way out of the village and to the river, which would lead her back home.

N'gai walked through the night, following the river southwest, her sounding stick her guide. As Solla rose the pain returned to her head, where her hard sandstone eyes met flesh, but the pain, she told herself, was a gift. It would urge her home. To her family, and to the one goddess-speaker who she knew wouldn't fail her.

The recent rain had helped to swell the meagre river, and goddess trees were more plentiful here, so N'gai did not thirst for water. One day, stooping at one of the trees, she found a clay statue in the shape of the mother-goddess. It was one she had made many moons ago, when she had first travelled this way with B'goro. N'gai sighed as she put the statue back. So much had changed since then.

N'gai's progress was slow but uneventful. Then one day, she understood that she was very close to home; she could smell it in the air.

Suddenly there was a shout – "N'gai!" – and the sound of running footsteps. Her siblings. She was being embraced and talked at and then there came a lull... Her eyes. What had happened to her eyes? And where was B'goro?

N'gai allowed herself to be carried along to her father and mother and her baby brother, who was fast asleep against his mother's chest. It was only when she found herself being held by her parents that she understood how much she had missed them.

N'gai's mother wept, first with joy, and then with sadness. "Tell us what happened."

So N'gai told them about what had happened to her eyes. Her father cursed B'goro and the goddess-speaker of the mountain village, and her mother stroked N'gai's hair as she wept her motherly tears.

"You are home now," said her mother. "That is all that matters. We will look after you. And tomorrow we will ask the goddess-speaker for her help."

So the next day the goddess-speaker came to talk to N'gai. She asked to be alone with N'gai, to give counsel with no one else present. N'gai said that she would allow this.

"Your mother has told me what happened to you." She sighed. "Sometimes, for some goddess-speakers, the goddess is not enough. They crave more. They make bargains with unworthy men and the unfathomable fire-god that have cruel outcomes. They end up hurting their sisters. I do not know why these things happen. But they do. However, I also sense that there is more to your story than you have told your family."

N'gai sighed. "I did not want to add to their sorrow."

"Go on," said the goddess-speaker.

"I almost died of thirst on the journey home. But then the goddess sent me help. I came across driftwood and made a fire with this orb that the mark-makers at the sea village gave me." N'gai took the smooth glass orb from her pouch and showed it to the goddess-speaker. "So I was able to turn seawater into freshwater. But then a fisherman, his blood poisoned with firewater, saw the fire. He... he tried to hurt me. But I managed to escape. I threatened to ink his flesh with B'goro's knife."

"I see." The goddess-speaker took the orb from N'gai and held it up to the light. "Go on," she said, studying it carefully.

"I made it to the sea village. The goddess-speaker there offered me *kratoma* plant leaves for the pain in my head."

The goddess-speaker shook her head. "It was stupid of her to offer that to you. It is like firewater, but more difficult to shake off."

"But I managed to. And now I am here."

The goddess-speaker took N'gai's hands. "You have been through so much, N'gai. And when so many have harmed you, your trust in me has remained intact. If I told you that there might be a way to help you, what would you think?"

N'gai thought for a moment. "I would be glad. It would mean that I was right to return home. But is there a way back? Can you return my sight?"

The goddess-speaker took a deep breath. "No. I cannot return to you your eyes as they once were. But I think I can turn the unnatural eyes you have now into something else. Something better. And the pain should go. But the process will hurt... and I cannot guarantee that it will work."

N'gai let go of the goddess-speaker's hands. "Well then, I must think about what you have said."

A few days later, and after speaking with her mother and father, N'gai made a decision.

"I do trust you," she told the goddess-speaker, "and I want you to try to help me. But I will only undergo what you suggest after my daughter is born."

"Very well," said the goddess-speaker. "That is a good decision. When you are ready, let me know."

So in the days that followed, the goddess-speaker busied herself with the preparations for N'gai's transformation, and N'gai focussed all her energy and determination on birthing her daughter.

Weeks passed, and as N'gai's baby thrived so did N'gai. Her spirit had returned in full force with the birth of her daughter, whom she had named N'solla, and with it, the determination to be rid of her stone eyes and the pain and darkness they brought her.

"Do it!" she ordered the goddess-speaker one day. "Before I change my mind." N'gai passed her sleeping daughter, who had just now suckled asleep, to N'solla's grandmother.

"She will be fine with me," said N'gai's mother, putting her arm around her daughter's shoulder.

N'gai sighed and then allowed herself to be led to the goddess-speaker's hut. It was perhaps better that she was not able to see the stone bed at the back of the hut that the goddess-speaker took her to; for with its leather straps on metal hooks, it was not a welcoming sight.

The goddess-speaker asked N'gai to lie down on it, which she did. "I must strap your arms down, N'gai, so that you do not try to touch your eyes. And I must also strap down your head." N'gai's heart began to beat quickly, but she acquiesced. She felt the straps going over her wrists, a strap tightening over her forehead. "For it is imperative that your head remains perfectly still." N'gai's stomach tightened.

"Now then," began the goddess-speaker. "You must keep your eyelids open so that I can make a fire on your eyes. I will do my best to protect your skin with the ointments I have prepared."

N'gai felt cool, oily cream being placed on her face and the skin around her eyes.

"But you will still feel the heat clawing at you. A great heat. But you must endure it for as long as you can. The longer the better."

N'gai heard the crackle of fire and then the goddess-speaker coming close. She made sure to keep her eyelids wide open. Still, when the first ember touched her solid eyes the heat, dulled though it was, frightened her. She cried out.

"Forgive me," said the goddess-speaker. "There is no other way to perform this transformation."

The goddess-speaker piled on more and more embers. N'gai clenched her fists and bit her tongue and tried to ignore the ghastly smell of smoke.

The goddess-speaker began to chant while stoking the flames. N'gai's whole body tensed, the heat at the skin around her eyes intensifying.

N'gai suddenly felt her head become warm, and the reek of burning hair was at her nose. She screamed and tried to touch her head, but of course her hands were restrained.

The heat at N'gai's head suddenly subsided; the goddess-speaker had poured water on the flames. "Forgive me again! I should have dowsed you earlier. This fire is desperate to escape."

N'gai struggled. "What else is to catch fire? How much longer? The heat is unbearable!"

"Longer!" said the goddess-speaker. "It needs to be as hot as the goddess herself!"

N'gai struggled and writhed as the goddess-speaker continued to pile on fuel and to chant and to add precious minerals to the fire burning on N'gai's sandstone eyes, which were now two glowing orbs.

N'gai cried out again. "I can stand it no longer!"

"Almost there! Just a little longer. Keep perfectly still."

N'gai kicked out and then heard herself scream. She was all pain, only pain, and there was nothing beyond the pain but more pain.

And then there was the whoosh of water and the shock of not-pain.

She blinked furiously as she heard the laboured breathing of the goddess-speaker and then the loosening of her restraints, the scraping of a stool.

Light began to flood into N'gai's eyes. But the images were white and otherworldly, tinged with blue and green, the objects strangely magnified and distorted.

N'gai raised herself and then looked about the smoke-filled hut. The goddess-speaker, exhausted, sat on the stool, her body bent double.

N'gai left the bed and helped the goddess-speaker off the stool. "We must get out of here. The air is filthy."

The goddess-speaker allowed N'gai to lead her out of the hut and back to N'gai's home.

"I don't know what you did to me," began N'gai, her voice trembling, "but... I can see. Everything looks strange... but I can see! What is it that you did to me?"

The goddess-speaker smiled wearily. "It was your orb that gave me the idea. You should look at your reflection one day. For your eyes are beautiful. Like... glass."

When N'gai reached her home, her family was astonished by her transformation.

"N'gai..." began her younger sister, N'giri. "You have the eyes of the goddess herself! You really do!"

They crowded around N'gai in wonder. They laughed and questioned N'gai and thanked the goddess-speaker over and over.

N'gai's mother, tears streaming down her face, passed N'gai's daughter back to her. "Can you really see? Then what do you think of your daughter?" she asked. "And the pain, is it gone?"

N'gai looked down at her daughter's face and began to cry soft, salty tears. "Yes, Mother," she said, "I can see my daughter." She smiled. "She is beautiful. And, yes, the pain has gone. And all that there is, is light."

Later, when the sun had set and the three moons, the children of the mother-goddess, shone bright in the night sky, rain fell. While the rest of her family slept, N'gai fed her baby, stroking her fuzzy black hair as she suckled away. She looked out at the three moons. How she had missed seeing them! As her new glass eyes focussed on the moons, she saw what no one else had ever seen before. The faces of three women: N'luna, N'lina, and N'lon. And they were smiling at her.

A Survival Guide for the Contemporary Princess

Like many girls, you dream of marrying a handsome prince. But princes are thin on the ground in Alabama. So as soon as you scrape together enough cash, you leave your drunk of a father and head north-east, never once looking back at the trailer park which has been your home for almost sixteen years.

You find yourself a job, cleaning up after rich people. Yet it's only after the third week of washing blood-stained shirts that you make the connection between your employer's Italian surname and their particular brand of family business. So when the boss's son takes an interest in you he's difficult to refuse. Besides, he *is* a prince. Of sorts. And it sure is nicer to be treated like royalty than the help.

But then there's an almighty shoot-'em-up between the rival families, and your prince shoots dead two innocent bystanders. Kids. The police can't ignore that. They ask you questions, and they know that with your cooperation they can get him put behind bars. "Testify," they say. "We'll give you protection, a new identity. Justice needs to be done."

You want to say yes, but you're scared. So they sweeten the deal by offering to throw in one of the new AI companions. He'll be your round-the-clock protector, capable of overwhelming anyone who tries to hurt you. And he's fully functioning, "In a number of physical capabilities, if you get my drift," says the cop. He also happens to be gorgeous. You say yes.

You never figure out how a being of metal and plastic and whatever his wonderful, soft skin is made of can be so beautiful. But you know your heart aches for him. You get one precious year with him as you build a life for yourself in Seattle, a place where it never stops raining. But then the cops want him back. You beg to keep him, say you wouldn't feel safe without him. They let you have him for another six months.

You know he cares nothing for you. That after you've made love to him he doesn't sleep. That he simply closes his eyes and goes into standby mode while you listen to the rain and dream of an impossible future in which the love you feel for him is reflected in his eyes. You know he's like a drug, and that you're addicted to him. What will you do when he leaves you?

An old woman at the diner at which you work says you'll manage. "I seen it all before," she says. "You're sick with love. But, this love you think you're feeling, it's all in your head. You created it all on your own. Pour it into yourself, into your life, instead."

You know she's right, but you don't know if you've got the courage to do what she says.

"You ever walked away from something real bad and never once looked back?" the old woman asks.

You nod. And then you smile.

You've got this. You *think*.

This Little Piggy

My mother once told me that Sartre was right. "You know, about hell. And people. How it's created by those around us." But then I remember her sighing and shaking her head. "No, that's not quite true. Hell comes from within."

She pulled her long cardigan tighter about her and then put her hand to her forehead. "The mind. The body. They're linked, of course."

I knew she'd been seriously ill years earlier, before I'd been born, and so I assumed she was referring to her illness. But shortly after I told her that Lizzie and I would be starting on IVF – I must've said something like *It's going to be hell* – she turned on me.

"Hell!" she hissed. "You've got to be joking, right? You're lucky to have that as an option. Don't go complaining about it, Anton. Can you even imagine what life was like for infertile women before IVF came along? Because *that* was hell. And believe me, I'm an expert on that."

Years of resentment clawed at my throat. "Well, go on, Mum," I said, my voice tight. "Share some of your expertise. Because I'm sick of the selfless martyr act. And why is it that Lizzie can't do anything right by you?"

"This isn't about Lizzie!"

"Really?"

"Really."

Suddenly, her shoulders slumped, and she took a wobbly step towards the kitchen table. I helped her into a chair and then took a seat myself.

"Do you honestly want to know about hell? My hell?" she asked.

"Yes," I said, angrily. "I do."

She looked at me with searching eyes, her frown lines deep, accusatory.

She began to toy with the gold cross on her necklace. "There've been so many times I wanted to tell you, but…"

"Go on, Mum," I said, more gently this time.

She took a deep breath. "There was this article, you see. In a woman's magazine. It must've been sometime in 1976. Two years before the first IVF baby was born. It was about the lengths some women would go to, to get pregnant. One woman had become fixated on visiting so-called 'fertile' places, you know, pagan sites. She and her husband would make love amongst standing stones and on chalk downs where ancient tribes had carved men and women, their sexual organs huge, swollen. After two years of this she finally became pregnant.

"Another woman pushed her body to all kinds of extremes, going on drastic diets and gruelling exercise regimes to make her body 'perfect'. She'd eat all kinds of strange things, like coal, caviar, raw meat, cough syrup – anything that was thought to enhance fertility. 'I went through hell to get my baby,' I remember her saying. 'But it was worth it.'

"I cut out the article and carried it around with me. I felt as though these women understood me. They knew about *the emptiness*. And the desperate, desperate urge, no, the *hunger*, to have a baby.

"The word 'hell' kept going round my head. Was I prepared to go through hell to have a baby? And that's when it struck me. Hell was a house. Specifically, the old Gascoigne house, down by the river Skerne."

An image of a mouldering Victorian mansion came into my mind. Along with some myth about women luring men to the river, to their deaths. "I think I remember it. Wasn't it turned into luxury flats?"

"Yes, but back then, it was this decrepit old building. Ivy was choking it to death, the windows were broken, paint was flaking off the walls and it was full of rubbish. A slum."

"You went inside?" I said, confused.

"Twice. The first time was when it was up for auction. Your dad, bless his soul, had this idea that we could do up the old place. Turn it into a fancy hotel. His job with the American firm was paying him good money. He said it could be a fun project for me.

"But before the auction, when we viewed it with some other people, I just remember feeling very frightened. There was something about the place, I mean, besides the rubble, broken glass, and what remained of the battered furniture, there was – how can I put it? – an atmosphere. As if there was something malicious about it. I remember a man whispering to his wife that the place used to belong to a doctor. But that he can't have been a very good one, because all his kids got sick and died.

"The estate agent was trying his best to stay enthusiastic, but when we came across a room that had 'This is Hell' spray painted in red across its door even he went silent."

A single tear rolled down my mother's face. I put out my hand but she didn't take it. Instead, she took a handkerchief from her pocket and dabbed at her eyes.

"Well, of course, Colin and I weren't interested in somewhere that was being used as the neighbourhood drug den, or whatever, so we never went to the auction. But after I read that article, I finally understood what I had to do. I had to spend a week in that house."

"What?" I said, incredulous.

"I wish I could say it wasn't that bad. But it was. It was the worst week of my life. And the number of times I've wished I could unmake that stupid, stupid decision. Well…"

She sniffed again, her eyes wet with tears.

"So what happened?"

She shrugged. "It's funny, isn't it? The things an old woman remembers. I can still recall debating with myself about whether I should take any food. A blanket. Some toilet paper. After all, should one prepare for hell? Wasn't that cheating? In the end I went empty-handed. Colin had just gone down to London for the week, so I knew he wouldn't miss me. He'd only ever phone the once, when he arrived, and I left a note for my neighbour saying that I'd be away at an old friend's. Which was kind of true. It would be just me and my old friend, the emptiness. Anyway…"

She paused, suddenly lost in thought, and then exhaled deeply.

"So, late that September night I walked along the river, found a way through the brambles, and there I was. It was easy enough to get into the place since the back door was rotten through, but when I was inside, I had my first fright. Rats. Scrabbling and skittering all about the ground floor. I nearly turned back there and then. I wish I had.

"Yet I persevered. I forced myself through the dark and went upstairs to make my 'camp' in one of the smaller bedrooms. I remember lying down on a filthy mattress, looking up at the moon and thinking about my own bed at home. The mattress was white – or

181

rather, it had once been white – with blue stripes. There was dust everywhere; whenever I moved, dust would swirl into the air and settle on my hair, get into my lungs. I cursed myself for not bringing any water. And that's how I got through the first night – with the promise that if I didn't find any drinking water the next day I would go home.

"But the following day, one of the outdoor taps sputtered into life. The water was filled with grey flakes. But it was drinkable. So I had to stay."

"Mum," I began. But she ignored me.

"The days were okay. I'd walk out to the orchard, enjoy the dust-free air, and eat apples and blackberries.

"But the nights... I hardly slept, of course. Every noise was a 'something' coming to get me. And when I did sleep, strange dreams, full of the murderous doctor and his dead babies, haunted me."

More tears rolled down her cheeks.

"But that was nothing to the horror of the last night I spent there.

"Because on the last night – it was a Friday – there was a noise to be properly scared of. Because it was a human noise.

"At first, there were voices outside, then the creaking of the back door. The sound of rats scarpering. Bottles clinking. A tape recorder playing a tinny pop song.

"I froze. The door to my room was half open. If anyone were to pass by I'd be seen. So, slowly and ever so quietly, with my heart beating so hard I thought it would burst, I crept to the wardrobe in the corner of the room and crawled inside. I curled myself into a ball and covered my ears with my hands. But it wasn't enough to muffle the sound I wish I could erase from my memory. A woman's scream.

"Panic, and fear, drove me deeper into the wardrobe, and myself.

"I kept saying the Lord's Prayer over and over, breathless, tears squeezing themselves out of my eyes. Urine seeping through my trousers.

"Hours must've passed. And, somehow, out of the delirium I had retreated to I re-emerged. Daylight streamed through the cracks in the wardrobe, and when I uncovered my ears there was silence. I was so relieved I began to cry all over again.

"Eventually, I ventured down, alert to every noise. But the house was empty. As I made for the back door – fresh litter, beer cans and empty syringes amidst the rubble – I suddenly paused. Escape was only a few metres away, but my gut twisted and wouldn't let me go any further. What if there *was* someone there? In the room with the red graffiti on the door? And they needed help? But I couldn't do it. I couldn't make myself look, so instead I ran. Just like the littlest pig – *'wee wee wee' all the way home*. And I never spoke to anyone about it. Ever."

She sniffed and then dried her eyes. She looked at me, a sad smile on her face, and I held out my hand again. This time she took it. "So now you know. And everything else that happened to me in the next year was like nothing, compared to the remorse that I felt, and which poisoned my every waking thought. Why hadn't I been brave enough to look in that room?

"Stupidly, I held onto the idea that I'd been through enough to become pregnant. And nine months later, when I began to feel sick and tired, my belly aching and my period all over the place, I just knew that this time I'd managed to conceive a child.

"It was a while before I went to the GP. Colin came with me. I remember him looking at me with worried eyes as I happily cradled my stomach.

"He was right to be anxious, though, because as it turned out the baby wasn't a baby, but a tumour. And an ugly one at that. Do you know what a teratoma is?"

I shook my head, a lump in my throat.

"It's a tumour that has bits of other body parts in it. Hair, eyes, teeth. A tiny hand.

"But I was lucky. At least, that's what everyone said. It was removed and I survived."

She let go of my hand and sighed. "All my life I've been selfish. Driven by two urges: to have a baby; to survive. I thought that maybe adopting you would be my first selfless act. When I saw a photo of you in that Romanian orphanage, wearing a babygro the colour of dust, in a cot with a filthy blue-and-white striped mattress, I thought I could save you. But it turns out I was wrong about that too. Because in the end, my precious boy, you gave me far more than I could ever have given you."

"Mum," I began, suppressing a sob, "don't say that. You did save me. My life as it is now… is all because of you."

I went to her and simply held her. "I love you, Mum," I said instinctively, my voice breaking. But for the first time in my life I realised those words weren't enough. For there was no one who could save my mother from her own personal torture but God. Yet I didn't think He was listening.

Tough Love

Home. The word was a trigger, causing my heart to pound, my thoughts to race in wobbly, anxious loops. Before our parents died our home was never silent. It had been a warm, noisy place full of laughter, bickering, the sound of the TV strident with adverts or whatever console game the twins were playing; the hum of radiators pumping out heat.

It also came with its own kind of Smell-O-Vision – the aroma a curious mix of Dad's cardamom-rich curries and Mum's suet puddings: spotted dick, treacle tart, jam roly-poly. But now that it was just me and Tushar, with Mum's sister Pauline dropping by with casseroles from time to time, it was as quiet and depressing as the pub on a Monday afternoon. So when my brother rolled up to the bar on a Thursday evening, just as I'd finished pulling a pint, saying that we had to bring the twins home, I told him to shut the fuck up.

He sighed heavily and then drummed his fingers on the arms of his wheelchair – his automatic response to anything that irritated him. "Okay, so you're not keen on the idea. But will you at least listen to what I've got to say? Just give me five minutes. And a Stella."

"How'd you get here?" I asked as I got him the lager. "Is Pauline in on this?"

"No, she's not. And I got a taxi. I wanted to catch you before you disappeared off to wherever it is that you're going nowadays."

I crossed my arms and gave him my most defiant little sister glare. "I'm staying at Nick's. He lives just round the corner."

"So he's your latest, is he? Okay, whatever. Look, I've had an idea. I mean, about how to get the twins out of that godawful place."

"Yeah, how?"

He glanced about the half-empty pub, suddenly shifty-looking, and then lowered his voice. "You know that epileptics aren't allowed to take part in virtual reality games, right?"

"Yeah. So what?"

"Well, recently, NeuralKEEP, actually, all the VR companies, have had to come up with guidelines for how to deal with gamers who experience 'distressing neurological episodes' as they like to put it, because there's been an increase in gamers having what are, basically, epileptic fits during VR sessions. The guidelines say that they've got to be sent home. And then banned."

"You're not suggesting... actually, fuck it, I know what you're suggesting." I turned to my boss, who was serving a gaggle of women – all big hair and lipstick – and asked him if it was okay if I left a bit early. "I have to get a cab for my brother."

Ken looked at Tushar. "You all right, mate?"

"Yeah," he replied, taking a swig of his Stella. "You know. Keeping on keeping on."

"Good lad."

"So…?" I asked of Ken as I hovered near the doorway where I'd hung my coat, desperate to get my vapes.

"Yeah, Manj, fine. I'll see you tomorrow."

"Cheers, mate," said Tushar.

"You see," Tushar explained as we made our way along the near-deserted high street and on to the taxi rank, "it's all there in the hundred-page long terms and conditions. Though I've never bothered to read it. No, Riz from security told me. In the canteen. He was complaining about all the climbing he'd had to do that day. So I humoured him and listened to him complaining about his back and shoulders. Turns out, he'd been up a ladder 'updating' the CCTV cameras in the factory. He'd been replacing the real ones with fakes. KEEP's doing it to make savings, apparently. But Riz's face wasn't saying that. More like they didn't want footage of gamers having fits. So I asked him what the difference was between the real and fake cameras, all nonchalant-like. He tapped his nose and said, 'That's for me to know and you to find out.' The high and mighty git. But he did tell me this. That he was up and down that ladder for most of the day."

"So you reckon that most of the cameras at NeuralKEEP are fakes?" I asked as I watched his wheelchair struggle across a particularly uneven bit of churned-up pavement.

"Definitely the ones where the gamers are. On the factory floor, as us cynical types like to call it. But not in the foyer or our offices. I never saw Riz anywhere near us coders."

"But how can we make them have a fit while gaming? And wouldn't it be, like, super dangerous to them?"

"I've done my research. The twins both have luxury capsules. God knows how they got the money for them, but Emma's got one too and her family, messed-up as it is, has got money. So what I reckon is –"

"Wait a minute. Are you saying that not only do you want to get our baby brother and sister out of there, but Emma too?"

I looked down at my brother and saw that his brow was furrowed, his expression spectacularly earnest. "Yes, Emma too."

"Oh yeah, now I get it. You had a thing for her a while ago."

"So what if I did? She's our friend! And she's addicted to the VR. We've got to help her."

"But isn't that her choice?"

"Yeah right, like our brother and sister have a choice?"

I shook my head. "That's different. They're family. We promised Mum and Dad that we'd look after them."

Tushar's voice was defiant. "We help her too."

I didn't have the energy, or the inclination, to argue with him. Besides, we were at the taxi rank and I wanted to finish my vape before a cab came. "Okay, whatever," I said, inhaling deeply, "what were you saying about the capsules?"

"Okay," he said, once more animated, "you see, the brain activity of each gamer is monitored remotely. But the settings on each gamer's capsule isn't. That's all done manually. Nurses come by every two hours to check the capsule settings, the IV drips and urine collection bags."

"Ew," I said, "so they're all like totally hooked up? They don't have to eat or piss for the whole time they're there?"

"Pretty much. Although there's rules about them staying for longer than a few days. I guess the rules get broken, though. Anyway, you and me are going down there on the weekend. When the three of them will be there for sure. I'll say that I want to show my sis round my workplace. That you're maybe thinking of having a go on the VR. Someone will come round with us. I'm betting that it'll be one of the new recruits who don't yet know the drill. But then, when we're on the factory floor, I'll say that I need the loo. The nearest toilets with decent access are at the back of beyond – at the far end of the luxury capsules area – and I'll tell our escort that you can take me there and –"

"But you can go yourself. You don't need me."

"They won't know that. Anyway, I'll tell them not to bother waiting for us, that I know the way back and that we'll only be ten minutes or so. And while I'm supposedly in the toilet you're going to turn up all the settings on their capsules. Temperature, glucose, saline; the brightness and sound on the VR. Just for a minute or two. It should be enough to cause a seizure."

I suddenly felt sick. "Jesus! And then?"

"I come out of the toilet, we leave, and we pray that it works. And that Riz wasn't lying about the fake CCTV cameras."

I exhaled heavily, working through the implications of what we'd be doing; the consequences of stuff going wrong… Even if we got them out of there safely, was this a secret me and Tush would have to keep for the rest of our lives? "Okay…" I said, slowly. "But is cold turkey the only way for them?"

"We've tried everything else. Reasoning with them. Arguing with them. Controlling what little money Mum and Dad left for them. And nothing, absolutely nothing has worked. Right?"

A memory of Mum and Dad confiscating the twins' consoles after a particularly bitter argument about the length of their screen time popped, Pokémon-like, into my brain. "And this way they'll be banned from all the VR factories, for good?"

"For good."

"And coming…" I hardly dared say the word, "home. But, listen," I went on, my voice shaky as I admitted something I'd never before said aloud, "we've got to give them something worth coming home for, you know. 'Cause it's not like it used to be. That's why I've been… staying at friends. And I guess that's why the twins have been doing what they've been doing. Escaping into their virtual world. It's as much a home to them as our four-bed semi, which is only full of…" I thought 'grief' but instead said, "tumbleweed."

Tushar sighed. "I know. But when we're all together again it'll be okay." Tushar took a deep breath, like this was a big speech he had to prepare himself for. "We need to start rebuilding… spending time together. Eating together. It's what Mum and Dad would've wanted. When the twins are back I'll make us some chana masala and you can microwave up a pudding or whatever. Invite that new bloke of yours. And we should ask Pauline to join us too. We'll talk. Watch a film. It'll be like… you know, before. Old times."

For a moment I heard that old soundtrack to my life; remembered the days when our family was knitted together with food and noise and love. Impervious to such catastrophic things as death.

"Tush," I began, "I mean… do you ever feel bad about the fact that it's your coding, your virtual worlds – all those AI characters you've created – that have got them addicted?"

I could see my brother's face tighten, his shoulders become stiff with dissonance. "Yes, no. But hey," he said, suddenly running a hand through his hair, "I'm good at what I do. But there's got to be boundaries between the gamer and the game. Right?"

"Yeah," I said, nodding. "Okay then, so it's tough love?"

"Tough love."

Everything worked just as Tushar said it would. Only the new recruit was chattier than he'd expected her to be. In the end he had to send her off to get us a couple of coffees while we made our way to the toilets. Thankfully, she went off all enthusiastic-like, no doubt completely oblivious to the fact that even an employee of NeuralKEEP wasn't to be left alone with the out-for-the-count gamers, and we knew we had just enough time to do what had to be done.

As we headed towards the toilets, I kept my eye on the numbers at the end of each long row of sleek-looking VR capsules, zoned-out human soul after zoned-out human soul, so that we could find where our brother and sister and Emma were.

"Row 62, just here," Tushar whispered, as he came to a stop. His face was beaded with sweat. "They're in pods 'R', 'S' and 'T'. Meet me by the toilets as soon as you're done, okay?"

I nodded and gave him a half-hearted smile.

"Wait," he said. "I should be the one to do it."

"No! We can't risk you losing your job. Besides, we don't have time to argue about this now. Go on, fuck off, I'll do it. Anyway, you're a better bullshitter than I am. If someone comes you can stall them."

Tushar passed a hand across his sweaty brow. "Okay, but you'd better be fast."

I was. I raced along the aisle, singing the alphabet through muted lips as I scanned the pods – each one a home to a zombified gamer, their mind only alive to the sights and sounds of the game which was more real to them than anything else.

I found them in their shiny white pods, motionless and in thrall to Tushar's lush coded worlds – alien, fantastical – the sexy-as-fuck AIs, and with trembling hands made the necessary adjustments to their environmental and physiological settings. I glanced up at a CCTV camera way up in the cavernous roof, hoping to God Riz was right and that it was blind to my actions.

And then I ran back down the row of pods and towards the toilets, praying that I hadn't just killed them, and saw Tushar who looked just as anxious as I felt.

"You did it?"

"Yeah," I said, breathless. "I did it."

A few moments later, we were approaching the foyer and our guide was handing us our coffees and asking if we wanted to see anything else. In the distance, there was the urgent sound of beeping.

By the time the new recruit realised that the prolonged beeping wasn't a good sign, a few nurses had rushed out to the factory floor.

"What's going on?" asked Tushar, all innocent, swirling his coffee cup.

"Oh um… I'm not really sure," said the young woman, frowning. "Sometimes, some gamers have, um, bad reactions. But it looks as though it's being dealt with."

She tried to chivvy us out the front entrance, telling us that we must be busy – and wasn't it a lovely day? – but Tushar insisted on staying.

"I want to show my sister my office. There's a fantastic view from up there."

The next half hour was agony. I was desperate to know if the three of them were okay. And I needed a vape. My hands were shaking like mad. Finally, Tushar got the call, and I listened in, hungry for news. Could we come pick up his brother and sister? They'd had an 'episode' during a VR session. They were okay, but they needed to be taken home immediately. And did he know an Emma Barnes? Her first emergency contact, her mother, was out of the country. And the number of her second, her father, wasn't a valid number. She had come in with his siblings. Could he take responsibility for her?

"Yes," he said, smiling up at me, "I will."

We went down to the foyer, and within a few minutes the three of them were wheeled out to us. It was strange to see them in wheelchairs, just like Tushar. But, unlike Tushar, they looked pathetic. Emma was sobbing and the twins appeared to still be in shock, their faces as blank as a pair of switched-off screens.

"So what happened?" Tushar asked the medic.

"Seizure. Unknown cause. It happens sometimes."

"Too much gaming?"

"Maybe. But's that not NeuralKEEP's responsibility." The medic thrust some papers into Tushar's hands. "You'll need to sign these."

"What do they say?"

"That you give us the right to share the information about their 'episode' with the other VR companies. They'll need to desist from all VR gaming. For the foreseeable future. It's all in the terms and conditions, of course."

"Of course," said Tushar, quickly signing the forms.

The nurses helped me wheel the three of them out to the car park, and between us we lifted them out of the wheelchairs and into Mum and Dad's ancient, roomy Volvo – a car that held a million memories.

As we drove home the sun emerged from behind a cloud. Tushar put on some music; it was a favourite album of Mum and Dad's which they used to play over and over when we went on holiday. When it was the six of us: Mum, Dad, me and Tushar, the twins.

I turned to look at the three of them on the back seat. Emma had stopped crying and was looking out of the window. And the twins were leaning against each other.

"It's all right," I said to them, my throat suddenly tight with emotion. "You're going to be all right. We're going home now."

"Home," repeated the twins, their umber eyes empty, unseeing. The word meant nothing to them.

The Sun is God

London, September 1844

"Good morning, Miss Beckwith!" says Mr Winsor, beaming at her from behind the wooden counter of his shop. "And what is your brother in need of today?"

Eugenie Beckwith looks about the tall wooden shelves thick with glass jars full of powdered pigments – ultramarine, verdigris, chrome yellow, vermillion, umber, lamp-black and Cremnitz white – and thrills with excitement. No matter how many times she's been to this colourman's shop, she will always feel joy when she looks upon the pigments. They silently sing to her; beseech her to transmute them into paint and form. She sees the sunsets and sunrises, landscapes and still lifes they might become under the guidance of her brush.

Tearing her eyes away from the jars, she tells Mr Winsor that her brother is after the usual, and so he instructs his assistant to fetch down the vermillion, the chrome yellow and Cremnitz white. But as she watches the young man weigh out the pigments, the jar of turquoise catches her eye and calls to her. It makes her think of the coves of Isola di Spargi, just north of Sardinia. Of swimming with Giovanni in the blue-green waters; of his naked body against hers.

"And an ounce of turquoise please," she adds.

"Of course," says Mr Winsor, making sure that his assistant has heard this. He then asks after her brother's health. "I heard that he's been rather poorly."

Eugenie frowns. "He was, but he's better now."

"And well enough to capture the sun on his canvas?"

"Indeed."

When Eugenie returns home with her purchases, her long-haired tabby cat, Emperor, greets her with a miaow.

"Hello, my love," Eugenie says as he sniffs at the hem of her skirts and then rubs against her legs. "And what have you been up to?"

Beth's head emerges from the kitchen door. "Miss Beckwith?"

"Yes?" says Eugenie, going to her.

"I was to give you a message from Edward. He said he was going out, and that it was likely he'd be away for most of the day. You'd have to show Mr Turner around the gallery."

Eugenie grimaces and then exhales deeply. "Doesn't he know I have work to do?" Another sigh. "Ah well, if I must."

Beth gives her a sympathetic smile. "Would you like a pot of tea?"

"Please," says Eugenie.

Emperor follows Eugenie into the studio, and after she has put down her parcels and taken off her coat, she stands in the large rectangle of autumn sunlight within the swell of the bay window and closes her eyes. The cat lounges at her feet, his fur aglow, and purrs loudly. Eugenie, appreciating the sun's warmth, its vitality, the way it graces each inch of her with its blessing, clasps her hands together and says a silent prayer. *Gracious Father, open my heart and mind and eyes to Your beauty. And let me be a vessel for Your Holy Spirit, so that through me, He can create what You wish me to create. Amen.*

Exhaling deeply, she opens her eyes and unclasps her hands. She fetches her apron; pulls it over her gown. "Now then," she says to herself, "which colour shall I make up first?"

Emperor turns his amber eyes on her, blinks, and lets out a small yowl.

"What was that? Yellow? Very well, chrome yellow it is."

Eugenie tips the pigment into a marble mortar which is stained yellow and begins to grind the coarse powder. "And what do you require of my body today?" she asks of the pigment.

Pausing for a moment to listen to its answer, she hears it say that it craves a dusting of her nails. And so she files down each of her fingernails, making sure to catch the fine dust in the mortar. She grinds the powder a little more and then tips it out onto the marble slab, adding some linseed oil and a small quantity of beeswax binder. This beeswax is incredibly expensive. Eugenie has it sent to her from a beekeeper who lives in Latvia. She met the woman on her travels, having heard of her great skill from a friend of a friend. The woman was more witch than apiarist – her unruly hair threaded with bees, her skin leathery, her mirthless laugh a cackle of buzzing – but as soon as

Eugenie held the beeswax in her hands she'd known that it would do something very special to her pigments.

Eugenie then mixes everything together with a metal spatula to make the paint. "And what of my spirit?" she asks, continuing with her folding and mixing, the linseed oil filling her nostrils with its sweet, nutty aroma.

The paint, coming into being beneath her spatula, desires a profound memory.

She closes her eyes for a moment, and sees the memory. As she mixes and smooths the yellow paint on the slab, she remembers the first time she became aware of the sun's power. She'd been riding in a phaeton with her brother and father, fields of sunflowers on either side of them, their yellow-petalled faces turned to the setting sun. Following their gaze, she'd looked at the sun intently, a great awakening occurring within her. It was as if she'd been filled with the certainty that here, before her, in all His magnificence was God. And – oh! – how much He loved her. This feeling was so intense, so overwhelming, that she began to cry. Her father, taking her hand, asked her what was wrong. "Are you thinking of your poor, dear mother?"

Eugenie, not wanting her father to think ill of her (she dared not admit that she could hardly remember her dead mother), sniffed loudly and looked up at her father, her eyes hot and tearful. To please him, she said that she was, and so he patted her hand and gave her a sorrowful smile.

"But she's in Heaven now, isn't she?" said Eugenie. "With God. And as the sun is God," she went on, pointing at the setting sun, "that must mean we see her every day?"

"The sun is God?" asked her father, confused.

Edward, alert to his father's discombobulation, took the opportunity to tell his sister that she was stupid. A kick reinforced his point.

"Ow!" cried Eugenie.

"Edward!" scolded their father. "There's no need for that."

Edward glared at his sister.

"No, Eugenie, that can't be right," her father said. "For God is the Almighty. And not the wayward star about which our planet turns." His face had suddenly brightened. "Ah, but you must mean Jesus, His son. Ess-*oh*-en. Although the two words sound the same, they are not the same. They are spelt differently. As the Greeks would have it: *omófonos*. That is, homophonous."

He had given her hand another pat and then sat back in the phaeton, a look of contentedness upon his face – as though he had passed on a great wisdom to his daughter. Eugenie, looking once more at the setting sun, felt her heart swell with emotion. She said a silent thank you.

There is a pause as Eugenie extricates herself from the memory, and returns to her present. The paint beneath her spatula is just the right consistency. She places some on her palette, and the rest goes into a jar. As she begins to clean the marble slab on her mixing table, Beth brings in a tray of tea things.

"Here you go, Miss," Beth says, placing the tray on a chair beside Eugenie's mixing table. Beth pours her mistress a cup of tea, adds some milk and passes it to Eugenie. Beth knows from experience that if she doesn't do this, it will remain untouched.

Eugenie, taking a sip of tea, looks at Emperor sprawled on the ground in the rectangle of morning sunlight. "Isn't he gorgeous?"

"He must be roasting," says Beth.

Eugenie laughs. "And they say that painters are the great devotees of light. But Emperor's the true disciple, prostrating himself before God hour upon hour."

"More like he's a lazy little beggar."

"Beth! Don't puncture my pretty metaphor."

"Sorry, Miss. I'm just saying what I see."

Emperor, irritated by the women's chatter, fills the momentary pause by exhaling deeply, exasperatedly.

"Oh very well, Emperor," says Eugenie, smiling wryly at Beth. "I will stop with the grandiosities."

"Is there anything else you'd like?" asks Beth.

"No thank you. I really must try to get as much done as I can before Mr Turner arrives."

Beth nods and then leaves the studio, quietly closing the door behind her.

Putting down her cup of tea, Eugenie returns her focus to the mixing table.

Now for the vermillion. As usual, it desires a drop of her blood. So she cuts into the little finger of her left hand and allows some of the blood to drip into the mortar full of pigment. It soaks into the coarse powder and vanishes. She pounds away at the pigment and then tips the fine red powder onto the clean marble slab. As she begins to mix the pigment with the linseed oil and beeswax binder, the vermillion asks her for a wound – a wound of her soul that has never, and will never, heal. Eugenie isn't at all surprised by the request, for the vermillion is a bloodthirsty beast. Still… what it asks of her causes a great deal of pain. For a moment she stands on a precipice, allowing herself to be empty of thought and feeling – ah, that is sweet balm indeed! But if her paintings are to come alive, she must plunge into the darkness. And so she thinks of the babe that had once resided inside her, the child whom she already loved with all her heart and soul; the purple-skinned babe that after eight months of growing within her had burned his way through her insides and then slipped out of her, covered in blood. The cord was wound tight about his neck and although she unwrapped it as fast as she could, she was too late. Her son was dead. And with him gone, his father – Giovanni – had died to her too. She'd held the cold, wee man to her breast for three days and nights, unwilling to let him go, until her brother had forcibly taken him away from her. Edward had insisted that she drink some water, eat a little food. He'd put a glass of water to her lips, a slice of bread in her hand. When she'd slaked her thirst and eaten the bread, she'd dragged herself out of her bloody, filthy bed and slowly washed herself.

Eugenie mixes the paint with vigorous, violent strokes. "Is that what you wanted to hear?" she demands of the vermillion, her face hard, her eyes bright. "Is that enough of a wound for you?"

The vermillion paint radiates her agony, and she knows it is satisfied. She puts a little of the vermillion on her palette and then scrapes the rest of it into a jar, slamming down the lid. With great vigour, she cleans the marble slab.

Sighing, she wipes her vermillion-spattered hands on her apron and then brushes away a tear. She takes a sip of tea, grateful for Beth's thoughtfulness. The tea is a balm, helping to compose her before she mixes the next colour.

"And what do you require of my body?" she asks of the turquoise as she tips the coarse pigment into the mortar. Through the silence, Eugenie hears the answer: *a tear.*

Well then, that's easy enough, she thinks, for her eyes are still wet with tears. And so she lets them fall into the mortar of turquoise, where they quickly vanish. She pounds the coarse pigment with the pestle and wonders what it will require of her spirit.

A wish for the future.

Ah, now that's a hard one.

Eugenie bashes away at the pigment for a little longer, wondering if the new paint tubes John Goffe Rand has invented will catch on. One day, she imagines, there will be great machines of steam to grind pigment and mix paint and imprison it within a metal tube. But as she tips the fine powder onto the marble slab and begins to mix it with the linseed oil and beeswax, she knows that although it will be time-saving, efficient, something will be lost. For the magic of her paintings does not come from the actual strokes of her brush – for anyone can smear paint onto a canvas – no, the magic comes from this painstaking preparation: the grinding, the mixing, even the cleaning of the slab. And into all of this she pours her very soul.

Shaking her head a little, Eugenie tries to focus on what the turquoise requires of her. A wish for the future.

She would like to wish for something that makes her feel noble – that her brother will cease to live such a debauched lifestyle. But, in truth, this is not her heart's greatest desire, for it suits her to have her brother gone from the house for most of the day.

There is a part of her that longs for recognition: for the public to know that it is she that creates these paintings, and not her brother. But, then again, she has been happy enough to go along with the supposition made many years ago that the paintings signed E. *Beckwith* have been created by Edward. It would be vain of her to wish for this recognition. And, besides, what would she do with the praise? It does not belong to her, but to God. As long as she is painting, and improving her craft, then she is happy. And if her work continues to find appreciative viewers (and buyers, for she and Edward must eat) then that is all that really matters.

Eugenie continues to mix the paint. She does so slowly and carefully, almost dreamily, and she once again thinks of the turquoise waters of Isola di Spargi, of Giovanni encouraging her to leap from his boat and into the warm, clear water.

It is then that she admits her heart's greatest desire: to once again be with Giovanni. She wonders if he'd recognise the woman she's become, for there's little of the shy, uncertain young lady about her any more. Indeed, the anxiety that used to consume her whenever anyone showed an interest in her art, causing her every fibre to tremble and nausea to sweep through her, is long gone. Now, she couldn't care less about others' opinions. For if a person judges her work and finds it wanting, then they judge God too. Which is hubris of the most abominable kind. And she can't be doing with people like that.

Eugenie remembers the first time she'd met Giovanni, the Italian sun beating down on her as though she were an ant beneath a magnifying glass, the low marble wall she'd been sitting on uncomfortably hard. She recalls the pencil sketches in her notebook which had caught his attention, and him asking her in his broken English if he could take a look; the touch of his hand on hers as he took the sketchbook from her and leafed through it. She'd been terrified of his disapproval, but none had been forthcoming. He'd gazed at her pencil sketches and wan watercolours – of the Sardinian coastline, the churches, the bowls of green and black olives – and had smiled. "These are very good," he'd said. "Very good."

She'd blushed, already madly in love with him, and then he'd said something that had made her insides churn with bile.

"Technically, they are very good." He'd then put his clenched hand to his heart and said, "But they lack *la passione.*"

"*Passione?* Whatever do you mean?"

"Heart. Love. Great feeling."

Eugenie had wanted to tear the sketchbook from his hands, to get up off the wall and walk away, but of course she did no such thing. She couldn't. She could no more leave his presence than the sun could stop shining.

He'd turned another page and found the picture of her late father, his ruddy face bloated, his eyes full of pain. There was also the sketch of his hands, one folded over the other, which she'd done after his funeral; the veins sinuous rivers of ultramarine. "Ah, but I see here a great feeling." Giovanni's eyes began to shine. "A great grief." He'd turned to look at her, and then held her hand. "I am sorry."

Eugenie had said nothing and simply acknowledged his condolences with a nod.

Giovanni continued to look through the sketchbook and then passed it back to her.

"You have, inside you, the ability to become a great artist. But to become a great artist you need to experience life. Not only grief, but love and laughter. And pleasure, and fear, and freedom."

He'd offered her his hand. "Come with me. I will show you the most beautiful places. The most fascinating people."

She'd wanted to take Giovanni's hand, was desperate to go with him, but she hadn't been brought up to wander off with strange men. And in a foreign country, too. "I will ask my brother if he can accompany us."

Giovanni had shrugged. "As you wish."

Yet Edward, ensconced in the nearby taverna, a glass of wine in one hand, a woman in another, said he wasn't going anywhere. "Go by yourself," he'd slurred. "After all, when in Rome, do as the Romans do." Amused by his own wit, he'd burst out laughing.

Eugenie, not knowing whether she should despise her brother or thank him, had hurried out of the taverna before he could change his mind.

"You will come with me?" Giovanni had asked, looking over her shoulder for her brother. "By yourself?"

Eugenie had nodded, and smiled at him, offered him her hand, which he bent to his lips and kissed. "Wonderful! Signorina, I promise you will not regret one single moment."

And she hadn't, even when she'd returned to England, every ounce of her soul pining for Giovanni. Even when Edward had discovered she was pregnant, prompting him to call her all sorts of slanderous names.

The only thing Eugenie had regretted was not telling Giovanni about their child. About his birth, and death. And now... who knew where Giovanni was? But if she were to see him again... or if he were to ever look upon one of her paintings, he would know. For he was right. She had to experience life – its many tones of pleasure and pain – so that she could capture it in her paintings. So that others would feel it too.

Eugenie sighs; returns to the paint before her. Her hand is now still, the turquoise beneath her spatula the perfect consistency. Scooping a goodly amount of it onto her palette (the rest goes in a jar), she then picks up her brushes and goes to the large blank canvas on its easel. She stands before the canvas for a moment, her eyes closed, seeing what she must paint. It is the Tyrrhenian Sea at noon, the pale sand visible through the shallow turquoise waters; the stone of the rocky coastline white, grey, sienna and vermillion. The sun itself is not in the picture, but it is fully present in the image – it is the heat that radiates off the sandy beach and cliffs; the jagged stripes of gold across the surface of the water; it is the very sky, the ultramarine blue suffused with light and warmth. The painting is of the moment in which a youthful Eugenie, deeply in love with Giovanni, wished summer would go on forever. The child had already taken root in her womb and her future contained only happiness. When Eugenie completes the painting, the viewer will see exactly what she saw at that moment; exactly what she felt. They will feel the sun on their skin, the water at their feet, the love in their heart, the naïve expectation that life would always be as perfect as this summer day.

Eugenie opens her eyes and begins to paint.

A few hours later there is a knock on the door of Eugenie's studio, but Eugenie doesn't hear it; she is lost to her painting. It is only when Beth comes in and stands beside her, pulling at her sleeve, that Eugenie notices her.

"Please, Miss," she says. "It's Mr Turner, come to look at the paintings."

Eugenie turns her head to Beth and looks at her with unseeing eyes.

"Mr Turner?" she echoes.

"Yes, Miss. Remember? Your brother's not here so you're to show him around."

Eugenie sighs. "Oh yes."

Reluctantly, she puts down her palette and brush; wipes her hands on her apron. "Let's just hope that he doesn't stay too long."

Mr Turner is already in the sun-filled gallery, and when Eugenie comes in he acknowledges her with a tip of his hat. He then returns his gaze to her painting of the white cliffs of Dover. The image is of the moment when, after a long trip abroad with her father and brother, Eugenie first sighted her homeland. She'd exclaimed, "Oh my beautiful country! My home!" much to the amusement of her father, who'd been charmed by her innocent patriotism. The painting has already been sold and is soon to be dispatched to its buyer.

Eugenie stands at the back of her gallery, working at the fingers of her left hand which are stiff from holding the palette for so long. But although she is physically present in the room, she is still at her painting, lost to the sand and the sea, the sky and the sun.

Mr Turner moves away from the seascape to another painting which has already been sold. It is of a heather moorland, the golden bees collecting nectar a striking contrast to the sky which is voluminous with pewter-coloured clouds. It was where Edward had taken Eugenie to recuperate after the birth and death of her son; it was the place she'd lost and then re-found God. She'd walked on the moor every single day for three months, no matter the weather. At first, there was nothing. Just emptiness. She'd trudge across the moorland for miles, not caring that her feet were blistered, or sodden, her skirts heavy with rain, or that her shawl had been bejewelled with mist. What did it matter? God had abandoned her when she needed Him most, and in her darkest hours she would curse Him to Hell. Gradually, she became aware of her physical discomforts; of the moorland about her. As the sunny days became more numerous, she would sit amongst the heather and watch the bees. They would hum to her, tell her of the joy to be found in the amaranthine sweetness of the heather; of the healing balm of good, honest work. In time, she took her notebook with her to the moors, and on one particularly fine day she began to sketch the moorland. It was then, as she was absorbed in her drawing, that she realised God was again beside her. Indeed, He had never left her, and she wept in relief. She begged for forgiveness, though He told her that there was nothing to forgive.

Mr Turner looks at this painting for a long time, an unreadable expression on his face, and Eugenie, rather unkindly, wishes that he'd hurry up. He then turns to the 'self-portrait' of Edward, who is seated at a table with Emperor at his elbow, and smiles wryly, for though Edward is known to almost everyone as a handsome, well-dressed and generous man (though one who likes his port a little too much), Eugenie has captured him looking distinctly ignoble. Despite the fact that he is wearing a contrite smile, every muscle of his face radiates resentment. Shame.

Eugenie had painted this shortly after Edward had one of his tantrums. One evening he'd been particularly put out by some recent praise of one of 'his' paintings, and unluckily for Emperor he'd been the first to cross Edward's path when Edward had decided to let fly his foul mood. Eugenie, startled by the sound of Emperor's screeching, had run out from the studio to find Edward in the corridor, kicking the poor cat who was cowering in a corner. "Stop it!" she'd cried, running at her brother and beating him with her fists, but Edward had ignored her protests and batted her away as though she were as insubstantial as a moth. Eugenie, wild with rage, had run back to her studio, picked up a jar of vermillion paint and run back out to the corridor. "If you don't stop, I'll cover you in paint!"

Not even turning to look at her he said, "You wouldn't dare."

But Eugenie *had* dared, and plunging her hand into the jar had leapt onto his back and smeared paint into his eyes and mouth and nose until he'd thrown her off. She'd crashed into the wall behind her, winded and bruised, and Edward had run, blindly, to the bathroom. As soon as he'd gone, Emperor had fled. He was gone for three days. When he did lope back, his fur matted with dried blood and mewling for food, she'd thanked God for his safe return and fed him all his favourite dishes. She'd then painted the portrait of Edward and inserted a knowing and superior-looking Emperor into the scene. If you were to look closely, you'd see tiny daubs of vermillion clinging to Edward's hair, the sleeves of his coat, the creases of his eyelids. The painting hung in the gallery as a warning: *restrain yourself*. Oh, she understood where her brother's rage came from – for it had to be awful to *not* have the desire to create, to paint; and to simply drift through life, blithely accepting the praise that was rightly hers as his own. Still, as she'd told him later, his torment wasn't an excuse for violence.

Mr Turner then strolls towards the painting of the field of sunflowers, which is not for sale. He stays there for a long while, simply looking at it, a serene expression on his face. "Miss Beckwith," he says, turning to look at her, and she goes to him and waits for him to say something more.

His eyes travel to her paint-stained apron, the crusts of paint on her fingers and beneath her nails; he glances at her right hand and notices the way the tips of her thumb, index and middle fingers are flattened from consistently holding a paint brush.

"You'll have to excuse my sorry state," says Eugenie. "I was just mixing some paint for my brother."

Mr Turner grunts; he isn't fooled by her lie. He pauses for a moment longer before saying, "I suppose you must tire of hearing this, but –" he pauses again "– these paintings are… without parallel." He returns his gaze to the fields of sunflowers, their necks craned towards the sun, their god. "When I look at this painting – at any one of these paintings – I am there. Actually there. And experiencing what the painter felt in that moment. Here, for instance," he indicates to the painting of sunflowers, "I am seated in a phaeton, the clop of horse hooves in my ear. A light breeze brushes my face and I can smell the faint aroma of sunflowers – vegetal, oily sweet – and the stronger scent of a bonfire. In the distance I can see a walled castle, and my left shin hurts from where I have been kicked by someone." He turns to look at her. "Edward."

Eugenie doesn't know how to respond, so she lowers her eyes and again wipes her hands on her apron.

"This feat alone is remarkable enough," he says, his gaze once again on the sunflowers, "however, this painting also speaks to me of a great insight. A divine revelation that I, myself, came to some time ago. And I believe that it is a revelation that all true artists come to, in time."

He turns to look at Eugenie, and she sees that his eyes are shining.

She nods, her eyes welling with tears, and for a while they are both silent, still; their mutual understanding as precious to them as the dawn.

And then Mr Turner moves towards one of the few still lifes in the gallery. It is of a white-and-blue china jug filled with open red roses on a rough wooden table. The jug's glazing is cracked all over and the handle looks to have been broken and inexpertly glued back on. A few fallen petals are scattered across the dark wood of the table. It is the closest that Eugenie has ever come to painting a self-portrait, and Mr Turner will know this. She suddenly feels dreadfully exposed, as though all her clothes have been wrenched from her body.

He gazes at the painting for some time but says nothing. Eventually, he mutters, "How can something so fragile, so broken and stuck-back-together, hold so much beauty?"

Eugenie blushes and wrings her hands. Oh, if only Edward had been here, then she wouldn't feel so naked! And yet, a part of her delights in Mr Turner's praise, his empathy. He doesn't say anything more for a while, but eventually, he turns to her and says, "Yet there is loss in this painting too. The loss of a child. Which is the worst kind of loss, isn't it?"

Eugenie looks directly into his eyes and says, "Yes. Yes it is."

He nods, a melancholy expression on his face. "Well, I won't take up any more of your time. I know you'll be wanting to get back to your work."

Without thinking, Eugenie puts a hand to his sleeve. "Won't you stay for a glass of port? Some tea?" Hunger suddenly claws at her stomach and she realises she hasn't eaten in a long while. "Or a bite to eat? You'd be very welcome to stay for lunch. Our dining arrangements are very simple, but if that does not concern you, then –"

"Miss Beckwith," he says, a smile suddenly lighting up his dour face, "I would be honoured."

London, December 1851

Eugenie is sitting at the kitchen table with Beth who is laughing at Emperor's antics. Desperate for the chicken on Eugenie's plate, he keeps attempting to steal a morsel. His paw hovers at Eugenie's hand, occasionally darting at the forkful of meat as it goes from her plate to her mouth. But then there is the sound of the front door slamming and footsteps along the hallway, and both women turn to the open door of the kitchen, to see what kind of state Edward is in.

He is drunk, but only mildly. And a little melancholy. He leans against the doorframe and says, "Well, the old duck's dead."

"Who's dead?" asks Eugenie, her heart racing.

"You know who. Your great admirer. Mr Mallard, or Mallord, whatever his middle name is. Was."

"William Turner?"

Edward nods.

She cannot process this, for although she knew that Turner had been in ill health for years, she had always thought of him as being immortal. Just like his paintings.

"And do you know what his last words were?" asks Edward, a sour expression on his face.

Eugenie shakes her head.

"The sun is God."

She is round-eyed, silent. They are all silent; the only sounds the crackle of the fire, the contented munching of Emperor who has finally managed to swipe a piece of chicken from Eugenie's plate.

Edward sighs, pushes himself off the doorframe and then takes a bottle of port from a cupboard. He pours out three glasses, and hands a glass to both Eugenie and Beth. "To Mr Turner," he says, raising his glass. "One of the finest painters ever to have lived. May he rest in peace."

"Rest in peace," echo Beth and Eugenie.

A few days later, Eugenie finds herself sketching a three-quarter view of Mr Turner. He is standing in the gallery, the sunflower painting behind him. His eyes are on hers. As she makes her first bold strokes in graphite, she already knows how the oil painting that it will become will look. When it is finished, she will ask him how he is. What he sees in his Heavenly home. He will tell her that it is like nothing he has ever seen. That it is beautiful beyond belief, and that they were right. The sun is God. And Eugenie will weep with gratitude.

Star Making at Sellafield

They make for an unusual pair – the young black woman, professional in her Chanel suit, and the old white man, thick-spectacled, his head bowed, reluctant to face the sea of journalists. It's a windy day. Some of the reporters would rather be indoors, yet the photographers aren't complaining. They appreciate the striking imagery gifted to them – the brilliant, beautiful businesswoman and the genius physicist against the backdrop of Sellafield, with its glittering dome and the decommissioned Windscale Piles. Taking dozens of shots, they make sure they've got enough blue sky in their photographs for the headline, whatever that might be, though it'll be something along the lines of: 'Nuclear Fusion Finally a Reality', 'Clean Energy from a Dirty Place', 'Northern Souls the Brains behind Forever Energy', or perhaps the somewhat jumbled 'Would You Adam and Eve It! They're Making Stars at Sellafield'.

The statement to the press goes well; Livienne is superb at communicating her vision and providing tweetable quotes. She deflects taunts masquerading as questions, sidesteps queries about finances and safety that are too probing, too dull, and coaxes some coherent sentences out of John, her deceased father's research colleague, about the science of the project, of how they'll be 'cleaning up Sellafield' by using spent radioactive material in the process of nuclear fusion. She ends with the statement that thousands of new jobs will be generated; the Cumbrian coast will be transformed. Never to be the same again.

Afterwards, Livienne is high on adrenaline and the memory of the awestruck faces, the clamour for more information. John, however, crumples into a chair as soon as he's back in her office. His right hand instinctively goes to his shirt pocket, though he hasn't kept his cigarettes there for a long time. He pats it over and over, as though he's drumming in a code that will somehow make them appear.

Livienne enthuses about the response; she checks Twitter and grins as she sees #Sellafield, #nuclearfusion and #SellafieldSaviours beginning to trend. She glances at John, still patting the left side of his chest, and notes his ashen face.

"It's over," she says. "You did well."

He smiles weakly. "I need a smoke."

Livienne sighs. There are a million things to do. But she can also see that John needs her.

"A smoke and a walk?"

He nods.

"All right, give me a minute."

She gives her assistant some hurried instructions, tells her to call if there's anything she can't deal with.

"C'mon, soft lad," she says to John. "Let's get you some ciggies."

Livienne's driver takes them to a newsagent in Seascale where John buys a pack of ten Marlborough Lights – *See, I'm cutting down,* he tells her – and then they go to the beach. They sit on a bench near the car park and watch the steel grey sea.

"D'you remember the time," says John, lighting up, "when your kite flew away, and you kept on crying till Kel made you a new one?"

"From his shirt, two sticks and wool from Mum's knitting bag," she recites, certain that her real memory has long vanished.

She smiles, nudges her shoulder against John's. "You tried to comfort me with an ice cream but I was having none of it."

"Smart girl," he says, with pride in his eyes. "You weren't one to be diverted easily. Thank goodness. Otherwise none of this – what're the media calling it? Freaky fusion? Money for old rope? – would ever have happened."

"You and Dad were the ones who made it happen."

John shakes his head. "The physics wasn't the hard part. Nuclear fusion's simple. But the engineering necessary... *That* was the real cutting-edge stuff. The bit your dad figured out. I only wish that Kel was here now. If only to see how you made it all possible."

Livienne waves away his praise, then blots a tear that is threatening to ruin her mascara. "Spinning a good story, persuading investors. Negotiating." She suddenly laughs heartily. "I'm just a hell of a good saleswoman."

John laughs too. "Like your mother."

Livienne nods. "Yep, just like Mum."

There is a comfortable pause. They watch a lone dog walker at the water's edge, gulls arguing over scraps of food.

"This was one of the few beaches Mum didn't hate," she says suddenly.

John furrows his brow, adjusts his glasses. "She never said."

"I think she never wanted to seem ungrateful. To speak ill of England, and its cold, flinty beaches. But when you and Dad were walking, discussing work, she'd tell me about her home. The beaches of white sand. The crystal clear turquoise sea. How it was paradise on Earth."

"And what do you think now?" John asks.

"That's she's right. The Caribbean *is* stunning. When I go to visit her I don't want to leave. But this place... Well. It'll always be special to me. It's where I got a custom-made kite, for a start."

John smiles, stubs out his cigarette.

"Fancy a stroll?" he says.

Livienne glances down at her phone. Nothing urgent. "Why not?"

They head north, towards Sellafield, past the car park and the empty playground. The tide is low, leaving the mostly sandy beach exposed. Livienne recalls her childhood, searches for a memory that hasn't been remade by others. She remembers building sandcastles, her mother, voluptuous in her red wool bikini, pushing pebbles into the sides, adorning turrets with feathers. She had wondered when her own skinny body would fill out and her breasts become large enough to fill a bra top. And always, Kel and John talking shop. Their conversation, though unintelligible to her, fascinated her. She knew she was listening to something impossibly exciting; that she was on the edge of something big, though she couldn't explain what. And she wanted in.

She doesn't tell John that there is little altruism in her makeover of Sellafield. She spent her girlhood dreaming of ways to escape her provincial hometown – of going someplace where she would 'fit'; of being somewhere not constantly in the shadow of the nuclear plant, her father's first love.

She found those places. First in London, at university, and then in New York, in the world of business, and of course Saint Lucia, where her mum now spent most of the year. But always, in her dreams, there was Sellafield, her father and his groundbreaking work. There was no escape. Even as an adult she wanted in. So she found a way in. Not through science, but business.

"Penny for your thoughts," says John.

"Oh, I…" she says, shaking her head. "Two months until lift off. Can you believe it?"

John looks down, puts his right hand to his shirt pocket. This time he finds the cigarettes there.

"You ever wonder what'll happen after the two months?" he says, extracting a cigarette from the packet and pausing to light it.

"We'll be in the news. Constantly. Share prices will rocket. We'll have more work than we can possibly cope with."

"No, I mean, what about the unintended consequences? Will we really cause a reduction in greenhouse emissions? Or will they go, 'Oh well, we've got clean fuel now, it's okay to chop down all the forests and poison the soil.'? That's what I mean. Biology. Human brains in human bodies. How people behave. I've never known anything so baffling."

"Have you been reading the comments on *The Guardian* again?" she says, with a laugh. "I thought I told you to never read the comments."

John shakes his head. "No. Maybe. But I can't help thinking about it."

Livienne is silent for a moment. "But that's not for us to worry about. We've done our bit. And we've got to keep doing it, *successfully*, so that other sites copy us. That's what will make the real difference."

John takes a deep drag on his cigarette, and then nods. "I suppose so." He stops walking, turns towards the beach. "Nice day, isn't it?"

"Yes," she says, taking his arm, "lovely."

John pats her arm. "It's not right that your dad died, and I stayed on. But I can say this: Kel would've been proud of you. *I'm* proud of you."

Livienne puts her head against John's shoulder. This time she lets her tears fall.

"Thank you," she says.

Two months later Livienne and John are wearing lab coats, just two of the many crowded around the stellarator in the heart of Sellafield. The prime minister is about to switch on the device. There is silence. Then: *clunk*. The fusion reactor hums and then jitters into action; there is clapping, cheering. Somebody whistles.

The noise pounds its way into John's head, muffles the sound of his heart imploding. He suddenly clutches his chest, then falls to his knees. Livienne sees him go down and is instantly at his side. She knows from his desperately pale face that this is serious. She calls to her assistant, tells her to call for the first aiders. For an ambulance. Two of John's colleagues help her to move him through the crowd and into an empty room.

"Help will be here in a moment," she says, holding his hand.

John's eyes are fixed on Livienne's. He tries to smile.

"We did it," he says, his eyes watering and losing focus. Everything becomes radiant. He is unable to tell her that the newspapers were right. That him and Kel *had* looked to the stars and wished to be like God.

Livienne nods, tears running down her face. "We did it," she says, smiling.

"Good girl," John manages to say, before his heart shuts down for good. The last thing he sees is a sunrise, a kite, free of its owner, in the distance.

The November Room
(or Leaving the Labyrinth)

As Indra walks along the sunlit marble corridor, the smooth white stone cool beneath her bare feet, she stretches her arms wide and runs her fingertips along the walls. The corridor continues straight ahead of her for what seems like miles. Glancing upwards at the cerulean sky she sees a flock of geese, and before she can stop herself she wishes they would swoop down and lift her up and out of the labyrinth. When she is thousands of metres high, the air about her thin and cold, she will let go and fall to her death. It is the only way to truly escape the labyrinth. But as soon as this wish has formed in her mind, goose feathers begin to drift down from the sky, into the marble corridor. It should be a beautiful sight but it isn't; she's learnt that everything she's ever invited into the labyrinth quickly turns strange, into something "other". She begins to run.

Her breath rattles in her throat and her legs shiver with exhaustion; her heart is like an overstretched skin on a drum and her soles are raw from running on the hard, unforgiving stone. She thinks there is a door in the distance and wills herself onwards. Yes, it is a door, and it is marked *June*. Vaguely, she thinks that June is okay, she can cope with June. Then she remembers that the accident was in June and pauses for a moment. But when she turns to look behind her she sees the creep of goose feathers. Each one of the many that have fallen from the sky and come into contact with the marble labyrinth has been turned into stone. There are heaps of marble feathers littered across the corridor, up and up the walls, so that the way back is completely blocked. There is no going back, she must go into the June room. She takes a deep breath and opens the door.

There is neither rhyme nor reason to the rooms within the labyrinth, or so she thinks. The calendar on the wall says it is the 3rd of June 1976. Her adult self falls into her ten-year-old body on the day that she plucked up enough courage to tell the first boy she ever liked that she wanted to kiss him. Her adult self – the self that is trapped within the labyrinth – is a voyeur to this romantic impulse, and when the boy says, yes, he would like to kiss her, she sneezes in his face and his glasses are spattered with snot. The children around them in the playground roar with laughter and she runs and runs and runs, her cheeks burning with shame, until she finds a gap in the hedge that skirts the school field and burrows her way into it. She stays there, wishing death upon herself, until the cling-clang of the bell. Her adult self wants to laugh off these feelings but she must experience them as if she were ten. She wipes away her burning tears and then returns to her schoolroom, sits at the wooden desk she has graffitied with the assertion that *I.S.* ♡ *A.T.* and tries to listen to Mrs Hall who is teaching them how to tell the time.

The next day is the day of the accident: 24th June 1991. She wakes, excited about the fact that today is the opening of her exhibition at the gallery, and hardly pays any attention to her small son and husband who are already at the kitchen table having breakfast. Her older self, trapped in her younger body, winces at how distracted she is; her heart aches as she helplessly watches this younger version ignore her son's request to walk him to school. Her mind is a tumult of preparations for the launch – there is extra champagne to buy, her business cards to be reprinted, her dress to be picked up from the dry cleaners.

"So what do you think?" asks her husband.

"Sorry, David, what did you say?" she replies, putting down her coffee cup.

"James wondered if you could maybe walk him to school?"

"Well," she glances at her watch, takes a last sip of coffee and then addresses her son. "I'm kind of in a rush today, pickle. Would it be okay if you just go with Daddy? I've got so much to do with getting everything ready for tonight. It's exciting isn't it?"

James isn't excited. In fact, he looks as though he is about to cry, and Indra suddenly worries that he will pick up his bowl and hurl it at her. But David puts his arm around his shoulders – does his particular brand of David 'magic' – and heads off the storm before it arrives. David says it's okay, they don't need Mummy today. They have a secret mission to accomplish on the way to school and she'll only get in the way. James looks questioningly at his father, who is wearing an enigmatic expression, grins at him, and then puts his cereal bowl to his lips and slurps down the last of the sugared milk.

"Oh James, for goodness sake, don't do that!" she snaps.

But her husband doesn't scold him. "Waste not, want not."

"Anyway, I'd better get going," she says, standing and giving them each a hurried kiss. "I've got so much to do, and there's so little time."

Later, when she is sitting in her stationary Ford Sierra, the last of many of a long queue of cars all waiting for a red light to turn green, her older self braces herself for the pain to come. Her younger self glances in the rear view mirror and sees a speeding truck behind her. Stupidly, her first thought is of the crates of champagne in the boot of the car. If the truck doesn't stop soon it'll break all the bottles and she'll have to buy more. She looks ahead, at the cars in front of her, at the stubbornly red light, and then again at the truck, which is accelerating. Panic takes hold of her as she realises the truck is about to plough into her car and she fumbles with the seatbelt in a desperate attempt to get out of the car. But she can't, and before she knows it, she is whipping forwards and her head is crashing into the steering wheel. Her body sings with pain.

For the next three days she is three months old, and utterly helpless. The year is 1966 and the days are June 1st, June 30th and June 22nd. Her mother is everything to her – warmth, food, comfort – but her mother has a habit of repeatedly placing her in a cold crib and then slipping out of sight. Indra cries. A lot.

The rest of the thirty days of June are mainly uneventful ones – she is either in London, at The Slade, or at secondary school or working in her studio. There is one glorious day, when she is in her second year at The Slade, which consists of nothing but desire and the fulfilment of desire. It is one of the hottest days of the year and she and David, whom she only met the week before, spend the whole day in bed, making love, until the sheets are damp with sweat. Eventually, they leave her flat to go and find some food in Soho. Her older self, reliving this day, basks in the bliss of their romance; the fact that she has no knowledge of the terrible thing that will derange their future.

Then there is the day when she is thirteen and her father says he needs to have a little chat with her. The expression on his face is hard to read. He sort of looks sad, but also not. He tells her he won't be living in their home any more. He's going to live with another woman.

215

A woman that he loves very much. But he'll always be her daddy. And Mummy and she will never ever need to worry about money. He'll see her as often as he can. Indra sobs, and when he tries to console her she thumps him as hard as she can with both fists and then runs to the toilet, locking herself in. He won't be able to go until she comes out, and she's never going to come out. But after twenty minutes or so, she hears his footsteps on the stairs, her mother flinging some last insults at him, and then the slamming of the front door. Her older self wants to comfort her childish self, but she can't. They are shut away from each other, locked into their own silent grief.

On four wonderful days James is with her. He is young – 3, 11, 9, 6 – and mostly untroubled. There is only one somewhat challenging day in which she has to collect James's costume for his last ever primary school performance. He is playing the Minotaur, and as everyone knows her to be the 'arty' mother she must get him the best. She does. A friend who excels in papier-mâché sculptures has made a bull's head for him. It is exquisite, but James doesn't like it and refuses to even try it on. She does her best to coax him into putting it on, but he doesn't respond to her pleas; they only result in him going from sullen to enraged and he throws himself on the floor, wailing and thrashing his limbs about. As she attempts to get him up off the floor, he screams and kicks her.

Indra, deeply embarrassed by her son's tantrum, clutches at the silk scarf about her neck. The scarf is as red as a bullfighter's flag, and for a moment she longs to wrap it about James's neck and pull it tight. Her older self cringes at the terrible impulse; she knows it is a thought that will haunt her for the rest of her life. Her younger self gives her friend, Ari, an apologetic look and tells her son that it's okay, that he doesn't need to try it on right now and that it's time they went home. But he doesn't budge.

It is only when Ari gets out a pot of bubble solution and begins to blow bubbles over his supine form that he becomes still. Fascinated, he watches the bubbles float upwards, to the ceiling.

"Would you like to make some?" asks Ari.

James says nothing and when Ari offers him the pot and wand, Indra is sure that he'll whack them away, but instead, he snatches them from Ari's hands and begins to blow bubbles; a mixture of his own snot and tears first coating the loop of the wand.

"That's right," says Ari, encouragingly. "Now you're just like your mother. Only *you're* a sculptor of air."

James doesn't say anything, but he is calmer now, and Indra is thankful for Ari's understanding, her patient handling of the situation.

After a while, Indra manages to coax James off the floor, and they leave, with him clutching the pot of bubbles and her the bull's head. Her younger self is exasperated, angry; full of self-pity. *Why does he always ruin things that should be joyful?* Her older self simply wants to hold James one more time.

The last day in the June room is June 16th 2005, the day when David said in a gentle voice that maybe it would be best if they went their separate ways. Her five-month younger self doesn't argue and watches him walk to the front door with a rucksack full of clothes and his portfolio full of charcoal sketches of their son.

He opens the door but then pauses on the threshold, turns to her and says, "But if you need me and ever want to talk… well, I'm here for you. Okay?"

She nods, willing herself not to cry. She wants to say something, anything, but when he speaks, says that considering what they've gone through it's understandable that they've drifted apart, she closes the door on him. As it slams shut, tears waterfall from her eyes.

She steps out of the June room still crying and sits with her back to one of the marble walls of the labyrinth, hugging her knees to her chest. As soon as her tears hit the floor they turn into smooth chips of marble. Looking at the door she has just now come through, she sees that it is already turning into stone. That part of the labyrinth is now closed off to her, reinforcing the fact that there is no way back or out; she is being shunted ever onwards. Endlessly trapped. She picks up the marble chips and screams as she hurls them at the opposite wall. They clatter to the ground and one splits in two as it hits the floor. It gives her an idea. She scrabbles around for the broken pieces and finds the two halves of the teardrop. One of them has a particularly rough, sharp edge, and before she can think her way out of the action she uses it to try to cut the artery in her neck. Desperately, she jabs, jabs, jabs at her throat, but her neck, though bruised, is otherwise unharmed.

She wonders how many rooms are ahead of her still, before the year is up. Running through the months in her head, she marks each one of them by slicing the skin on her upper arm with the sharp marble chip. Beads of blood form at each incision, and though each cut is shallow, she is pleased with her handiwork; it is then that she fully realises she's been in eleven rooms already and none of them was the month of November. It's the one room she can't face, and she sobs, sorrow welling out of her, and she longs to cry a river – an ocean – and to drown in her own tears. As soon as she has thought this, the marble floor begins to undulate, roll, crest. It is bubbling up like water from a spring, and rippling and breaking against her feet. With a pounding heart she realises what she's done: she's summoned a river of marble to come drown her. But though a part of her would like to remain here and be suffocated in stone, another part recoils from the roiling river, from the waves that are already as tall as the walls of the corridor. She runs.

She follows the labyrinth, turning left, then right, then left and left again until she meets with a door. It is the November room. The room she doesn't want to enter. But she can hear the rushing of the marble river behind her and there is nowhere to go. As the water flows towards her, trickles of living stone brushing against her feet, a great wave rises up in the river and she panics. It is going to engulf her and she will be crushed, drowned, suffocated. Turned to stone. She tells herself that she doesn't care, that she deserves this death, but an instinct to survive – to live at all costs – betrays her, and she reaches for the handle of the door and tumbles into the November room.

Of course, the first day she falls into is November the fifth 2002, the one day she has never wanted to relive. Most of the day is spent in the studio, using a rasp to refine the sculpture she is working on. When the air is full of marble dust and her arms are spent with fatigue, her assistant helps her out of the climbing harness. Attached to the criss-cross of wires and pulleys up in the rafters, the harness enables Indra to get up close to the tall block of marble she is sculpting. Unclicking the various clips and safety harnesses, her assistant helps Indra into her wheelchair and brings her a cup of coffee. She then tells her about the phone calls she's dealt with while Indra was working. They are numerous and important – involving commissions, requests for interviews, a television appearance; an update on a purchase of a spectacularly large slab of marble she made some weeks ago. When her assistant hands her the local newspaper and shows her an article about one of her *obscene* sculptures that was bought for a huge sum, she tries to laugh off the mean little write-up, but the word lodges in her mind, her heart, and she tells her assistant that she's had enough for the day, would she please take her home?

Later, drinking gin and tonic in her study and still thinking about that rotten article, her thoughts occasionally interrupted by the noise of fireworks, she hears James at the front door. She calls to him and after a few moments he opens the study door, immediately asking her where Dad is.

"Probably stuck in traffic on the M25. Don't you remember? He was giving a lecture in Cambridge today."

James sighs and then turns to go.

"Wait up. How was college? Any better?"

He shrugs, as sullen as ever; yet through the eye holes of his *don't give a fuck* mask she thinks she sees some genuine emotion. It is anger, though it quickly disappears, folding in on itself, crumpling. Her younger self is proud of the way James deals with his anger nowadays, though a small voice insists that she's kidding herself. Anger folded inwards hasn't gone, it's still there but more concentrated. Denser. She ignores the voice, and her older self sobs. Longs for release.

There is the sound of another firework, *fwoosh-bang!*

"Bloody rockets," she says. "Can't stand them."

James seems to think this comment the conclusion of their conversation and goes upstairs. The small voice prods her to call to him as he does so. "Only two days to the big birthday, eh? And what about Amy? Can she make it?"

He slams his door just as another rocket goes off, and it seems to Indra as though the whole house shudders violently.

For the Indra trapped in the labyrinth, in the November room, and in the body of her younger self on November fifth 2002, the next hour is pure torture. She tries shouting at her younger self, hitting, kicking biting – anything – that will get her to go up to James. But she is powerless to exert any influence on her younger self who continues to brood over the article and the way in which the reporter shoved in a comment by an oft-quoted critic who calls her work *Damer meets Duchamp*. It's a lazy comparison. Yes, she works in a traditional manner, but a toilet only featured once in her sculptures. Still, she's famous for

219

the piece – "Sex on Loo" – and she knows she mustn't begrudge the fame (or is that infamy?) it's brought her. The older her screams herself hoarse in trying to intrude on her younger version's egocentric reflections. But it's only when three years younger Indra hears a thump from James's room above that she wheels into the hallway and calls up to him. Silence. She goes to the stairlift and hauls herself out of her wheelchair and into the seat. As she slowly rises up the stairs, anger claws at her throat. Why does he never reply? He knows she can't just walk up the stairs like other people. When she gets to the top she lifts herself out of the seat and into the wheelchair waiting on the landing. She's going to have to lay down the law; she can't be doing with this shouting-from-downstairs-only-to-be-ignored nonsense.

But when she tries opening the door to his room and finds it jammed, she is consumed by fear. She shouts for him, shoves the handle down as hard as she can. She uses her fists to try bashing down the door, but it's no good. She needs something heavy. So Indra goes to a spare bedroom which she knows is crammed full of her early works and picks up a marble bust. On returning to his room she lobs it at the door and it smashes right through, showing her the chair that was propped up beneath the door handle. She clears the obstacles and wheels herself into the room and the moment that will change her life forever. The scene is too awful for her to comprehend; she can only take in small snatches of it, and so it morphs into the unreality of a cubist painting: James's neck at an absurd angle, his dangling body, the shoelaces of his trainers skimming over the carpet, the brown leather belt attaching his soft throat to the ceiling light *forever forever forever.*

Her older self could never remember exactly what happened in the moments after her son's suicide, but now she gets to watch her younger self – hysterical, physically useless – in the aftermath: feeling for a pulse; trying (and failing) to get James down; going downstairs to the phone while cursing the uselessness of her legs, the torturously slow stairlift; phoning for an ambulance; phoning David who doesn't immediately reply. Just before the ambulance gets to the house he answers the phone and says, "Sorry, I was doing 70 when you called earlier but now the whole bloody motorway's jammed."

It is only now, three years later, when she is stuck in the November room of the labyrinth, that she considers what David must've gone through in the two hours it took him to get home to his dead son. She cries until she can't breathe and wishes for it to turn midnight.

When it does, she is plunged into a day that she knows has to be infinitely better; and though it is not – for it is the day when her alcoholic mother tells her that she's been diagnosed with liver cirrhosis and doesn't have long to live – she at least gets to hold her mother, tell her that she loves her, that she'll be there for her.

The next day is the launch of David's exhibition – his last ever before James's suicide – and though teenage James is clearly not comfortable about the fact that he is his father's muse, there is a small flicker of pride in his smile as he greets his friends in the gallery and they point to a large canvas that bears his face. As Indra goes about the gallery she overhears two women who are, ostensibly, considering a painting of a flock of white geese entitled "The Imprisoned Brothers", but actually gossiping about David. How he's a real dish. And how it must be so annoying for him to have his wife's awful work lauded when his is so much better... prettier...

She laughs soundlessly at their remarks – David is the least egotistic artist she knows. His mastery in oils is unparalleled, though his paintings don't tend to draw the attention of the critics because of his choice of subject matter. Its lack of controversy. He's inspired by fairy tales, mythology, and often takes elements of these timeless tales and places them in a contemporary setting. His art sells, too. There are plenty of people who will pay good money to have one of David's paintings in their homes. Or the next best thing: a print. It makes her smile to think of the number of homes that have on their walls one of his most popular works, "Icarus Dreams" (the title came from a poem written by a writer-friend) which took months to paint, what with James grumbling about the huge, white wings his father made him wear for short periods of time.

And as to him being a dish, well, of course, that's true. But David is *her* dish, so the women can fuck off. Still, she's thankful to them for showing her David in a new light. She looks across at her husband of eighteen years, champagne glass in hand, and considers his still-handsome features, his thick, black hair which is just beginning to be threaded with grey, and almost bursts with a fierce kind of pride. He sees her and raises his glass in acknowledgment. She raises her glass too and grins.

The next day is November 8th 1984, the day she gave birth to James. She wakes at four a.m. suddenly overwhelmed by pain and fear, and the day rushes onwards in a blur of midwives, doctors and downright barbaric procedures which leave James with a crushed head and her with a mutilated vagina. But when James is finally placed on her chest, *before* is suddenly no longer relevant. Later, she thinks, she will give her experience a shape, a form in marble, but for now there is only James's warm wriggly body, and the incredible food that is toast. Close to midnight, she falls asleep, exhausted but happy. Her older self is grateful for each exquisitely painful moment of the day.

The next fifteen days are all intense: she is either caring for a howling newborn or grieving for her grown-up son. Indra is sure that the way the labyrinth interchanges these two radically different kinds of day will break her; though they do show her something important which she failed to see at the time: David's devotion to both her and James. He is always there for her in the baby days, offering to help change nappies, cooking food or making her cups of tea. When she is grieving he brings her yet more tea, cooks, deals with the paperwork. Offers her a listening ear. But she is ridiculously stubborn and refuses his help. Turns in on herself. She must do this alone.

Just when she thinks she cannot take a single more day of being in the November Room, it brings her a beautiful day. She is in the Caribbean, with David. It is the day of her father's wedding to *the bitch*, as her mother always called Sonia. Indra and David are recently married themselves and David has hinted that maybe next year would be a good time for them to become parents. It's a gorgeous, sunny day, and though Indra's never particularly liked Sonia – how could she when her mother blames her for driving her to drink? – she can see that she makes her father happy. The wedding ceremony is unexpectedly sweet, and she and David drink far too much champagne and make fools of themselves on the dance floor but don't care. They end the day by strolling along a moonlit beach while David sings "Underneath the Mango Tree" to her. He doesn't know most of the lyrics, so he makes up his own. She laughs with each stupid line. Eventually, they fall into each other's arms and make love in the sand.

The next two days she is back in the studio in London, a year after James' death, two years after, urging herself to create; to make something out of his suicide; to give him a solid form. But nothing other than his lifeless body comes to her mind's eye, and she refuses to capture him in marble in this way. She doesn't make any sketches, or a preliminary figure in clay, or pick up her hammer or chisel. Instead, she drinks glass after glass of gin and tonic.

The penultimate day of the month she spends in the November Room is a good day. She is young, seventeen, and wildly in love with art. She is visiting the studio of a well-known sculptor with her father, who has arranged the meeting, and after the sculptor has talked about his process, and shown her a little of how he uses traditional tools to gouge into a block of marble to extract the form within, she is itching to have a go herself. As he places a hammer and chisel in her hands she has a sense that this is a significant moment, and as she begins to chip away at the stone she experiences a deep contentment – a *rightness* – within herself. This is what she will do with her life.

The last day of November is, of course, the day of James' funeral. She wouldn't have expected anything less from the cruel labyrinth. It is raining and she is wearing black, David is wearing black, everyone is wearing black and carrying a black umbrella, and they come to her with their sorrow, their mute faces, the women's mascara running, unable (or unwilling) to even try to express the inexpressible. For what is there to say? Nothing. Yet, slowly, a pointillist picture of the why behind James' suicide emerges. Dots of deep depression, violent mood swings, his recent break-up with Amy, his bad grades at art school which he told no one about, his assertion that he just couldn't do art, unlike his famous parents, dabbling in drugs, the pages and pages of stream-of-consciousness writing in which he kept asserting that he was a loser, a weirdo, that his mind was a maze in which he was trapped, that everyone would be better off without him; they all come together to build a sort-of narrative that she can just about make sense of. But the grief, and guilt, well, there's no making sense of that. As she looks upon the sea of umbrellas stretching before her, Indra locks herself away into a room of her own making.

Indra falls out of the November Room sobbing. Turning to look at the door behind her, she sees that it is turning into stone. Why isn't she home?

"That was the last fucking month!" she screams into the marble corridor.

"What more do you want from me? There's only twelve fucking months in a year!"

She stops then, her mind reeling. Why should there be only twelve rooms in the labyrinth? It doesn't give her the months, or the days of the months, in any kind of chronological order, so why on earth did she think she only had twelve months to get through and then she'd be home? Stupid, stupid woman! She could be here for the rest of her life, running through her out-of-sequence past until her mind, itself, shatters like stone beneath a chisel.

"All right then," she shouts, suddenly defiant. "Bring it on! A minotaur, rain, umbrellas, I'll take the fucking lot!"

And sure enough, a small boy wearing a bull's head of papier-mâché suddenly runs past her, pelting down the corridor ahead of her as fast as he can. In one hand he is carrying a small yellow plastic bottle, in the other a bubble wand. A trail of soapy bubbles stream after his fleeing form; the rainbow-shimmered spheres float upwards.

After a moment of disbelief, which keeps her frozen to the spot, she cries, "James!" and runs after him.

But rain is now falling from the thunderous sky and into the labyrinth, where it morphs into droplets of marble which hammer into her head, her shoulders, her bare arms and feet and shins and calves, making her wince with pain; slowing her down.

She thinks that she could, indeed, do with an umbrella right now, and as she looks up into the grief-coloured sky, a black umbrella floats down to her, and then another and another – as though she is on the set of *Mary Poppins*. Indra catches hold of one, and though it turns to white marble on her touch, it is curiously light; more bone than stone.

She runs on, desperate to get to James, yet fearful that the strong and capable legs the labyrinth has given her will let her down; become too tired to continue the chase. When she sees a turn in the corridor ahead, she thinks he will disappear down it. But he doesn't. He stops running and then stands there, waiting.

Indra runs up to him and, breathless, drops the umbrella. She falls to her knees by his feet, oblivious to the fact that it's no longer raining.

"James," she asks, her voice breaking, "is it you? Really you?"

He doesn't say anything, but the outsized bull's head wobbles a little, giving her a small nod.

She clutches him to her, sobbing. "Are you all right? Oh God, how I miss you! I'm so sorry," she says, "for everything. I want you back. We all do. Can you come home?"

Indra feels him squirming, trying to extricate himself from her embrace. She doesn't want to let go of her son, but eventually she loosens her grip and he steps away from her. He seems to shake his head.

"But are you okay? Please, just let me know you're okay. We're not, I mean your dad and I. But how can we be, when you're no longer with us?"

He hands her the pot of bubble solution and the small looped wand, and she takes them from him wordlessly, confused as to why he is doing this. James then points to something behind her in the corridor.

Indra turns to see a great line of marble umbrellas behind her. But why is he pointing to them?

When she turns back to him he has gone, though the sound of his footsteps tell her that he's disappeared down the turn. Replacing the wand in the pot of bubble solution, she gets up and runs after him, left, right, straight, on and on, right, right, straight, left. But it's no good, he's going unnaturally fast, and she can't keep up with him. She collapses in a heap, and gazes upwards at the sky which is slowly turning from one of her favourite shades of watercolour – Payne's grey – to lavender blue. Bubbles, presumably from earlier, are floating up into the fast-changing sky.

Still holding the pot of bubbles, she hugs herself tight, encouraging herself to go on. She must follow her son, and she will follow her son, until the very end, until her feet are bloodied stumps and her heart is too weak to go on beating.

Slowly, Indra stands and then limps along the corridor in the direction that James has gone. But soon she hears the patter of footsteps behind her – from the way she has just now come. Confused, she turns around and back-tracks and, yes, there he is, though she cannot understand his seemingly slipping past her without her noticing. He leads her all the way back to the corridor full of umbrellas.

"Why are we here again?" she asks, going to him.

But he skips away from her, and then points at the umbrellas. The moment she glances at where he's pointing, he vanishes.

"Don't go!" she cries, looking about her. Unsure where to go or what to do, she simply stands there, utterly lost. He doesn't want her. Her son doesn't want to be with her.

She slumps onto the floor, heavy with this awful knowledge, and cries, her arms about her shuddering chest, until she can cry no longer; until she reaches a tremulous and terrible dry-eyed calm.

She looks back to the umbrellas. There are soap bubbles in the sky above the corridor full of white marble umbrellas, and for a moment they shape themselves into a door.

Indra gasps, understanding coming to her now. It wasn't that he didn't want her… he was trying to help her.

"Of course!" she mutters, and she stands and smiles. How ridiculous to only think in two dimensions! She consciously thinks of umbrellas and, instantly, more come floating down from the sky and into the corridor. But in her mind she arranges them in an overlapping manner, so that they become a stairway going upwards, to the door she can see in the bubbles. It is slowly becoming more substantial now – a free-floating door of wood and white gloss paint, just like the door to James's bedroom. The umbrellas have formed a graceful, curved stairway into the sky, and she scrambles up it, way past the tops of the walls of the labyrinth. She climbs and climbs until she is only a short way from the door. But it's just out of reach, and no more umbrellas are floating downwards, despite her best efforts to will them into existence. Frustration threatens to overwhelm her. She is so close!

A honking sound breaks into her thoughts and she realises that the geese are back. The beautiful white geese who will help her up so she can reach the door. And they do. Taking hold of her cotton dress with their orange beaks, their great, powerful wings beating about her, they lift her to the door.

"Thank you!" she cries as she grabs the handle, falling through the open door and onto solid ground. Ground that is carpeted, with wooden floorboards underneath. The door shuts behind her and she knows that she has finally escaped the labyrinth. She clutches at the thick pile of the ivory-coloured carpet outside James's room, tears seeping from her eyes, and laughs hysterically at the fact that she's never been happier to see a piece of carpet. She is out. Out!

"Indra!"

It is David, and he is rushing up the stairs to her. "Oh God, what's happened? I was so worried when you didn't answer my calls. Are you all right? How did you get up here? I thought the stairlift was broken? And there's no wheelchair up here!"

He sits beside her and takes her into his arms; it is then that he notices the dozens and dozens of white pills scattered about the carpet; one has been split into two, and Indra is clutching one of the halves. In her other hand is a plastic pot with a label that reads *Bubbles*. Her neck is bruised and there are scratches on her upper arm which are still oozing blood.

"Oh God, oh God," he mutters. "Please tell me you're okay, that you haven't taken any tablets, please Indra."

"I'm okay," she manages to say. "I'm okay. James saved me. So did you. And I'm out now. I got out."

David doesn't know what the hell she's talking about, but when she tells him that she's sorry, that she's sorry for everything, he holds her even tighter, and they both cry tears that have the power to bind them together in something other than guilt and grief.

It is then that Indra sees in her mind's eye the white marble sculpture she will make. It will be huge, the largest sculpture she's ever created; it will be of a curving stairway made of overlapping umbrellas, a door supported by flying geese at the top; tucked in a shadowed corner beneath the stairway will be a small boy wearing a bull's head. He will be holding a small bottle and a bubble wand. Thin glass bubbles, their curved surfaces like those of puddles sheened with rainbow-swirled petrol will float about the sculpture. They will hang in the air, unsupported. She has no idea how she's going to make them do that, but as she grips the plastic bottle she knows she can do it. She can do anything now.

Indra will call the sculpture, "The November Room" or "Leaving the Labyrinth". Maybe both.

Acknowledgements

My sincere thanks to all the lovely people of the Northampton SF Writers Group who have critiqued my short stories over the past few years – your insightful and encouraging feedback is very much appreciated. Thanks as well to my Nottingham SFF writer friends: Victoria Haslam, Andy Hedgecock, Michael Krawec, Hilke Kurzke and Maureen Neal, who read some of the earliest stories within this book. I have many fond memories of us meeting at the Nottingham Writers' Studio or other places in the city to critique each other's work. Thanks also to Andrew Kells for organising the monthly daytime socials at Nottingham Writers' Studio which are always a boost, and for regularly asking me how my writing is going. Likewise, my thanks to Rogelio Fojo for taking the time to read and offer generous comments on my short fiction.

Also, I am deeply grateful to all the editors who have published and championed my writing, gifting me with the encouragement I needed to keep writing my strange, little tales. Especial thanks go to Noel Chidwick, the founder of *Shoreline of Infinity*, Donna Scott, editor of the *Best of British Science Fiction* series, Steve J. Shaw of Black Shuck Books, Gareth Jelley of *Interzone*, and, of course, Ian Whates, editor of *Parsec* and NewCon Press publisher-extraordinaire. You are all stars!

My gratitude also goes to my wonderful husband, Tom, my first (and bestest) reader, my children, Rebecca and Jerome, who always cheer when I tell them that I've placed a story, and my mother, Ludmila, who is extraordinarily proud of whatever I do. Finally, I give thanks to God for planting within me the storytelling seed, and for all His blessings.

About the Author

Teika Marija Smits is a UK-based writer and freelance editor. She writes poetry and fiction, and her speculative short stories have been published in *IZ Digital, Parsec, Reckoning, Shoreline of Infinity, Best of British Science Fiction* and *Great British Horror 6*. Her debut poetry pamphlet, *Russian Doll*, was published by Indigo Dreams Publishing in March 2021. A fan of all things fae, she is delighted by the fact that Teika means fairy tale in Latvian. She can be found at: https://teikamarijasmits.com/ @MarijaSmits

ALSO FROM NEWCON PRESS

Polestars 1: Strange Attractors – Jaine Fenn
First full collection from the award-winning author of innovative science fiction and off-kilter fantasy; features her finest short stories, selected by the author, drawn from more than two decades of publication, including the BSFA Award-winning "Liberty Bird", a Hidden Empire story, and a new tale, "Sin of Omission", written specifically for this collection.

Polestars 3: The Glasshouse – Emma Coleman
Contemporary tales of rural horror from one of genre fiction's best kept secrets. An avid haunter of libraries, Emma's fiction is steeped in local colour and rooted deep in her native Northamptonshire, drawing on her love of nature, her passion for literature, and her keen eye for detail. Her fiction is atmospheric, mesmeric, and frequently disturbing.

The She – Terry Grimwood
A devil's dozen of outstanding stories from one of the UK's most consistent writers of short fiction. Witness the fall of Adam and the rise of Lillith; discover what really happened to band leader Glen Miller's plane; meet the third man on the moon, whose name will never be remembered; and see who the true survivors are in a post-apocalyptic world…

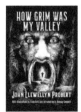

How Grim Was My Valley – John Llewellyn Probert
After waking up on the Welsh side of the Severn Bridge with no memory of who he is, a man embarks on an odyssey through Wales, bearing witness to the stories both the people and the land itself feel moved to tell him, all the while getting closer to the truth about himself.

Best of British Science Fiction 2022 – Donna Scott
Editor Donna Scott has scoured magazines, anthologies, webzines and obscure genre corners to discover the very best science fiction stories by British and British-based authors published during 2022. A thrilling blend of cutting-edge and traditional, showcasing all that makes science fiction the most entertaining genre around

Milton Keynes UK
Ingram Content Group UK Ltd.
UKHW010725270823
427545UK00004B/178